BEST NEW
WEREWOLF TALES
VOLUME 1

TABLE OF CONTENTS

EDITED BY
CAROLINA SMART

BOOKS of the DEAD

LIKE PART OF THE FAMILY
JONATHAN MABERRY

"My ex-husband is trying to kill me," she said.

She was one of those cookie-cutter East Coast blondes. Pale skin, pale hair, pale eyes. Lots of New Age jewelry. Not a lot of curves and too much perfume. Kind of pretty if you dig the modeling-scene heroin chic look. Or if you troll the anorexia twelve-steps or crack houses looking for easy ass that's so desperate for affection they'll boff you blind for a smile. Not my kind. I like a little more meat on the bone, and bit more sanity in the eyes. This one came to me on a referral from another client.

"He actually try?"

"I can *tell*, Mr. Hunter."

Yeah, I thought and tried not to sigh. *What I figured.*

"You call the cops?"

She shrugged.

"What's that mean? You call them or not?"

"I called," she said. "They said that there wasn't anything they could do unless he did something first."

"Yeah," I said. "Can't arrest someone for thinking about something."

"He threatened me."

"Anyone hear him make the threat?"

"No."

"Then it's your word."

"That's what the police said." She crossed her legs. Her legs were on the thin side of being nice. Probably were nice before drugs or stress or a fractured self image wasted her down to Sally Stick-figure.

Skirt was short, shoes looked expensive. I have three ex-wives and I pay alimony bigger than India's national debt. I know how expensive women's shoes are. I was wearing black sneakers from Payless. Glad I had a desk between me and her.

"Your husband ever hurt you?" I asked. "Or try to?"

"*Ex*," she corrected. "And—yes. That's why I left him. He hit me a few times. Mostly when he was drunk and out of control."

I held up a hand. "Don't make excuses for him. He hit you. Being drunk doesn't change the rules. Might even make it worse, especially if he did it once while drunk and then let himself come home drunk again."

She digested that. She'd probably heard that rap before but it might have come from a female case worker or a shrink. From the way her eyes shifted to me and away and back again I guessed she'd never heard that from a man before. I guess for her men were the Big Bad. Too many of them are.

It was ten to five but it was already dark outside. December snow swirled past the window. It wasn't accumulating, so the snow still looked pretty. Once it started piling up I hated the shit. My secretary, Mrs. Gilligan, fled at the first flake. Typical Philadelphian—they think the world will come to a screeching halt if there's half an inch on the ground. She's probably at Wegmans stocking up on milk, bread and toilet paper. The staples of the apocalypse. Me, I grew up in Minneapolis, and out in the Cities we think twenty inches is getting off light. Doesn't mean I don't hate the shit, though. A low annual snowfall is one of the reasons I moved to Philly after I got my PI license. Easier to hunt if you don't have to slog through snow.

"When he hit you," I said, "you report it?"

"No."

"Not to the cops?"

"No."

"Women's shelter?"

"No."

"Anyone? A friend?"

She shook her head. "I was—embarrassed, Mr. Hunter. A black eye and all. Didn't want to be seen."

Which means there's no record. Nothing to support her case about ex-hubby wanting to kill her.

I drummed my fingers on the desk blotter. I get these kinds of cases every once in a while, though I stayed well clear of domestic disputes and spousal abuse cases when I was with Minneapolis PD. I have a temper and by the time they asked for my shield back I had six reprimands in my jacket for excessive force. At one of my IA hearings the captain said that he was disappointed that I showed no remorse for the last 'incident'. I busted a child molester and somehow while the guy was, um, resisting arrest he managed to get mauled and mangled a bit. The pedophile tried to spin some crazy shit that I sicced a dog on him, but I don't *have* a dog. I said that he got mauled by a stray during a foot pursuit. Even at my own hearing I couldn't keep a smile off my face to save my job. Squeaked by on that one, but next time something like it happened—this time with a guy who whipped his wife half to death with an extension cord because she wasn't 'willing enough' in the bedroom—I was out on my ass. He ran into the same stray dog. Weird how that happens, huh? Long story short, I already didn't have the warm fuzzies for her husband. We all have our buttons, and when the strong prey on the weak all of mine get pushed.

"Did you go to the E.R.?"

"No," she said. "It was never that bad. More humiliating than anything."

I nodded. "What about after the divorce? He lay a hand on you since?"

She hesitated.

"Mrs. Skye?" I prompted.

"He tried. He chased me. Twice."

"*Chased* you? Tell me about it."

She licked her lips. She wore a very nice rose-pink lipstick that was the only splash of color. Even her clothes and shoes were white. Pale horse, pale rider.

"Well," she said, "that's where the story gets really—strange."

"Strange how?"

"He——David, my ex-husband—*changed* after I filed for divorce. He's like a different person. Before, when I first met him, he was a very fastidious man. Always dressed nicely, always very clean and well-groomed."

"What's he do for a living?"

"He owns a nightclub. *The Crypt*, just off South Street."

"I know it, but that's a Goth club right? Is he Goth?"

"No. Not at all. He bought the club from the former owner, but he remodeled it after *The Batcave*."

"As in Batman?"

"As in the London club that was kind of the prototype of pretty much the whole Goth club scene. David's a businessman. There's a strong Goth crowd Downtown, and they hang together, but the clubs in Philly aren't big enough to turn a big profit, and not near big enough to attract the better bands. So, he bought the two adjoining buildings and expanded out. He made a small-time club into a very successful main stage club, and he keeps the music current. A lot of post-punk stuff, but also the newer styles. Dark cabaret, Death-rock, Gothabilly. That sort of thing. Low lights, black-tile bathrooms, bartenders who look like ghouls."

"Okay," I said.

"But this was all business to David. He didn't dress Goth. I mean, he wore black suits or black silk shirts to work, but he didn't dye his hair, didn't wear eye-liner. Funny thing is, even though he was clearly not buying into the lifestyle the patrons loved him. They called him the Prince. As in Prince of—"

"Darkness, yeah, got it. Go on."

"David was more fussy getting ready to go out than I ever was. Spent forever in the bathroom shaving, fixing his hair. Always took him longer to pick out his clothes than me or any of my girlfriends."

"He gay?"

"No." And she shot me a 'wow, what a stereotypically homophobic thing to say' sort of look.

I smiled. "I'm just trying to get a read on him. Fastidious guy having trouble with a relationship with his wife. Drinking problem, flashes of violence. Not a gay thing, but I've seen it before in guys who are sexually conflicted and at war with themselves and the world because of it."

She studied me for a moment. "You used to be a cop, Mr. Hunter?"

"Call me Sam," I said. "And, yeah, I was a cop. Minneapolis PD."

"A detective?"

"Yep."

"Okay." That seemed to mollify her. I gestured to her to continue. She took a breath. "Well—toward the end of our relationship David stopped being so fastidious. He would go two or three days without shaving. I know that doesn't sound like the end of the world, but I never saw David without a fresh shave. Never. He carried an electric razor in his briefcase, had another at home and one in the office at the club. Clothes, too. Before, he'd sometimes change clothes twice or even three times a day if it was humid. He always wanted to look fresh. Showered at home morning and night, and had a shower installed in his office."

"I get the picture. Mr. Clean. But you say that changed while you were still together?"

"It started when he fell off the wagon."

"Ah."

"When I met him he said that he hadn't taken a drink for over two years. He was proud of it. He thought that his thirst—he always called it that—was evil, and being on the wagon made him feel like a real person. Then, after we started having problems, he started drinking again. Never in front of me, and he always washed his mouth out before he came home. I never smelled alcohol on him, but he was a different person from then on. And he started yelling at me all the time. He called me horrible names and made threats. He said that I didn't love him, that I was just trying to use him."

"I have to ask," I said, being as delicate as I could, "but was there someone else?"

"For me? God, no!"

"What set him off? From his perspective, I mean. Did he say that there was something that made him angry or paranoid?"

"Well—I think it was his health."

"Tell me."

"He started losing weight. He was never fat, not even stocky. David was very muscular. He lifted a lot of weights, drank that protein powder twice a day. He had big arms, a huge chest. I asked him if he was taking steroids. He denied it, but I think he was trying to turn into one of those muscle freaks. Then, about a year and a half ago he started losing weight. When he taped his arms and found that his biceps were only twenty-two inches, he got really angry."

"David has twenty-two inch biceps?" Christ. Back in his Mr. Universe days, Arnold the Terminator had twenty-four inch arms, fully pumped. I think mine are somewhere shy of fifteen, and that's after three sets on the Bowflex.

"Not anymore," said Mrs. Skye. "He lost a lot of muscle mass. Really fast, too. I was scared, I told him to go to a doctor. I thought he might have cancer."

"Did he go to the doctor?"

"He said so—but I don't think he did. He kept losing weight. After six months he didn't even have much definition. He was kind of ordinary sized."

"Was he drinking by this point?"

"I'm sure of it."

"That when he started putting his hands on you?"

"Yes. And he became paranoid. Kept trying to make it all my fault."

"How long did this go on?"

"Well—after the first time he, um, *hurt* me, I gave him a second chance. After all, he was must husband. I figured that he was just scared because of his health. But then it happened again. The second time he knocked me around pretty good. I couldn't go out of the house for a few days."

"Was that when you left?"

It took her so long to answer that I knew what her answer would be. I've done too many interviews of this kind. If self-esteem is low enough then victimization can become an addiction.

"I stayed for two more months."

"How many times did he hurt you during that time?" I asked.

"A few."

"A few is how many?"

Another long pause. "Six."

"Six," I said, trying to put no judgment in my tone. "What was the straw?"

She looked at her hands, at the clock, at the snow falling outside. If there'd been a magazine on my desk she would have picked it up and leafed through it. Anything to keep from meeting my eyes. "He choked me."

"I see."

"It was in the middle of the night. We were—we were—"

I almost sighed. "Let me guess. Make-up sex?"

She nodded, but she didn't blush. I'll give her that. "He'd been sweet to me for two weeks straight without getting mad or yelling, or anything. He acted like his old self. Charming." She finally met my eyes. "David has enormous charisma. He makes everyone like him, and he always seems so genuine."

"Uh huh," I said, wondering how that charm would work on a blackjack across his teeth.

"We sat up talking until late, then we went to bed. And in the middle of the night—things just started happening. You know how it is."

I didn't, but I said nothing.

"I was, um—on top. And we were pretty far into things, and then all of a sudden David reaches up and grabs me around the throat. I thought for one crazy moment that he was doing that auto-whatever it's called."

"Autoerotic asphyxiation," I supplied.

"Yeah, that. I thought he was doing that. He talked about it once before, but we'd never tried it. He's really strong and I'm pretty small. But—I guess I thought he was trying to change things, you know? Create a new pattern for us. A fresh start."

Naivety can be a terrible thing. Jesus wept.

"But it wasn't sex play," I prompted.

"No. He started squeezing his hands. Suddenly I couldn't breathe. It was weird because we were so close to—you know—and David kept staring at me, his eyes wide like he was in some kind of trance. I tried to pull his hands apart, but it just made him squeeze tighter. That's when he started calling me names again, making wild accusations, accusing me of destroying his life."

"How did you get away?"

Her eyes cut away again. This was obviously very hard for her.

"I threw myself sideways and when I landed I kicked him in the, um—you know."

I smiled.

"Good for you," I said, but she shook her head.

"I grabbed my clothes and ran out. Next day I drove past the house and saw that his car was gone. I had a locksmith come out and change all the locks and change the security code on the alarm. I hired a messenger company to come and take a couple of suitcases of his clothes to the club. Next day I rented a storage unit and hired a moving company to take all of his stuff there. I used the same messenger service to send him the key."

"I'm impressed. That was quick thinking."

"I—I'd already looked into that stuff before. Until that last stretch where he was nice I was planning to leave him. I'd already talked to my lawyer, and I filed for divorce by the end of that week."

"What did David do?"

"At first? Nothing except for some hysterical messages on my voicemail. He didn't try to break in, nothing like that. But after a while I started seeing his car behind mine when I was going to work."

"Where do you work?"

"I'm a nurse supervisor at Sunset Grove, the assisted living facility in Jenkintown. Right now I'm on the four to midnight shift. I've spotted David's car a lot, sometimes every night for weeks on end. I've seem him drive by when I'm going into the staff entrance, and he's there again when I get back home."

"What makes you think he's planning to do more than just harass you?"

"He's said so."

"But—"

"He didn't say or do anything at first—but over the last couple of weeks it's gotten worse. About three weeks ago I came out of work and stopped at a 7-11 for some gum, and when I came out he was leaning against my car. I told him to get away, but he pushed himself off the car and came up to me, smiling his charming smile. He told me that he knew who I was and what I was and that he was going to end me. His words. '*I'm going to end you*'. Then he left, still smiling."

"Did anyone see this?"

"At one in the morning? No."

Convenience stores have security cameras, I thought. If this thing got messy I could have her lawyer subpoena those tapes. I had her write down the address of the 7-11.

"That's how it went for a couple of weeks," she said. "But last night, he really scared me."

"What happened?"

"He was in my bedroom."

"How?"

"That's it—I don't know. The alarms didn't go off and none of the windows were broken. I heard a sound and I woke up and there he was, standing by the side of my bed. He's really thin now, and as pale as those Goth kids at his club. He stood there, smiling. I started to scream and put a finger to his lips and made a weird shushing sound. It was so strange that I actually did shut up. Don't ask me why. The whole thing was like a nightmare."

"Are you sure it wasn't?"

She hesitated, but she said, "I'm positive. He pointed at me and said that he knew everything about me. Then he started praying."

"Praying?"

"At least I think that's what he was doing. It was Latin, I think. He saying a long string of things in Latin and then he left."

"How'd he get out?"

"The same way he got in, I guess—but I don't know how. I was so scared that I almost peed myself and I just lay there in bed for a long time. I don't know how long. When I finally worked up the nerve, I ran downstairs and got a knife from the kitchen and went through the whole house."

"You didn't call the cops?"

"I was going to—but the alarm never went off. I checked the system—it was still set. I began wondering if I *was* dreaming."

"But you don't think so?"

"No."

"Why are you so sure?"

She fished in her purse and produced a pink cell phone. She flipped it open and pressed a few buttons to call up her text messages. She pointed to the number and then handed me the phone.

"That's David's cell number."

The text read: *Tonight.*

"Okay," I said. "Let me see what I can do."

"What *can* you do?" she asked.

"Well, the best first thing to do is go have a talk with him. See if I can convince him to back off."

"And if he won't?"

"I can be pretty convincing."

"But what if he won't? What if he's—I don't know—too crazy to listen to reason?"

I smiled. "Then we'll explore other options."

* * *

The Crypt is a big ugly building on the corner of South and Fourth in Philadelphia. Once upon a time it was a coffin factory – which I think would have been a cooler name. Less trendy and obvious. The light snow did nothing to make it look less ugly. When we pulled to the corner, Mrs. Skye pointed to a sleek silver Lexus parked on the side street.

"That's his."

I jotted down the license plate and used my digital camera to take photos of it and the exterior of the building. You never know.

"Okay," I said, "I want you to wait here. I'll go have a talk with David and see if we can sort this out."

"What if something happens? What if you don't come out?"

"Just sit tight. You have a cell phone and I'll give you the keys. If I'm not out of there in fifteen minutes, drive somewhere safe and call the name on the back of my card." I gave her my business card. She turned it over and saw a name and number. Before she could ask, I said, "Ray's a friend. One of my pack."

"Another private investigator?"

"A bodyguard. I use him for certain jobs, but I don't think we'll need to bring him in on this. From what you've told me I have a pretty good sense of what to expect in there."

As I got out my jacket flap opened and she spotted the handle of my Glock.

"You're not… going to *hurt* him," she asked, wide eyed.

I shook my head. "I've been doing this for a lot of years, Mrs. Skye. I haven't had to pull my gun once. I don't expect I'll break that streak tonight."

* * *

The breeze was coming from the west and the snow was just about done. I squinted up past the streetlights. The cloud cover was thin and I could already see the white outline of the moon. Nope, no accumulation. Typical Philly winter.

I crossed the street and tried the front door. Place didn't do much business before late evening, but the doors were unlocked. The doors opened with an exhalation of cigarette smoke and alcohol fumes. There was probably an anti-smoking violation in that. Something else to use later if I needed to go the route of making life difficult for him.

It was too early for a doorman, and I walked a short hallway that was empty and painted black. Heavy black velvet curtains at the end. Cute. I pushed them aside and entered the club. Place was huge. David Skye must have taken out the second floor and knocked out everything but the retaining walls of the adjoining properties. The red and white maximum occupancy sign said that it shouldn't exceed four hundred, but the place looked capable of taking twice that number. Bandstand was empty, so someone had put quarters in to play the tuneless junk that was beating the shit out of the woofers and tweeters. Whoever the group was on the record they subscribed to the philosophy that if you can't play well you should play real god damn loud.

There were maybe twenty people in the place, scattered around at tables. A few at the bar. Everyone looked like extras from a direct-to-video vampire flick. The motif was black on black with occasional splashes of blood red. White skin that probably never saw the sun. Eyeliner and black lipstick, even on the guys. I was in jeans and a Vikings warm-up jacket. At least my sneakers and my leather porkpie hat were black. Handle of my gun was black, too, but they couldn't see that. Better for everyone if nobody did.

The bartender was giving me *the look*, so I strolled over to him. He knew I wasn't there for a beer and didn't waste either of our time by asking.

"David Skye," I said, having to bend forward and shout over the music.

"Badge me," he said.

I flipped open my PI license. "Private."

"Fuck off," he suggested.

"Not a chance."

"I can call the cops."

"Bet I can have L and I here before they show. Smoking in a public restaurant?"

Another smartass remark was on his lips, but he didn't have the energy for it. He was paid by the hour and this had to be a slow shift for tips. I took a twenty from my wallet and put it on the bar.

"This isn't your shit, kid," I said. "Call your boss."

He didn't like it, but he took the twenty and made the call.

"He says come up." The bartender pointed to another curtained doorway beside the bar. I gave him a sunny day smile and went inside.

There was a long hallway with bathrooms on both sides and a set of stairs at the end. I took the stairs two at a time. The stairs went straight up to his office and the door was open. I knocked anyway.

"It's open," he yelled. I went inside and as I looked around I hoped like hell that the office décor was not modeled after the interior landscape of David Skye's mind. The walls were painted a dark red, the trim was gloss black. Instead of the band posters and framed '*look at who I'm shaking hands with*' eight-by-tens, the walls were hung with torture devices and S and M clothes. Spiked harnesses, leather zippered masks, thumbscrews, photos from Abu Graib, diagrams of dissected bodies. A full-sized rack occupied one corner of the room and an iron maiden stood in the other, one door open to reveal rows of tarnished metal spikes. The only other furniture was a big desk made from some dark wood, a black file cabinet and the leather swivel chair in which David Skye sat. He wore a black poet's shirt, leather wristbands, and a smile that was already belligerent.

"The fuck are you and the fuck you want?"

The man was a charmer. I could just taste the charisma his wife had mentioned flowing like sweetness from his pores.

I flipped my ID case open. "We need to have a chat. It can be friendly or not. Your call."

"Go fuck yourself."

So much for *friendly*.

"That whore send you?" he demanded.

I smiled but didn't answer.

He had a handsome face, but his wife was right when she said that he'd lost weight. His skin looked thin and loose, and he had the complexion of a mushroom. More gray than white.

"Did my wife send you?" he said, pronouncing the words slowly as if I'd come here on the short bus.

"Why would your ex-wife send me?"

His eyes flickered for a second at '*ex*-wife'. I strolled across the room and stood in front of his desk. He didn't get up, neither of us offered a hand to the other.

"She makes up stories," he said.

"What kind of stories?"

"Bullshit. Lies. Says I slapped her around."

"Who'd she say that to?"

He didn't answer. He did, however, give me the ninja secret death stare, but I manned my way through it.

"What are you supposed to be," he said.

"Just what the license says."

"Private investigator. Private *dick*."

"Yes, and that was funny back in the 1950s. Why do *you* think I'm here?"

"She's probably trying some kind of squeeze play. The club is doing okay, so she wants a bigger slice."

"Try again," I said, though he might have been right about that.

"Oh, I get it—you're supposed to scare me into leaving her alone."

"Do I look scary?"

He smiled. He had very red lips and very white teeth. "No," he said, "you don't."

"Right—so let's pretend that I'm here to have a reasonable discussion. Man to man."

Skye leaned back in his chair and stared at me with his dark eyes. It was a calculating look and I'm sure he took in everything from my slightly threadbare Vikings jacket to my cheap black sneakers. Put everything I was wearing together and it would equal the cost of his shirt. I was okay with that. I don't dress to impress. Skye, on the other hand, smiled as if our mutual understanding of my material net worth clearly made him the alpha.

I smiled back.

"What does she want?" he asked.

"For you to leave her alone."

"What is she afraid of?"

"She thinks you're trying to kill her."

"What do *you* think?"

"What I think doesn't matter. I'm not a psychic, so I don't know whether you're trying to kill her or if you're playing some kind of mind-game on her. Whatever it is, I'm here to ask you to lay off."

"Why should I?"

"Because I asked real nice."

He smiled at that.

"Because it's illegal and I could build a harassment case against you and you could lose your club and sink a quarter mil into legal fees. Because I know inspectors who can slap you with fifteen kinds of violations that will hurt your business. I can have your car booted by *accident* three or four times a week, every week."

"And I could have you killed," he said, the smile unwavering.

"Maybe," I said. "You could try, and I might fuck up anyone you send and then come back here and fuck you up."

"Think you could?"

"You really want to find out?" When he didn't answer, I took a glass paperweight off his desk and turned it over in my hands. A spider was trapped inside, frozen into a moment of time for the amusement of the trinket crowd. I knew he was watching me play with the paperweight, wondering what I was going to do with it.

I put it back down on the desk.

"Really, though," I said, "how long do we need to circle and sniff each other? We don't run in the same pack and I don't give a rat's ass what you do, who you are, or how tough you think you are. We both know that you're either going to stop bothering your ex-wife and go on with your life; or you're going to make a run at her—either because you have some loose wiring or because I'm pushing your buttons by being here. If you back off, we're all friends. I'll advise my client not to file a restraining order and you two can let the divorce lawyers earn their paychecks by kicking each other in the nuts."

"Or—?" he asked. Still smiling.

"Or, you don't back off and then this is about you and me."

"Nonsense. You're no part of this. This is about me and—."

I cut him off. "I'm *making* this about you and me. Maybe I have a wire loose, too, but once I tell a client that I'm going to keep her safe, I take it amiss if anything happens to her."

"Amiss," he repeated, enjoying the word.

"But that's a minute from now. We're still on the other side of it until you give me an answer. What's it going to be? You leave her alone? Or this gets complicated."

"What were you before you started doing this PI bullshit?"

"A cop."

He grunted. "You sound like a thug. An asshole leg-breaker from South Philly."

"Thin line sometimes."

He steepled his fingers. It was one of those moves that looked good when Doctor Doom did it in a comic book. Maybe in a boardroom. Looked silly right now, but he had enough intensity in his eyes to almost pull it off. He gave me ten seconds of *the stare*.

I stood my ground.

His cell phone rang and he flipped it open, listened.

"I'm in a meeting," he said and closed the phone.

His smile returned.

I heard the footsteps on the stairs even though they were quiet.

I sighed and turned. There were four of them. All as pale as Skye, but much bigger. "Really? You want to play that card?"

"It's one of the classics. Though, to be fair, it'll be more than a typical beating. I—, am I wrong in presuming you *have* had your ass kicked?"

"That cherry was popped a long time ago."

The four men entered the room and fanned out behind me.

"So, our challenge, then," Skye said, "is to put a new spin on this. Something surprising and fresh so that you'll be entertained."

"Mind if I take my jacket off first?"

"Go right ahead."

I heard a hammer-cock behind me.

Skye said, "You can put your jacket on my desk here, and take off your shoulder holster and put that—and your piece—on top of it."

"Sure, whatever," I said. I shrugged out of the jacket. I bought it the year the Vikings took their eighteenth division title. I'll buy a new one if they ever win the Super Bowl. Or when pigs sprout wings and learn to fly, whichever comes first. I folded it and set it down, unclipped my shoulder rig, set that down. If I was going to ruin my clothes, then at least nothing I was currently wearing had sentimental value.

I leaned on the desk. "Let's agree on a couple of things first, okay?"

"Sure," he said with a grin.

"When I'm done handing these clowns their asses, then you and I dance a round or two."

"That would be fun," he said, "but I doubt I'll have the pleasure."

"Second, if I walk out of here on my own steam, then it's with the understanding that you will leave the lady alone."

"If you walk out of here? Sure. But, tell me something," he said, and he looked genuinely interested, "why do you care? What is she to you?"

"Maybe I'm the possessive type, too. Maybe now that she's asked for my help, it's like she's part of the family. So to speak."

"Part of the family? You fucking kidding me here?"

"Nope."

"You Italian? This some kind of dago thing?"

"I said it's *like* she's part of the family. My family," I said, "and I protect what's mine."

"That's it? It's just a macho thing with you?"

"No, it's more than that," I admitted. I gestured to the torture and pain motif in which his office was decorated. "But, seriously, I doubt you would understand."

"Mmm, probably not. I'm not into sentimentality and that bullshit. Not anymore."

"What happened? What changed you?"

His smiled faded to a remote coldness. "I learned that there was something better. Better than family, better than blood ties. Better than any of this ordinary shit."

"You found religion?" I said.

"It's a 'higher order' sort of thing that I really don't want to explain and I doubt *you'd* understand."

"I might surprise you."

"I don't think that's possible. But *we* might surprise you. In fact I can pretty fucking well guarantee it."

"Rock and roll," I said.

I straightened and turned toward the four goons. They took up positions like compass points. The office was big, but not big enough to give me room to maneuver. They were going to fall on me like a wall, and they knew it. The guy with the gun even snugged it back into his shoulder rig. They were *that* confident, and they were smiling like kids at a carnival.

"You shouldn't have bothered Mr. Skye," said the guy in front of me. He was the gun who'd holstered his gun. He stood on the East point of the compass. "You should have—"

I kicked him in the nuts. I really didn't need to hear the speech.

I'm not that big but I can kick like a Rockette. I *felt* bones break and he screamed like a nine year old girl. Dumbass should have kept his gun out.

I stepped backward off of him and put an elbow into West's face. It had all of my mass in motion behind it. That time I heard bones break and he went down so fast that I wondered if I'd snapped his neck.

That left South and North. South spent a half second too long looking shocked, so I jumped at him with a leaping knee—the only Muay Thai kick I know—and drove him all the way to the wall. By the time North closed in I'd grabbed South by the ears and slammed him skull-first into a replica of a torture rack. Blood splattered in a Jackson Pollack pattern.

I pivoted and rushed to intercept North who was barreling at me with a lot of furious speed; so I veered left and clothes-lined him with my stiff right forearm. He did a pretty impressive back flip and landed face down on the black-painted hardwood floor.

If this was an action movie everything would switch to slow motion as the four thugs toppled to the ground and I turned slowly looking badass, to face the now startled and unprotected villain.

The real world is a lot less accommodating.

I caught movement behind me, figuring it for Skye going after my gun, so I whirled and made ready to launch into a diving tackle.

Only it wasn't Skye.

It was East and West getting to their feet. West's face was smeared with blood from his broken nose, but he was smiling. As I watched he took his nose between thumb and forefinger and *snapped* it into place, then spit a hocker of blood and snot onto the floor.

North was chuckling as he rose; and behind me I could hear South shifting to stand behind me again. I turned in a slow circle. They were all smiling. They shouldn't have been *able* to. They should have been sprawled on the floor and I should have been giving some kind of smart-ass speech as I closed in to lay a beating on Skye. That was the script I'd written in my head.

What the hell was this shit?

"Surprise!" said Skye dryly.

"What the hell are these fuckers *taking*?"

"You wouldn't believe me if I told you?"

"Try me."

"Blood," he said.

"What the—"

And I looked more closely at the smiles. Lots of white teeth. Lots of long, pointy white teeth.

"Oh, balls," I said.

"Yeah, kind of cool, huh?"

"Vampires?" I said.

"Yeah."

"Actual vampires?"

Skye laughed. The four—well, let's call a spade a spade—*vampires* laughed with him.

Even I laughed.

"Geez. When shit goes wrong it goes all the way wrong, doesn't it," I said.

"On the up side," said Skye, "you did win the first round. Nice moves."

"Thanks."

The four of them circled me. My pulse jumped from 'uh-oh' to 'oh shit'. It was cold in his office but I was starting to sweat pretty heavily.

"I guess I shouldn't be surprised," I said. "You're one, too? Am I right?"

"A recent convert," he admitted.

"So—that whole weight lose, going all weird on the missus that was—?"

"A transition process. It's not like they show in the movies, you know. Takes weeks. The whole metabolism changes."

"No kidding."

One of the vampires faked a lunge to psyche me out and I jumped a foot in the air. I'm pretty sure I didn't yelp like a Chihuahua, but I wouldn't swear to that in court. They all laughed at that, too. I didn't.

"Which explains why you lost all that weight."

"Who needs steroids and free-weights," he agreed and spread his hands. "This package comes with honest to God super strength. I'm like Spiderman and Wolverine rolled into one. Super strong and I heal from damn near anything."

"Could you be more specific on that last point?"

"Cute."

"Worth a try." I looked at them, at their grinning, evil faces. My nuts were trying to crawl up inside of my chest cavity. I mean—*fucking vampires?*

"Weird thing was," I said, "I was starting to build a case in my head about your wife. You losing weight and getting pale, blaming her for it all, saying you know what she is… is she a vampire, too? Is she the one who bit you?"

Skye laughed. "Christ no. And she's not a succubus either. She's just a nagging, soul-draining, passive-aggressive codependent bitch."

"Wow. You're really a chauvinistic prick, aren't you?"

"Better than being pussy whipped."

I dropped it. I had bigger fish to fry than trying to bring this macho jackass into the Twenty-first century. Namely the fact that I was in a roomful of vampires.

I know I keep harping on that, but really—it's not the sort of shit that happens all the time to me. Or, like—*ever.*

"Say, man," I said to Skye, "any chance we can roll back this tape to the point where we were still friends? I just walk out of here and we all call it a day?"

Skye made a face as if pretending to consider it. "Mmm—no, I don't see that happening."

"You want to make a deal of some kind?"

"Nah," he said. "You got nothing I want. Except the O-positive."

"AB neg," I corrected.

"Never tried that."

"You wouldn't like it. Goes right to your hips."

The wattage on his smile was dimmer. Jaunty banter can buy only so many seconds and then it's back to business.

I tried to keep my face neutral, but my pulse was like a jazz drum solo.

"I'm going to throw something out here," I said. I could hear a tremor in my voice. Fuck it.

"Oh, please." He gestured to the four killers and they started forward.

"Wait! Just hear me out. What have you got to lose?"

The thugs looked at Skye. West gave a 'why not?' kind of shrug.

Skye sighed. "Okay, what is it? Last words? A little begging?" he suggested.

"Mm, more like last threat."

"This I got to hear."

The five of them looked genuinely interested.

"Okay, so here you are, five vampires. That's some really scary shit, am I right? I mean creatures of the night and all that."

He nodded, nothing to disagree with.

"To most people that's enough to make them go apeshit crazy. I mean… vampires. Not your everyday thing. It opens up all kinds of metaphysical questions. If vampires exist, what *else* does. If there are supernatural monsters, does that mean God and the Devil are real. You follow me?"

"Sure. We get that a lot."

"And I'm outnumbered here. Five to one. Tough odds without you fellows being the undead. So—why ain't I scared?"

His eyes narrowed.

"I mean, yeah, my pulse is racing and I'm sweating. But do I look as scared as I should be? I don't do I? Now—why is that?"

"So you put up a good front. It'll be a good anecdote later," he said. "For us."

"Maybe he's got a hammer and stake," suggested West.

That got a laugh.

"Nope."

My heart rate had to be close to two hundred. It was machine-gun fire in my chest.

"Coupla garlic bulbs in your pocket?" asked East.

"Nah. I don't even like it on my pizza."

"You don't have any backup," said North. "And you don't got your gun."

My blood pressure could have scalded paint off a battleship. I wiped sweat off my brow with my thumb.

"Okay, jokes over," snapped Skye. "What's the punch line here? Why aren't you as scared as you should be?"

I smiled.

"I'll show you."

The first time it happened, way back when I was thirteen, it took almost half an hour. I screamed and cried and rolled around on the floor. First time's always the hardest. Each time since it was easier. My grandmother and her sister could do it in the time it took you to snap your fingers. My best time was during a foot chase back when I was with Minneapolis PD. I was running down the guy who'd beaten his wife with the extension cord. He saw me coming and ducked into his apartment, I kicked the door and he came out of the bedroom with a gun and opened up. I went through the change in the time it took me to leap through the doorway. Like the snap of my fingers. One minute me, next minute *different* me.

I tore the shit out of him. I lost my badge and pension and had to make up all sorts of excuses. On the plus side, I didn't die, which *would* have happened if I hadn't managed the change so fast. I'm only mortal when I look like one.

That night in Skye's office wasn't my best time. Maybe third or fourth best. Say, two, three seconds. It felt like an explosion. It hurts. Feels like my heart is bursting, like cherry bombs are detonating inside my muscles. It starts in the chest, then ripples out from there as muscle mass changes and is reassigned in new ways. Bones warp, crack and re-form. Nails tear through the flesh of my fingers and toes, my jaw shifts and the longer teeth spiked through the gums. It's bloody and it's ugly and it hurts like a motherfucker.

But the end result is a stunner. A real kick-ass dramatic moment that wows the audience.

I think all four of the thugs screamed. They jerked back from me, looks of shock and horror on their faces. If I wasn't so deeply into the moment I would have smiled at the irony. Monsters being scared by a monster.

I crouched in the center of the room, hands flexing, claws streaked with blood, hot saliva dripping from my mouth onto my chest.

It would have been cool and dramatic to have said, "Surprise!" to them the way Skye had said it to me, but my mouth was no longer constructed for human speech. All I could do was roar.

I did.

And then I launched at them.

Vampires are strong. Four or five times stronger than an ordinary human.

Werewolves?

Hell, we're a whole different class.

I slammed into West with both sets of front claws. He flew apart like he was made of paper and watery red glue. North and East tried to take me high and low, but they'd have done better to try and run. I brought my knee up into East's jaw as he went for the low tackle and his head burst like a casaba melon. I caught North by the throat and squeezed. Red geysered up from the stump of his neck as his head fell away. South backed away, putting himself between me and Skye, arms spread, making a more heroic stand than I'd have thought. I tore the heart from his chest. Turns out, vampires *need* their hearts.

Skye had my gun in his hands. He racked the slide and buried the barrel against me as I leaped over the desk. He got off four shots. They hurt.

Like wasp stings.

Maybe a little less.

I don't load my piece with silver bullets. I'm not an idiot.

He looked into my eyes and I would like to think that he saw the error of his ways. Don't fuck with the innocent. Don't fuck with my clients. My clients are *mine*, like members of my pack. Mess with them and the pack leader has to put you down. Has to.

So I did.

* * *

She saw me coming from across the street, her face concerned and confused. I was wearing a different pair of pants and different shoes. My own had been torn to rags during the change. Stuff I was wearing used to belong to the bartender. He didn't them anymore. He'd been on the same team as Skye and the four goons.

I opened the door and climbed in behind the wheel.

"Are you all right, Ro?" she asked, studying my face. "Are you hurt? Is that blood?"

I dabbed at a dot on my cheek. Missed a spot. I pulled a tissue out of my jacket pocket and wiped my cheek.

"Just ketchup," I said.

"You stopped for *food?*" she demanded, eyes wide.

"It was on the house. I was hungry. No biggie."

She stared at me and then looked at the club across the street. The snow was getting heavier, the ground was white and it was starting to coat the street.

"What happened in there?"

I put the key into the ignition.

"I had a long talk with your ex. I told him that you were feeling threatened and uncomfortable with his actions, and asked him to back off."

"What did he say?"

"He won't be bothering you anymore."

"Just like that? He agreed to leave me alone just like that?" She snapped her fingers.

"More or less. I told him that I had some friends on the force and in L and I, and made it clear that I could make his life *more* uncomfortable than he was waking yours. He didn't like it," I said, "but—" I let the rest hang.

"And he *agreed?*"

"Take my word for it. He's out of your life."

She continued to study me for several long seconds. I waited her out and I saw the moment when she shifted from doubt and fear to belief and acceptance. She closed her eyes, sagged back against the seat, put her face in her hands and began to cry.

I gripped the wheel and looked out at the falling snow, hiding the smile that kept trying to creep onto my mouth. I was digging the P.I. business. Fewer rules than when I was on the cops. It allowed me to be closer to the street, to go hunting deeper into the forest.

Even so—and despite what I'd said to Skye—I *was* pretty rattled that he'd been a vampire. I mean, being who and what I am I always suspected other things were out there in the dark, but until now I'd never met them. Now I knew. How many vampires were there? *Where* were they? Would they be coming for me?

I didn't have any of those answers. Not yet.

I also wondered what *else* was out there? I could feel the excitement racing through me. I wanted to find out. Good or bad, I wanted to find out.

I reached out a hand and patted Mrs. Skye's trembling shoulder. It felt good to know that one of the pack was safe now. It felt right. It made me feel powerful and satisfied on a lot of different levels. I knew that I was going to want to feel this way again. And again.

The snow swirled inside the thickening shadows.

Inside my head the wolf howled.

JAMES ROY DALEY

"Wait!" Jennifer said, somewhat urgently. She was standing in the door-way with a white coffee mug in her hand, looking excited and worried and absolutely beautiful. The cute little hearts on her silk pajamas were shiny and red, complementing the cherry polish on her fingers and toes. Her dark hair was cut boldly short. If her face wasn't so stunningly gorgeous the cut may have looked terrible because she had a boy's haircut, really. It was brave and it worked, but somehow it seemed best suited for a nine-year-old brat with ice-cream stains on his t-shirt and the knees knocked out of his blue jeans.

Richard, standing on the driveway next to his car, turned towards his wife. Complementing his bright green eyes and his slender nose was a smile that seemed more dimple than lip. With a smirk, he said, "What is it?"

"Just come here for a minute."

"But—" Richard had a travel bag in his left hand and his car keys in his right. He lifted them up and flaunted them, as if doing so was a statement onto itself.

"I know, honey," Jennifer said, using her 'baby-needs-some-loving' voice. "I know, but I have to tell you something. It's important."

Richard unloaded a hearty laugh. "Now? You need to tell me something important, now? The clock is ticking and I've got to go! Steve is probably wondering where I am already."

"Please, hon. I thought it could wait but now I don't think it can." She tilted her head to one side, scrunched up her expression and stood on her tippy-toes. Coffee splashed inside the mug.

Richard placed his luggage on the driveway and dragged his feet towards his wife. With his shoulders slumped, his eyes sad, and his face long, he looked like he was visiting his mother on death row. Should have been a stage actor. "What is it?"

Jennifer wrapped her arms around his waist and kissed him on the lips. Once the kiss was planted she nuzzled into him, and said, "I love you."

Richard laughed. "Well that's fantastic. I love you, too."

"No, I want you to *really* hear me. I love you, Richard Beach. I love you with all my heart. You're the best thing that ever happened to me, and I'm unconditionally yours."

"Aww…" Richard felt his belly flip as an unexpected batch of tears threatened to break free from their hiding place. She had said that very thing on their wedding day; it was part of her vows. Hearing it again was wonderful, and—*my Lord*, he treasured this woman. She was everything he wanted and more. She was artistic and beautiful; she knew how to make him feel like the luckiest man alive. Every hour they spent together seemed better than the one before it. And sure, his friends might argue that they were still in that honeymoon stage; they might even point out that things were bound to change, but still—if Jennifer wasn't the perfect woman he wasn't sure such a thing existed. With his eyebrows raised and his arms around her, he granted her a soft and loving squeeze. "You're so sweet."

"Tell me that you love me."

A smile blossomed. "I love you."

"No… really *tell* me. Make me understand."

Richard kissed his wife with as much passion as he could muster. He ran one hand along the center of her back while caressing her neck with the other. He whispered, "I love you Jennifer Samantha Beach. I love you more than you'll ever know. I'd die for you in a heartbeat, because you are the very best part of me. You are my everything; my center; my one. I'm so lucky to have you in my life, Jenn. I know it and I'll never forget it. I love you, baby-doll. I love you; I love you; I love you." He kissed her again.

Exploiting his emotions felt liberating and fabulous. He wanted the moment to last forever. It didn't. Jennifer pulled away while their lips were connected. She took him by the hand and looked him in the eye.

All business, she said, "I'm pregnant."

Richard flinched. "What?"

"You heard me. I'm pregnant and I want to keep the baby." Her eyes stayed with his, and when he tried to look away she gave his arm a yank. "How do you feel about that?"

Feeling manipulated, which wasn't a feeling his wife evoked very often, Richard allowed a moment of undisciplined honesty. "Shocked."

"That's a far cry from being overwhelmed with joy."

"Yeah, but—" A fumbling of words led to: "I thought the doctor said you'd never have children? What happened to that?"

Jennifer huffed, offended. "This is good news, right? You love me more than I'll ever know, correct?"

"I'm just—"

"You're not happy."

"I'm surprised, is all—of course I'm happy."

"You don't look happy. You don't *sound* happy either."

Richard turned towards his car, ignoring the fact that his wife was perturbed. He needed get behind the wheel and drive, because continuing this conversation was dangerous and disturbing and an assessment of his thoughts wasn't going to help anything. He *wasn't* happy; that was the truth of the matter. He wasn't the slightest bit pleased. If anything, he felt scared. And maybe a little sick.

He said, "I've got to get going."

"Just like that? You're leaving me?"

Richard swallowed back whatever emotions were bubbling to the surface. He could feel a cold shiver sashaying up his spine as his stomach churned into concrete. "Look," he said, faking a smile. "I'm happy. This is great. We're going to start a family and I think that's excellent, but I have to go—Steve's waiting. Let's talk about it later."

Jennifer's eyes morphed into slits. She wasn't thrilled but she didn't want to fight. "Will you call me?"

"I'll try, but you know how work gets. If I don't get a chance to call you tonight I'll see you in three days."

"Are you mad?"

"Mad?" Richard smiled, and this time he didn't fake it. "I'm not mad. This is great news, honey… really. Like I said, I'm just surprised. I thought we were going to adopt." He kissed her then. It was uncomfortable and clunky and the opposite of affectionate. And although he wanted to restate the fact that he loved her, somehow he couldn't find the words.

He turned away with a sigh, made for the car, and tossed his travel bag into the trunk. After he jumped behind the wheel he gave his wife a little nod and hit the road. Lips pursed, dimples lost, he didn't look back. He didn't even wave. Five minutes later he parked against the curb so he could cry his eyes out without driving into a tree.

* * *

They'd been sitting next to each other for thirty-five long minutes and Steven Wendelle knew damn-well that something was bothering Richard from the moment he sat down in the car. He could see it in Richard's eyes and hear in his voice, which wasn't exactly non-stop with discussion. The pain appeared to be rooted directly into the lines of his face, chewing at him like a virus, turning him into an old man before his time. But Steven was a good friend, his *best* friend, and sometimes a best friend must bite his tongue. He figured this was one of those times. Besides, the conversation would happen sooner or later. It always did, once Richard was ready. He wasn't the type of guy to bottle things up forever.

Thirty-five minutes became forty-five. Forty-five became an hour and fifteen. The grace period was over; it was time to put dinner on the table.

"Okay," Steve said. "Spill it."

"What's that?" Richard's voice was little more than a croak.

"I'm not blind, you know. I'm not stupid either. Clearly, something's wrong. Tell me what's bothering you, otherwise the rest of our journey is gonna be painful."

Richard took a moment, not because he didn't want to talk with his friend but because he needed a moment to put his thoughts into words. Finally he settled on, "It's Jenn."

"I figured. You guys fighting?"

"I wish it were so simple. No, we're not fighting. In fact, we've been getting along wonderfully."

Steven's face turned grave. He tapped a hand against his leg, saying, "She's sick." It wasn't a question.

"No, that's not it."

"No?"

"No. She's not sick, she's—oh, this stinks."

"What is it?"

Fingers tightened around the steering wheel. "She's pregnant."

"What?"

"You heard me. She's *pregnant.*"

"Oh shit."

"I know."

"I thought you said she couldn't get pregnant?"

"That's what the doctor told us. Twice."

Steve looked absolutely stunned. Time rolled by. Finally the question was asked, the one Richard had been asking himself all morning. "What are you going to do about it?"

"I don't know."

"Are you going to tell her?"

A deep breath. "I don't think I can. It'll ruin everything."

"You can't let her have the baby, you know. Don't even think it."

"Oh, I know. Letting the pregnancy continue isn't an option, but she won't have an abortion. I can't even ask."

"Are you sure?"

"Yes, I'm sure. An abortion is out of the question."

"If not that, what? What's left?"

"Well, to be honest, I was thinking of poisoning her. I'd be careful not to kill her, of course. But a high dose of those-morning after pills might, well—you know. Maybe I could crush them up and slip 'em into her food for a week or two."

"Will that work?"

Richard's voice suggested it was a long shot, when he said, "Honestly, I can't really say. I think you're supposed to take them the next day, after sex. I don't know—I don't know what to do, Steve. I'm lost."

They drove for another hour, stopped for lunch, and continued on. Conversation was minimal and for the most part, light-hearted. At one point Steve offered, "If there's anything I can do, just ask." But there was nothing he could do, nothing obvious anyhow, and both men knew it.

Day became evening.

They drove along a forgotten highway that few cars traveled. Cedar trees to the left of them, cedar trees to the right. A large hawk flew overhead as they turned onto a dirt road that led to a pathway that could hardly be deemed a trail. Deep in the woods, they were. Lost with the black bears and the insects, the crows and the deer. Lost in a place they called their own. Steve had purchased the land years earlier. *Picked it up for a song,* he said. *The money he paid his lawyer to square the deal was equal to value of the land,* he said. Steven Wendelle was no bullshit artist, and Richard knew he spoke the truth. Twenty acres of nothing—it was absolutely perfect.

As the sun began setting and the moon began to rise, they stripped down to their underwear and placed their clothing in the car. Sitting on a log, hands in their laps, they waited. Quietly. Peacefully. The August air was warm. It was fresh. The fact that Richard lied about working for the week-end wasn't relevant. He loved his wife and she loved him. He also loved the sounds of the forest, which were comforting and serene. All thoughts concerning Jennifer and the seed in her belly was set aside. Other things were swiftly becoming more significant.

Richard was the first to feel the change coming on. He felt it in his spine and in his teeth. His knees popped and his shoulders buckled. Then, as he watched his hands grow long and his fingers turn to claws, he tried to articulate how much he enjoyed the transformation. What escaped his throat could only be described as a growl. Animal thoughts consumed him. A thirst for blood boiled inside his brain.

Steve didn't notice these things happening to Richard; he was too busy becoming a monster.

The hunt would soon begin.

* * *

On the third day, right around the time Jennifer was expecting her husband to arrive home from his monthly trip, there was a knock on the door. She looked out the window and was surprised to find a police car in the driveway. She opened the door cautiously, wondering if she had done something wrong.

Two officers stood by the door. Expressions were solemn. The one that spoke first looked young enough to be in high school. He was lanky with eyes that bugged out of his head. The other cop, thirty years his senior, had a chocolate complexion and dark hair.

Jennifer sized them up quickly: the veteran was showing the rookie the ropes; they probably didn't have a thing in common.

"Mrs. Beach?" The rookie said, clasping his fingers together.

"Yes?"

The veteran stepped forward with his chin raised, taking control of the situation. In his hand was an envelope, which he gripped very tightly. "Are you Mrs. *Jennifer* Beach?"

Jenn nodded. "What seems to be the problem?"

The older cop removed his hat and held it near his chest. The rookie followed suit.

"Mrs. Beach, my name is Officer Wright and this is Lieutenant Moscowitz. I'm afraid we have some bad news for you."

Jennifer's eyes danced from man to man. She looked at the hats in their hands and the way they were standing. She looked into eyes brimming with shame. The rookie's shoulders dropped an inch as his stare found the floor. Oh, shit. They were about to say something terrible. They were about to say—

"There's been an accident."

Something inside Jennifer collapsed. Or died. The earth tilted on one corner and the air thinned. As the room began to spin she managed to say, "It's Richard."

"I'm afraid so."

"There's been an accident."

"Right again, Mrs. Beach—on highway 78. I'm sorry to inform you—

(oh please God no)

—that your husband—

(don't say it, for the love of God)

—is no longer with us, Mrs. Beach,—

(I don't want to hear this… please tell me I'm dreaming)

—I'm afraid that he's dead."

A question tumbled from her lips: "What happened?"

"It happened this morning around seven-thirty; a head-on collision. There were no survivors."

A one-sided conversation was laid out like brickwork. Officer Wright explained and described and enlightened and in the end it didn't amount to a hill of beans. Richard was dead, gone forever. Nothing else mattered.

At some point the envelope was placed inside her trembling fingers and the officers offered condolences that came from the heart. A short while later they left her to grieve. Alone. She couldn't be more alone if she tried.

And when she closed the door on a world that was eternally altered, she wondered how she'd ever find the strength to face the day.

* * *

The next three days were arguably—or perhaps not so arguably—the hardest days of Jennifer's life. She was still a young woman, twenty-nine this past March, and her life had been cruising along rather smoothly. On paper it may not have seemed that way. Her mother died when she was barely eight years old. The death had been hard on her, of course. But that was twenty-one years ago and twenty-one years is a long time for a woman not quite thirty years old. She could remember her mom's face, but mostly from photographs. She could remember her mother's voice, somewhat, and she had the memory of her mom gardening in the backyard. After that it was just little clips and snippets, not full-blown memories, really. More like recollections.

Her father was a different story.

He was an alcoholic she visited twice a year; his name was Ted. He wasn't a terrible man; he never intentionally hurt Jennifer or abused her physically, but he prayed at the altar of intoxication and was very devoted to his religion.

Ted took a bus into town on the day of the funeral and offered what he was able in terms of condolences. But Jennifer could smell the whiskey coming from his mouth and see it in his blood-red eyes. And when he announced that he couldn't stay Jennifer felt a weight lift from her shoulders that was heavier than she realized. She was already dealing with one catastrophe. When she looked into her father's slack-jawed face she felt like she was dealing with another.

It wasn't a perfect life, as no life is. Her mother was dead and her father was—for lack of a better word—gone. But it wasn't a bad life either, and she wasn't an only child. She had a younger sister named Kate who was just as bright and beautiful as she was. And it was Kate that embraced her after the funeral, although the reasons for it were not what Jennifer expected.

* * *

It was a day of tears. Richard and Steven were buried in the same cemetery at the same time. A double funeral at noon, two separate wakes shortly after. Jennifer hosted one; Steven Wendelle's parents hosted the other. For Jennifer, the last of her guests didn't leave until almost seven. And when they did, Jennifer and Kate found themselves sitting at the kitchen table, surrounded with food and beverages. The refrigerator had already been filled to capacity; the countertops were equally loaded. Jennifer was grateful for the generosity of her friends and family, but what she was supposed to do with so many provisions was beyond her.

Kate said, "I'd like to stay with you, if that's alright."

Jennifer was drinking rum and coke, unlike Kate who was drinking gin. Alcohol wasn't something they indulged in often due to the negative influence it had on their childhood. But here, now, it was just what the doctor ordered.

Jennifer took a drink, then said, "It's okay. I'll be fine. Honest I will. You should be home with Mike, not here with me."

Mike was Kate's husband. They had been married four years.

Kate, who was looking a little tired, said, "Actually, no. I don't think so. I want to stay here. Do you mind?"

"Why? Is everything alright?"

Eyes fixed on the table, Kate fought against a faltering voice. She tucked a lock of hair behind her ear and said, "I'm not offering charity, I'm asking for a favor." She looked up, expecting her sister to press for details. When it didn't happen she reluctantly explained her situation. "Mike and I are finished. He's been cheating on me, and we've been fighting, and our fights have been getting physical."

Jennifer was shocked. "He's beating you?"

"Not exactly." Kate shrugged. She took a drink. Ice cubes clinked inside the glass, accentuating the silence of the room. "To be honest, we've been beating on each other. He never hit me first, but he hit me a few times after I hit him. And I *have* hit him. *Hard.* And he deserved it. But I can't do this any longer. I can't sit in the house alone, wondering when he's coming home, or *if* he's coming home. I've been following him around at night and he's been—oh, God. It's so bad. Everything is *so* screwed up." Kate swallowed back a sob, before saying, "If Richard was still, well—you know— *alive* (the word came out in a whisper), I wouldn't ask. I'd probably just deal with my problems until Mike kicked me out or moved out himself. But if you're going to be *here* alone, and I'm going to be *there* alone—crying, or fighting with my asshole husband, well—" A tear rolled down her face. "I want to be here with you. I'm asking if I can stay."

Jennifer took Kate by the hand. Nobody would call her selfish at a time like this, but somehow, that's how she felt. She had been so caught up in her own life that she failed to glimpse into her sister's. Kate's world had been falling apart for however long and she didn't even realize it. It was shameful, really. And yes, it *was* selfish. Worst of all, Kate was more than just family; she was Jennifer's truest friend.

Voice miserable, Jennifer said, "Of course you can stay with me. Oh, hon. I'm so sorry."

"I'm sorry too.

"This sucks, doesn't it?"

Kate wiped a tear from her face using the palm of her hand. "It sure does."

They cried and drank and talked for hours. Later they watched *Legally Blonde*. Much like the alcohol, an hour and a half of Elle Woods seemed to be just what the doctor ordered. Kate stayed the night. The next day she went home and packed her bags. And three months later, when Richard showed up at the door, dressed in the suit he was buried in, it was Kate that let him inside.

* * *

Kate was living with Jennifer full time now, and her relationship with Mike was officially over. They talked on the phone. They went out for coffee. They slept together one final night and it was during sex that Kate discovered her love for the man was truly gone. The trust had vanished, the bond was destroyed, and the bed they shared seemed to be carrying some terrible secrets—secrets that would haunt her for as long as she allowed them to. Her future felt like a better place without the damaged remains of her marriage clinging to it like a bad smell. So she asked her 'soon to be ex-husband' not to call, and although there were many nights that he wanted to, he respected her wishes and left her alone.

When the doorbell rang, Kate was cleaning up the kitchen and Jennifer was, unfortunately, in the hospital. She had been having problems with her pregnancy—reoccurring pains were getting worst as time moved on.

The last batch of agony was almost four weeks ago, three and a half weeks into her second trimester. It lasted nearly three days. During that time she found herself buckled over on the floor, screaming at the top of her lungs, one hand clutching her belly, the other tightened into a fist that was pounding on the hardwood like a jackhammer. And although Kate was absolutely furious with her, Jennifer wouldn't visit the doctor until well after the pain had subsided. Kate didn't understand why; she *couldn't* understand why. And Jennifer couldn't explain it. But deep inside she knew something was terribly askew in a way that made her feel nauseous with fright. The child inside her body was scaring the hell of her, not just because of the pain she felt but also because of the atrocious thoughts that had been swirling around inside her head like a cyclone.

Jennifer was having nightmares—*terrible* nightmares on a nightly basis. She kept thinking about *Rosemary's Baby*, not the movie but the book. She had started reading it the day before she told Richard she was pregnant. She finished it forty-five minutes before the policemen gave her the news. Being the type of person that enjoyed Christmas stories in December and spooky stories on Halloween, she thought it'd be fun to read Ira Levin while pregnant. How unfortunate. Now her days were spent wondering if she'd find herself surrounded by doctors and nurses that were chanting "Hail Satan" after she gave birth to a child with a forked tail, little horns, and eyes that belonged to a goat.

When Jennifer finally found the courage to have her herself examined—a full week after she was sprawled out on the floor, kicking, screaming, and drowning in pain—the doctors were seriously concerned. Not just for the welfare of the unborn child but for Jennifer as well. For reasons they couldn't explain Jennifer's uterus had been torn in several places and she was bleeding internally. She also had bruises on her fallopian tubes, a pair of swollen ovaries, and a cracked rib. Needless to say, she was at risk of losing the baby. Worst than that, her life seemed to be in jeopardy as well.

Her stay in the hospital lasted for five days. During that time she had two minor operations. After that, Dr. P. Hollis, the head physician, made her promise that she'd return immediately if the abnormal pain started to flare up again. She agreed.

Earlier in the day the pain returned. And although she was afraid to have the baby examined while the aches were progressing, the fear of the unknown had taken control of the situation. She left for the hospital alone, informing Kate by phone hours after she arrived.

Kate swung the door open without looking through the window. Had she looked, things would have played out differently.

Richard was there, leaning a dislocated shoulder against the wall. He looked bad. Beyond bad. His back was twisted; his neck was broken. The top half of his skull had been crushed like an orange that had been stepped on by a very large foot. Both of his eyes were still in place, but one had turned dark and the other sat deep within its damaged socket. Parts of his brain bulged through a long crack in his face and his bottom lip had been torn free.

Kate stepped back, fingers on her mouth, eyes like baseballs. Her jaw dropped as her heart rate accelerated. She was going to scream—*had* to scream, because screaming was the only logical thing to do.

Surely, this *couldn't* be Richard. It *couldn't* be the man she considered a perfect match for her sister. Not him.

She looked away from his face.

Hanging from his shattered frame was a suit that must have been worn by the Incredible Hulk because it was tattered and frayed in ways that didn't make sense. The pale, dehydrated skin on Richard's hands seemed to belong on a living corpse. More so when he lifted those hands—hands that were covered in a thin layer of dirt, hands that were connected to arms with unnatural looking joints and elbows, hands that were reaching out.

Oh God, he was reaching out.

Kate's mouth was still wide open, but the scream she was looking for was hiding deep inside. Soon she'd find it, and when she did she would set it free. She would—

"Wait," Richard said. He tried to smile but with half his teeth smashed out he looked absolutely ghastly. "Please wait. Don't scream. I'm still alive––so help me, Kate. For the love of God, help me."

"Oh shit," Kate said, staggering back another foot. Her hand remained on her mouth; her bottom lip began to quiver. "What the hell is this?"

"I'm not dead—I was *never* dead." Richard dragged his left foot forward. His balance was reassigned and his right foot followed. The movement alone looked painful. "Help me come inside."

Just like that, Kate started crying. She couldn't help it. Her body was shaking and her knees trembled and full-sized tears were running down her cheeks. Had she not just used the bathroom she may have suffered an accident. To say Richard's presence was making her nervous would be like saying a pitchfork in the face might leave a mark.

She babbled, "But—but—"

"Help me Kate, I mean it." Richard slumped into the house and tossed a broken arm around his sister-in-law.

Kate screamed then. It slipped out before she knew it would happen. She screamed long and loud and when she was finished she screeched, "Oh, I'm sorry. Oh Richard, I'm *so* sorry. What do you want me to do?"

"Help me get to bed—and I need some water."

Despite the way he looked, and despite the fact that he smelled worse than death, Kate helped Richard into the bedroom and assisted him onto the bed. Doing so made her skin crawl, but what else could she do? Running away was possible, but this was *Richard*. He was family *and* friend. And most of all, he was in dire need of help. Besides, the notion of running came with an unsettling side-thought: *what if he chased her? What would happen then?*

Once Richard was settled Kate turned away, planning to fetch the water. Mostly she just wanted to be somewhere else, away from him, away from the monster.

Richard grabbed her by the arm. "Where's Jennifer?"

Still terrified, Kate said, "At the hospital. I was on my way to see her." This wasn't entirely true but in another thirty minutes it would've been.

"Why?"

"She's having complications with her pregnancy."

Richard mumbled, "I bet she is." Then he looked out the window, sizing up the darkening sky. "Do you know what time is it?"

"Seven-thirty? Maybe eight?"

Richard groaned. "Listen, Kate. Listen to my words and hear me well. Don't tell anyone I'm here. Don't call the doctors; don't phone the police.

Don't explain things to your husband and don't go yapping to your father. It's got to be our little secret, Kate. You understand me? Nobody can know I'm back."

"But why?!" Kate's emotions were getting pulled in every direction now. She felt like laughing and screaming and yanking the hair from her head in bunches. "You need help, Richard! You need medical attention right away!"

"No!"

"Are you serious?! Look at you, Richard! You look like—" She was going to say that he looked like a goddamn stiff but instead she asked: "What happened? I was at the funeral, you know... I was there!"

Richard coughed. Greenish-brown pus-like drool dribbled along the place his bottom lip should have been. He said, "Me too. I was inside the box, Kate. Inside that fucking coffin, unable to move, unable to scream." Richard paused. His thoughts twisted this way and that. Suddenly he wanted to explain everything. He wanted to tell her that he was alive when they scraped him off the road, and when they brought him into the morgue and embalmed him. He wanted her to know that he was alive when they boxed him up and covered him in dirt. He wanted her to understand what type of man he *really* was, and that he couldn't be killed in traditional ways. There was so much he wanted to say, so much he needed to explain. Choosing his words carefully, he said, "They thought I was dead, and I might have *looked* dead, but a car accident can't kill me. Not ever. And in time I get better. I *always* get better."

Kate couldn't believe what she was hearing. It was impossible. It was *insane*. But she knew what she was *seeing*, and what she was seeing had to be some type of sick joke. She asked, "How can this be happening?"

"Doesn't matter. What happened to Steven?"

"Who?"

"Steve, the—"

Kate realized what Richard was asking. She said, "Oh. He died in the accident." As an after-thought, she added, "With you."

Richard's thoughts turned a corner. He wondered if Steven was still trapped in his coffin, scratching the silk, trying to get out. He pushed the thoughts aside and said, "You've got to call Jennifer... tell her to come home right away. Can you do that for me?"

"Of course, I'll call her right now. But Richard, what in God's name should I tell her?"

"Tell her to come home. If she wants to know why, say I need to talk with her. It's very important."

* * *

When Jennifer hung up the phone her face had become pale. *Richard was back. He was alive. He wanted her to come home. It was important.*

She couldn't believe it.

Alone in her hospital room, she pulled herself from bed and dressed quickly. She ran her fingers through hair that no longer looked stylishly brave, but messy and without a hint of fashion sense. She made for the exit with her shoes untied, her skirt on sideways, and her travel bag hanging wide open. A car-ride later she shuffled through the front door of her home, sun setting in the west, moon rising in the east, clutching her belly with her fingers.

The child was kicking; the pain was getting worse. If it didn't soon subside she was going to find herself buckled over on the floor, screaming bloody murder. Again.

As she staggered down the hallway towards (her late husband) Richard, the bedroom door blasted open and Kate stepped into view. Her eyes were entirely different now. They looked swollen and red, like she had been screwing her fists into her sockets for the last five years.

She grabbed Jennifer by the shoulders and said, "You need to brace yourself."

"Let me see him."

"No! Listen to me Jenn; you need to prepare for what you're about to see. Richard is back, but he looks bad. He looks *really* fucking bad."

Jennifer cringed. She hadn't heard her sister use the F word since she was fourteen years old. She said, "I'll be alright."

"Brace yourself! I'm not kidding about this."

Jennifer pushed Kate away forcefully and plowed into the room. She figured she'd be able to handle it. No problem. She was a grown woman, for crying out loud. Besides, how bad could it be?

Richard was on the bed. His body was angled unnaturally and his suit was covered in dirt. Chunks of brain were resting on the pillow. A large bug ran across the sheets as another scurried up the wall. To summarize, he looked like an embalmed corpse that had been smashed to pieces with a sledgehammer and pulled from the earth he'd been buried in. And Jennifer, truth be told, didn't brace herself for what she was about to see; she didn't brace for anything.

"Oh my God!" she shrieked, with eyes growing wide. "Richard, is that you?"

Looking like a zombie, he said, "Listen to me, baby-doll. This is critical."

The thing living inside Jennifer kicked.

She staggered, clutching her belly.

At the same moment, Richard felt his spine expand. He said, "You need to kill the baby inside you. You need to do it right now. Get a clothes hanger; push it in. Abort the child."

Kate stepped into the room, quite literally trembling and pulling at her hair. She said, "What are you talking about—abort the child? *Now?!* What the hell is happening here?!"

Richard's knees popped and his shoulders buckled. His teeth elongated as his fingers turned to claws. "Hurry!" he managed. "Before it's too late!"

Eyes on her husband, Jennifer groaned. She could feel something chewing her apart. Then her knees faltered and she dropped to the floor. Pressing her back against the nearest wall, her body convulsed. Not once, but three times quickly.

"My baby," she whimpered.

She ripped open her blouse; buttons popped in different directions. Looking at her stomach, and seeing the strange way the child was moving beneath her skin, she almost understood. *Almost.* Then when she looked at Richard an important piece of the puzzle clicked into position. It felt like a hard slap in the face, and it was horrifying. She had a monster living inside her, a goddamn monster, trying to get out—Richard's child.

And Richard was—

Gone.

In his place was something most people will never see: half man, half wolf, bones mending, muscles growing, nose becoming snout, arms becoming legs, hair morphing into fur, hands turning into paws, eyes still green, still the windows to the soul of a man that's able to comprehend the situation. But his mouth was growing larger and more dangerous with each passing moment. Teeth seemed to be everywhere. Jaws opened far too wide and words escaped like hostages. They were hard to recognize, but much harder to ignore:

"Abort. The child."

Kate, standing in the center of the room with her hands in the air, looked away from Richard in horror. She saw Jennifer leaning against the wall with her blouse pulled open and her skirt hiked up. Her knees were shaking and her pink underwear had turned red. She had one hand cradling her belly as blood leaked from a long tear in her skin, through her trembling fingers, over her wedding ring (a ring she couldn't bring herself to remove), and across her unpainted nails. She said, "Please Kate, Richard's right. Get a clothes hanger. Help me abort the child."

Kate watched her sister endure two quick spasms before a mist of blood sprayed from her mouth. It ran a line down her chin and dripped onto an exposed breast. There was blood between her legs, a dark red puddle. It was growing larger. Kate didn't understand what was happening and she didn't understand why, but she knew one thing for sure: her sister was dying, being ripped apart from the inside.

Yes. They had to abort the child.

She looked across the room and her eyes locked on the closet door. In no time at all the door was open and she was standing in the doorway, pushing bags out of the way with her left hand while pulling shirts off hangers with her right. But there was a problem: all the hangers were made with plastic. She couldn't see any of the old-fashion metal kind. She grabbed a jacket and a vest and threw them to the ground in a pile.

Jennifer screamed.

Richard growled.

And Kate, cursing under her breath, saw what she was looking for: a rusty old hanger, nastier than a snake. She snagged it from the rack and stepped towards her sister, trying desperately to keep her eyes away from the huge thing that was laying on the bed, covered in fur, snapping its jaws, eying her like a fresh meal after a long day.

She said, "We need to get out of here!"

"No," Jennifer whispered. "Just hurry, Kate. Hurry!"

There was no time to argue so Kate bent the hanger this way and that, playing it like an accordion, trying to snap it. She didn't think she'd be able to unravel it fast enough, and time was so important now. Oh yes it was. She thought about running for the second time that evening, but Jennifer was in no position to follow her lead, and she couldn't leave her sister behind.

Richard growled, sounding like a grizzly bear.

Jennifer screamed again. And Kate screamed too, frustrated with the time she was spending. Her hands were working as fast as they could but it wasn't fast enough. She didn't think the hanger would ever break but suddenly it did. It broke right where she wanted. It almost seemed like a miracle.

Straightening the wire, she turned it into a long, narrow spear. Then she dropped to the floor, positioning herself between her sister's legs.

Jennifer's eyes widened. She looked desperate now—desperate and in serious pain. She lifted her knees, stretched her legs apart, and grabbed a hold of her blood-soaked underwear. She pulled the dripping cloth to one side, exposing her vagina. Gasping and begging, she said, "Do it, Kate. Kill it. *Kill* it!"

Kate caught a frightful glimpse of her sister's belly before pushing her labia apart with her fingers and plunging the wire in. But one glimpse of Jennifer's stomach getting ripped open was enough: skin splitting, muscles tearing, blood pouring to the floor in generous amounts. There was a coil of flesh that appeared to be growing and when Kate saw it her stomach clenched and she thought she might pass out. It was too late to perform a back-alley abortion. It *had* to be too late.

Looking Jennifer in the eye, Kate forced the wire deep inside.

And Jennifer, gasping her final breaths, writhing in agony, looked up. Not at Kate. Oh no. There was a monster in the room now, standing high above, gazing down at the girls with its terrible green eyes, teeth like daggers, bloodlust boiling inside its brain.

Richard was gone.

And although Jennifer knew that her husband had become something entirely different—something bred without love or affection—memory of the man she married seeped into her heart and she managed to say, "I love you with all my heart, Richard Beach. You're the best thing that ever happened to me. I'm unconditionally yours."

ANNIVERSARY
JOHN EVERSON

Margaret looked at the calendar rune and tickled her lips with her tongue. Full moon tonight. She'd been pressing her thighs together in anticipation of this day all month long. Charles only came on the night of the moon, and though her body ached for his visits, she knew that once a month, realistically, was all she could handle. There was so much to prepare for—and so much to recover from, afterwards.

She made the bed, called in sick to work—did anyone notice her sick days always coincided with the phase of the moon?—and went to the closet to find what Charles called her "ice cream" outfit.

"Those guys all think you're a cone waiting to be licked and caressed," he'd grin, evilly. "But I know better. You're a tigress. And I screeeeeem for you!" He'd howl as he said it and she'd strip out of the skin tight catsuit before letting him lay a hand on her.

"You don't want to be licking the napkin around your cone, do you?" she'd tease.

Staring at herself in the mirror, she could feel her body starting to sweat and moisten, just thinking about Charles. Her average 34 A-cup breasts looked like 36 Cs in the immodest display of the sheer, deep blue suit, and she knew her butt jiggled tantalizingly as she walked, every dip and tuck bouncing. She was not a well-endowed woman, but she made the best possible use of her assets. One of which, she realized staring at her reflection, her hair was currently not. Charles forbade her a shower on the day of the full moon, and her hair hung in flat, lazy twists across her shoulders. She'd dyed it auburn this month for a change and prayed he'd like it. Running her hands through it in a useless attempt at styling, she decided she'd have to rely on her other allure tricks. Charles wouldn't allow hairspray, either. Made him sneeze.

At the vanity in the corner of the bedroom she applied a heavy coat of electric red lipstick to match her nails, and lined her eyes in sooty black. She was ready.

First stop was the Kmart. More than a few graying heads turned her way in shock as she paraded through the white, tiled aisles. To any close stare she was stark naked in a coat of blue spray paint. An old woman stood fingering a fuzzy pink nighty in the underwear department and happened to look up as she passed. The nighty dropped to the floor. "Young lady," a scratchy high pitched voice chased her. There was a strong element of chastisement couched in those two simple words. Margaret glanced over her shoulder and flashed a crinkle eyed look. "You keep your man your way and I'll keep mine my own way," she smiled sweetly.

God, she hated people, she thought, picking up a white cotton tank. Confront them with the truth—a human body, un or thinly veiled—and they went to pieces. Religions had been built on hiding the truth of the human form. Laws had been passed on how it should be shielded and where it could be kissed. Human beings lived in denial of what they were, and she hated them for it. She knew what she was, and she was unashamed.

Shaking her head, she took the cotton t and matching bottoms, grabbed a box of popcorn, and went to the register. A high school-aged girl with braces and plastic framed glasses rang her up, pausing every few seconds to stare at her chest when she thought Margaret wasn't paying attention. "Yeah, you'll have them soon," she thought wickedly. "And you'll bind them and hide them and offer them in trade for a chain noosed around your lover's neck. Happy hooking, hon."

Striding purposefully from the store, she drove to a park nearby. The sun shone golden bright through the trees as she tossed handfuls of popcorn to the pigeons. They crowded her feet, scrambling over each other in their haste to eat. Others swooped down from the trees periodically, disturbing the complex pecking order of feeding. "Whoever pecks the most ruthlessly rules the dinner table," she thought, and wondered if she and Charles stood at the top of the food chain.

A pickup pulled into the parking lot a few yards away, and a middle-aged man stepped out. He was maybe 5'6, white, looked like a going-to-seed blue collar. Handleable. With a deliberate stretch, Margaret put her hands on the back of the bench, thrust out her chest, and spread her feet far apart on the ground. Within seconds the man answered the call.

"Mind if I sit down?" a tremulous voice asked. She did her best Madonna. "Sit or spit, I don't care," she answered, calculatedly bored. It was best not to act too forward—only look that way. She felt his weight settle onto the end of the bench, but didn't look at him.

There were only the noises of the scuffling birds for a few moments, and then he tried again.

"Um, my name's Bill," he said. She turned to meet his gaze. "Hi Bill."

"You, uh, come out here and feed the birds a lot?" he pressed on.

"Now and then."

"Married?" he braved.

"No."

Quiet again. Probably time to help him a little.

"You want to toss some," she offered, holding out the bag of popcorn.

His face lit and he slid closer to her.

"Sure."

* * *

It barely took an hour. Bill was an electrician, supposed to be at a job site. Sometimes, he admitted, he came here during lunchtime, looking for "company." She got the impression he didn't care what kind, as long as he got off. He let it slip that he was married, while his eyes massaged her chest and crotch guiltily.

"Sometimes," she said, "I like a little company, too."

She stretched, put her arm around his shoulder and trailed a nail down his biceps. He stiffened, and then looked at her face in unveiled lust. She leaned over, kissed him, and then stood.

"Want to come back to my place?"

It wasn't always this easy, but it was never that hard.

* * *

She led him by the hand down the stairs through the basement and into a nearly bare room. The walls were black painted cinderblock, the floor black tile. A white vinyl couch stood out in violent contrast in the room's center.

"I like to pretend it's night when it's day," she explained when he looked in dawning fear at the oddly decorated room. His suspicions evaporated when the blood rushed from his head to his cock as she knelt at his feet. She stripped them both, moving her supple body sinuously around his thickening waist and wrinkled rear. Laying him on the couch, she twisted and turned atop him, rubbing every inch of herself on his skin. No baths, and the scent of the man she'd brought him, that was what Charles asked. Smells drove him wild. She would not let the "other man" enter her. When he began to grow anxious for the act, she slid from the couch and worked him with mouth and hands as his own beefy palms grabbed and kneaded her flesh.

This was always the hardest part for her. Having to touch some disgusting strange man in the unclean places. She was not turned on by this—rarely did she pick up a man to whom she was sexually attracted. But she did this for Charles. She thought of the first time they'd met, when in her forward passion she'd reached inside his jogging pants in the very same park she'd picked Bill up in. Charles had kissed her lightly, and with a firm hand, had pulled her probing fingers from his crotch.

"I can only cum beneath the light of a full moon," he said softly. She was not convinced—other women just hadn't been as skilled as her, she thought somewhere deep in her lust clouded brain. His eyes looked sad as he watched her ego-deflating, vain attempts to prove him wrong. Filled with stubborn pride—and a telling, nagging wetness between her legs—she stuck out her chin and challenged, "Then visit me on the night of the full moon."

His strong features both grinned and frowned at that invitation. "I will," he promised.

She laughed inside now at her foolish naivety in extending that offer. She knew he had struggled not to accept—he'd liked her, and knew what would come of such a tryst. Ultimately, he had lost his internal battle. At her doorstep, 8 p.m. on the night of the moon he had appeared, a thin wiry man in a black t-shirt and jeans. He'd brought her roses and asked if she'd reconsidered her invitation. In answer, she'd leaned into his body, inhaling his musky, woodsy, animal scent and inserted her tongue between his lips. In moments, they'd been naked and rutting on the couch in the living room.

Beneath her absent ministrations she felt the warm stream that signaled an end to her duty. As Bill groaned in ecstasy, she reached a hand beneath the vinyl cushions searching for the chain. She needed a new couch, she thought. The cushions were cracked with age and scored with scratches. Her hand grasped what she was looking for. With a fast pull and snap, she efficiently cuffed Bill's right arm to the couch.

"Huh?" he exclaimed and grabbed for her with his free hand. She skipped easily out of his reach, watching in sad amusement as his cock deflated instantly. "What are you doing? Let Me Go!" he ordered in false bravado.

There was fear in his voice, but nothing like the tremors that would shake it as the day wore into night.

"Sorry Bill, but I need you tonight. Get some rest why don't you."

Ignoring his angered yells and curses, she picked up the clothes that littered the floor and left the room. The door clicked shut to leave Bill in blackest darkness. His bellows diminished to murmurs as she climbed the stairs to wait for the night.

* * *

When the doorbell rang at eight, Margaret was ready. Dinner was in the fridge, a crisp medley of carrots, spinach, lettuce, onions and other vegetables. The house was spotless—her only means of passing the time between locking up her guests and meeting her lover in the evening was to clean. You could eat off her floors. And maybe they would tonight, she thought entertaining erotic designs. Maybe he would spill the salad across the tile and feed each chopped vegetable to her with his lips.

Her body pulsed with anticipation as she crossed the room to let him in. She wanted this night to be perfect—it was their first anniversary. A carafe of deep ruby wine rested on the coffee table—his favorite vintage. She wore only the thin cotton underwear she'd bought this afternoon.

"Margaret," he whispered, admiring her near naked figure from the stoop. He held out a bouquet of red roses. She took them and pulled him inside. "Your hair is beautiful," he complimented, warming her to the bone.

"I need you so bad," she said, staring up into his face. He had those eyes that shifted, looked green one moment, brown the next. His face was smooth, but sharply drawn. She leaned to kiss him, and in her hurry, caught the roses between their bodies. "Ouch," she jumped and stepped back. A thorn had pricked her thigh. A thin line of red ran from the puncture to a crimson tear.

"Let me," he breathed, and knelt to lick her leg. His tongue was hot, but felt sandpapery, like a cat's. She shivered at his attentions, tousled his hair with her free hand. "Come have a drink, baby," she said, stepping back to break their contact. A few more minutes of this and they'd be fucking right there on the floor, and she wanted this night to be slow, thick—a steady building to perfect passion.

He stood, and flashing a row of gleaming white teeth, fingered her nipples, which poked like nails through the thin material.

"Whatever you say, lover."

She trembled at his voice. So much power there. A quick look at him would not give this impression. A thin nose, deep set eyes, smooth white face on a fit but not obviously muscled body. He was Joe Average, but she could sense the strangeness, the exotic reeking from his pores. Maybe that's what had attracted her to him in the first place.

They clinked glasses of heavy bordeaux together, and Margaret felt the sweat begin seeping from her body as he rumbled in his sexiest deep tone: "to us."

She drank deeply, closing her eyes to feel the fuel of the wine mixing with the fire of her lust. God, it was so hard to wait. The days between grew longer and longer and once he was here, she struggled every moment to stop herself from ripping his clothes off and mounting him without a word. At the same time, she wanted these moments before, when they could talk and just be together as the musk of their mutual lusts rose around them like a fog.

When she poured the last drops of the bottle into his open mouth, Margaret could wait no longer. His features were wild with the pull of the moon, his movements jerky as a palsied man. He licked his lips and husked the word as she pounced.

"Now."

His hands wrapped around her body in a bear hug, drawing her close. "You smell divine," he growled and proceeded to lick her arms and legs, his nose chasing cool trails across her skin. Leaping from his lap, she dragged him to his feet and in fumbling haste undid his belt and pants as he unbuttoned and shed his shirt. He stood before her then, naked, yet covered with a manly down. His public thatch was thick and long, almost braid-able. Its wildness couldn't hide the scope of the tool that hung hungry there. With a rough finger he traced a red line up her thigh.

"So, have you missed me this month?" he said from between gritted teeth.

She smiled at the ritual, and nodded affirmatively.

Tucking his finger inside the cotton panties," his voice dipped even lower. "So I feel." His hand cupped her, made her tingle, his head dipped to inhale her smell. "So I smell."

She scratched the thickening hair on his chest, her hand resting on his engorged cock. "You're the only meat for me, Charles. Let me eat you."

Acceding to her request, he dropped to the floor. Her tongue lashed him then, her teeth threatening to chew him to a bleeding pulp. He only scraped his nails deeply into her back, shredding the cotton shirt and staining it in spots with drawn blood.

He was panting then in the thick of the moon's pull, and she knew the change would soon be complete. Moving from his crotch, she posed on hands and knees beside him. He was quick to rise. With an excited tear of cotton he freed her breasts from the remains of the t-shirt, and at the same time shredded her panties, leaving a waistband dangling around her middle and swollen trails of blood on her behind. Her sex only ached more at his rough violations, and then, at last, he was mounting her doggy style there on the floor. She could feel him changing faster now, as he pounded his cock between her thighs. The nails gouging her shoulders grew sharper, the flesh meeting her butt grew prickly, as if she were being slapped by a bristled broom. Even within her, his cock altered, grew, until she screamed in spasms of ecstasy and collapsed on the floor as his frenzied motions peaked in a warm, wet rush.

"God," she huffed, "God, God, God."

A strangled "No," answered her, before turning into a howl. She felt his teeth gripping her leg, breaking the skin, sinking into the soft flesh of her calf. She had to get up, she thought, or he'd devour her. In this state, his desire overruled his mind and it didn't matter who she was.

Kicking out with her free foot, she slammed his head from her leg and launched herself down the stairs, a trail of blood marking her passage. He followed, raking claws at her thighs, tearing skin from her back as he tried to bring her down. She knew some part of him was fighting for restraint— or else she would not make it down the stairs.

With a twist she turned the knob of the door as his teeth sank into her arm. She felt a rush of wetness between her legs in answer to the pain and laughed out loud. If she let him, she'd cum again as he ripped the flesh from her bones. One day, she thought, that's exactly what would happen.

But... not... now, she grimaced, and pushed the door open.

"So you came back, finally," Bill's voice trembled from within the pitch black room.

Margaret felt Charles' weight shift as he heard the voice. She could see his ears pricking up, feel his paw leave her back as, for a second, he pointed, and then sprang.

Bill screamed his loudest then, because Charles generally went for the throat when he was really hungry.

She remembered hers' and Charles' first time, when, as she watched the hair growing from his limbs like cheese from grater, she'd realized how it had to end and as his wolfen cock had spurted its seed within her, she'd called out to her roommate.

"Cathy," she'd bellowed, in the midst of an orgasm herself, "I want you to come down and meet somebody."

Charles had flipped her over with a huge hairy paw and was going for her jugular when Cathy had cautiously peeked into the room, mere seconds later. "Bitch was probably was listening to us," Margaret had thought, and with all her strength she'd pushed Charles' muzzle in Cathy's direction.

"Get HER," she'd screeched, and somehow, even that early in their relationship, Charles had been trying to hold back the beast he was. He'd sprang and ripped out Cathy's throat in seconds and so, their monthly routine had been born.

Behind her, Charles' growls and Bill's wails were fading.

"Shoulda stuck with the noose you knew, Bill," Margaret thought as she limped up the stairs to the kitchen. The gurgled "helps," "stops" and "oh Gooooods," quit before she'd even pulled her salad from the fridge.

She went back down to eat with him, flicking on the light and sitting naked on the floor. Feral eyes looked up at her from the disemboweled carcass on the couch. She didn't share his meal. She trapped his food out of necessity, but she herself was a vegetarian.

Across the room, he slurped and chewed, wolfen head disappearing in and out of the gory chest cavity. She wished she didn't have to handle his food so much beforehand, but Charles said the scent of the other man on her was what ultimately, kept him from killing her. It got in his nose as he made love to her, and when that wolfen olfactory sense picked out the origin of the smell, his instincts took over and he was after it instead of her.

Crunching a carrot between her teeth, Margaret melted inside at the sight of her werewolf. Five feet of iron bone and sinewy strength, his paws shredded and picked apart the man on the couch as if he were butter. Her body warmed again in anticipation as she thought of him returning to her at the end of his meal. Before she uncovered the drain beneath the vinyl couch and hosed down the slaughter room (and herself), Charles would pad across the tiles to her, green eyes filled with lust. Then he'd hold her down with a vaguely human paw, and lick her clean with that rough and tumble tongue. He'd mount her again, fast and hard, before disappearing up the stairs and into the night.

She didn't have to cuff him to the couch and he didn't wear a collar, but she knew he'd be back. Real men didn't fight their chains. Sated and re-laxed, she propped herself up off the cold floor with one arm, and watched protectively as Charles enjoyed his meal.

She lived for the nights of the full moon.

THE VIRGIN O' FULL MOON FALLS
JAMES NEWMAN

Stand right there, asshole.

Does the gun make you nervous? Good. I'm glad. At least I know you ain't gonna try nothin' funny.

Don't you dare move a muscle. Don't even blink.

Now. Listen. I want to tell you a story—

* * *

There was this girl back in Full Moon Falls. Town in North Carolina, where I grew up.

Rayleen Estelle Connelly. Prettiest lil' thing you ever did see.

Rayleen had just turned sweet sixteen when all o' this happened, but she was so tiny a lot o' people used to insist she didn't look a day over thirteen or fourteen years old. Fiery red hair, pigtails, face full o' freckles like God's own game o' connect-the-dots. She used to wear these cute frilly dresses all the time, with flowers and honeybees and butterflies all over 'em. Pink and yellow ribbons in her hair.

The thing Rayleen was most well-known for, though, throughout the town o' Full Moon Falls: she prided herself on bein' a virgin. Rayleen even founded that CT4A group at the First Baptist Church o' Full Moon Falls her family attended: *Christian Teens For Abstinence.* I gotta admit, we were all mighty surprised at just how big the whole thing got, drawin' in fifty or sixty members within just a two or three months o' Rayleen startin' it. I remember seein' kids all over town wearin' those bright blue and yellow buttons Rayleen made in her spare time, buttons with slogans on 'em like *SEX IS GR8 WHEN YOU W8!*, or *I'M IN NO HURRY: I'VE MADE A SPECIAL PROMISE TO MY FUTURE HUSBAND* (or *WIFE*). I reckon you get the picture.

Lookin' back on it all now—I think maybe that was what got Rayleen in trouble in the first place. Advertisin' it so. Lot o' her fellow students at Full Moon High accused her o' thinkin' she was better than everybody else. The girls called her "Miss Goody-Two-Shoes." Boys her age—the ones who weren't members CT4A members, o' course—used to say she wasn't nothin' but a "dang cock-tease."

Rayleen heard the whispers behind her back. Sure she did. How could she help it, in a town the size o' Full Moon Falls?

Thing is, Rayleen Connelly never gave a damn what anybody thought about her. That's just the way she was. She just kept smilin', skippin' down the block past her daddy's gun shop and the Big Pig grocery store where her mama worked, on her way to and from her CT4A meetings every Tuesday night and the rallies every third Saturday mornin' o' each month, so excited about spreadin' the word to anyone who wished to listen.

That is, until what happened.

After that night, nothin' was the same. Nothin' was ever the same for any of us.

* * *

One cool October night, a bunch o' dirtbags from the white-trash side o' town got all jacked up on pot and crank and Jim Beam, decided they was gonna have 'em—these are *their* words, not mine—a "pussy party".

At sweet lil' Rayleen Connelly's expense.

Story goes, it was just after sunset, and Rayleen was makin' her way home from another CT4A meetin' (how's that for irony? I've always thought the Man Upstairs can be *beyond* cruel sometimes, and what happened to Rayleen cinched it, forever and ever amen) when all of a sudden this big, loud, mud-spattered Chevy 4x4 full of a half-dozen local troublemakers pulls up in front o' Rayleen. It pulls right up on the sidewalk, blockin' her path.

"Where you goin', purdy lady?" the dickhead behind the wheel asks Rayleen, shoutin' to be heard above Metallica on the Chevy's shitty stereo system.

He swigs from a can o' Pabst Blue Ribbon sittin' between his legs. Some of it dribbles down his big stubbled chin, but he don't bother wipin' it away. He looks *rabid,* and most likely—what do ya bet?—that's intentional.

"Answer me, girly. I asked you where you was headed?"

Buck Cooter was his name. He was the group's leader, I suppose. Big hairy sumbitch, flabby arms and face always smeared with grease thanks to his job at the Oil Well over on Talbot Lane. Sideburns straight outta the 'seventies, teeth like a rickety yellow picket fence that's barely survived a tornado.

"Get out of my way, *please,*" Rayleen replied. Polite, but in that tone o' hers some folks used to consider *snooty.*

And I guess that was all it took.

Them pieces o' shit were out o' Buck's truck and on little Rayleen before she knew what was happenin'.

That poor child—she never stood a chance against 'em—

* * *

Make a long story short—plus, I'm sparin' you the gory details 'cause I don't rightly care to dredge 'em up myself—the things them bastards did to Rayleen Connelly would go down in local history as one o' my hometown's worst crimes ever recorded.

Buck Cooter and his gang ignored Rayleen's screams for mercy as they drove into the thick, black woods borderin' Full Moon Falls. In fact, I think her shrieks might've been, to them animals' ears, like high-pitched cheers goadin' 'em on.

They proceeded to have their way with her.

All six of 'em.

Again and again. And again. *All night long.*

When they was done, they dumped her on her daddy's doorstep. Left here lyin' there like yesterday's garbage, all bloody, bruised, and barely breathin'.

* * *

That's not the worst of it, though. Oh, no—

What them sumbitches did to Rayleen that night was just the beginnin' o' her ordeal.

Ya see, there was somethin' the citizens o' Full Moon Falls never knew about Buck Cooter and company.

We knew they was trouble. No doubt about it. What the old-timers called "bad news."

What none of us had known, before that night—was that them bastards wasn't even *human.*

They was a pack. A pack of—*things.* Supernatural, hell-spawned creatures that ain't supposed to exist outside o' Stephen King books or them cheesy monster movies we all used to love watchin' over at the Full Moon Drive-In.

Poor lil' Rayleen. Nobody deserves what happened to her.

It shouldn't have even been *possible.*

* * *

So—what's all this got to do with you?

Oh, I think you know.

Here—I want you to put the barrel o' my gun in your mouth.

Yeah. That's it. Slow and easy—

Suck on it. Just like you made her do.

It took me thirteen long years to find all o' you. Travellin' from state to state. From Kentucky—to Tennessee—Georgia—South Carolina.

The huntin' skills my daddy taught me when I was younger? They've come in purdy handy throughout my quest, as if I have to tell you.

Some o' you were already down n' out, by the time I got to you. Gut-shot in bar brawls, shanked in prison. Livers eaten away by a lifetime o' hard drinkin'. All that was just fine with me, o' course, though I'd be lyin' if I said I didn't wish I'd got there sooner, so *I* could be the one who pulled the trigger, or stuck the blade in and twisted it.

Funny, though, ain't it, how every single one o' your gang *survived* such confrontations unless they involved *silver*. Maybe you just *barely* survived, but you were still alive—

At least till I came callin'.

Now—finally—there's just you. And me. Right back where we first started. I should have known *you* would never leave Full Moon Falls. You love it here, don't you? Wouldn't wanna live anywhere else in the world than here. You've got your truck, your trailer, your case o' Pabst Blue Ribbon, and your black-and-blue wife back home (does *she* know what you are, I wonder?). This place—this life—it's all you ever wanted.

You're gonna die here too, ya know.

You're the last. The last o' your pack, you piece o' shit.

I found you.

* * *

Rayleen couldn't help what you fuckers did to her. She couldn't help endin' up pregnant, with a litter o' lil' monsters squirmin' around inside o' her belly—yippin' and whinin' every time the moon was full—

You want to know what they did to her, when they was ready to come out?

There were *nine* of 'em.

Them things ripped her apart.

They chewed their way right out of her.

* * *

Open wide, Buck.

Eat my last silver bullet.

This is for my sister.

THE TROJAN PLUSHY
DAVID BERNSTEIN

The courtroom was silent, the air thick with anticipation, as the foreman stood. The elderly man looked at the judge who was peering over his spectacles awaiting a verdict. All eyes of the room rested on the foreman. He cleared his throat, breaking the room's silence like a sad drum roll before a dangerous act.

"We, the jury, find the defendant, not guilty." Brad Raling closed his eyes, putting his head to the table. He heard none of the reactions from his side or the defendant's. He'd gone to another place, a place only he could reach, deep in his mind. He felt his attorney pat his arm, bringing him back to reality. Brad shrugged the man off. "Leave me be," he grumbled.

Brad thought he had the man who murdered his family. The police arrested him; all the evidence pointing a guilty finger at the man, but an unthinkable act swooped in and ruined it all. A fucking recall. The damn breathalyzer—a new model, recalled due to failed meter readings. The man who killed his wife and daughter—Brad's reasons for living, was free.

Brad lay in bed for the next few weeks, drinking, throwing up and then drinking some more. He had vacation time and cashed it all in. With the bereavement leave, he totaled a little over a month of time off from his job.

People came to his house, dropped off food, cards, and gave their apologies. He hated looking at them, their sorry faces. What did they care, they simply got to return to their wonderful lives, grateful they weren't him.

One visitor, his neighbor Marcy Conrad, proved different. The woman hardly left her house. She was a hermit, a recluse. The neighborhood kids thought her to be a witch. She wasn't a witch, but she certainly knew one.

"Oh, Miss Conrad," Brad said startled, as he opened the door to retrieve the morning paper.

"Morning, Bradley," she said, her voice scratchy as if damaged from years of smoking. "I baked you a pie, apple." She held out a plastic bag, revealing yellow-stained teeth as she smiled.

"Thank you," Brad said, accepting the gift. His mouth began watering as the sweet aroma of baked apples and cinnamon entered his nostrils. The pie smelled delicious, but there was no way in hell he'd eat anything from that woman.

"Good day," she said before turning around and walking away.

Brad had always thought the woman strange, but at least she had a caring heart.

Inside, Brad went over to the trash-can, opened the lid and was about to toss the bag with the pie into it, when he noticed a card inside the bag. He removed the card, placing the pie on the counter. Taking a seat at the kitchen table, he read the card.

Neighbor,

I can only imagine how you're feeling. Your sweet, sweet, tender daughter and loving wife were savagely mauled by a monster. There are more paths to finding justice and avenging the dead than the means of which our flawed legal system allows. I know how you're feeling. You want justice! Vengeance! I know of someone who might be able to help you. Go to 105 Cremlock Wood Lane and ask for the righteousness you and your dead loved ones deserve.

The old bat was crazy; a smirk breeching his face as he tossed the letter into the trash along with the pie. Grabbing a bottle of gin, he meandered over to the couch and flicked on the television. He began gulping the liquor until he nearly choked at the image he saw—Martin Biggs, the man who slaughtered his family. He turned the volume up. Each word the man spoke sent shivers of ice down Brad's spine.

Martin was smiling, happy. He had his arms wrapped around his wife's and daughter's shoulders as they stood proudly at his sides. He spoke about the legal system and its just ways.

"I'm indeed sorry for Mr. Raling's loss, but my family and I just want to move on. We're looking forward to our lives returning to normal. Thank you." He took no questions, turning away from the cameras, got his family into a car and drove off.

Brad's fists were clenched, his right hand wrapped around the bottle's neck. His face had become a deep shade of burgundy, salvia dripping from his mouth, like that of a wild, mongrel dog. He stood; the image of a content Martin Biggs—family man, the person responsible for his family's demise, branded into his mind forever. Brad reached back, muscles tensed, and threw the gin bottle across the room. The glass shattered as it collided with the wall, knocking a picture of his family to the floor.

He walked over to the picture—the glass in the frame cracked—stepping on fragments of broken gin bottle, unaware and feeling no pain. Picking up the picture, he stared at it, tears welling in his eyes. He brought a finger to his daughter's face, caressing it, then his wife's. "I shall avenge you both," he whispered. He walked to his bedroom, hugging the picture to his chest, leaving a trail of bloody footprints behind.

Two days later, Brad found himself knocking at the door of 105 Cremlock Wood Lane.

* * *

Martin left his office shortly after six p.m., coming down from the highrise on 23rd Street and 5th Avenue. His week had been filled with catch-up work, his own court case having taken up much of his valuable time.

It was his daughter's birthday and he hadn't personally gotten her a thing. His secretary purchased the card, his wife bought the bicycle, but he felt he needed to get her something, something from him to her.

As he turned left to walk up the sidewalk, he saw an elderly woman standing behind a small cart filled with plush animals. He'd never seen her or her cart before and thought himself in luck—his daughter, like all children, loved stuffed animals.

As he approached the cart, the old woman's features presented themselves with clarity. Her skin was weathered like rough leather, and she had large sunken bags under her eyes as if she hadn't slept soundly in months, but it was the grotesquely hairy mole on the end of her nose that attracted the most attention. If Martin didn't know better, he'd thought she was a witch. Shaking the crude thought from his mind, he stopped within a foot of the cart.

"Hello," the old woman said.

"Hi," Martin replied quickly, his eyes on the merchandise.

"Shopping for your daughter?"

Martin paused, looking at the old woman. "Yes, how'd you know?"

The woman cackled. "Why else would a handsome young man such as yourself be looking at stuffed animals?"

Martin smiled. "Got me there." He saw tigers, dogs, cats, bears, zebras, lions, turtles, rabbits, and dolphins. "Quite an assortment you have here." The old woman grinned.

As Martin continued to search, his face scrunched in indecision, the old woman spoke.

"Here," she said, holding out what appeared to be a cute little dog. "Girls love stuffed animals, they should all have one."

Martin hadn't a clue as to what kinds of stuffed animals his daughter liked or had, but a doggy seemed like a safe bet—and essential to a young girl's collection. "I'll take it," he told the woman, reaching into his pocket and handing her a ten dollar bill, as the sign indicated the price.

Later that night, Martin and his wife presented their daughter Mindy, with her gifts—the card, the bike, and the plush doggy. The young girl was excited, jumping up and down and telling her parents how much she loved them.

"So you like the doggy?" Martin asked.

"It's not a doggy, Daddy. It's a wolf."

"Oh," he said, clearly having had no idea what type of animal he'd purchased. "Well, do you like your wolf?"

She smiled up at him, her face bright with joy. "Yes, I love him very much."

* * *

Brad sat on his sofa; his .45 resting next to him. He flipped through the channels looking for, and not finding, a certain news story. It had been two weeks since he'd paid—dearly—for the witch's services. He wanted results. Angered and half in the bag, he dialed the old hag's phone number.

"Yes?" she asked, answering the phone.

"When's it going to happen?" Brad asked, his speech somewhat slurred.

"Soon."

"I paid a lot," he said, staring at his left wrist, where his hand used to be.

"Patience my dear. All in good time."

"I'm not sure how much longer I can wait. I need this to be over. I've marred my body for this, sacrificed more than enough. I want results."

"Losing an eye and a hand is a small price to pay for what you asked."

Brad felt as if tiny spiders were crawling across his flesh, his anger quickly fading. "Fine," he said, trying to sound stern. "Just get it done."

* * *

Mindy rode her new bicycle every day and slept, hugging Bumpkins— her new teddy-wolf, close to her heart every night.

Three weeks after his daughter's birthday, Martin and his family sat at the kitchen table, enjoying a splendid, home-cooked meal.

As darkness fell across the land and the full moon glowed brightly in the night sky, Bumpkins began to stir. Its nose twitched as its limbs wiggled; unnatural life starting to flow.

The plush animal was nestled, like a newborn, between two fluffy pink pillows on Mindy's bed. Its body began to grow—arms and legs elongating. Claws, like fine daggers, protruded from its paws. The soft brown fabric that was its fur, lengthened, becoming shaggy like a mangy dog's. The onyx button eyes turned crimson, as if filled with blood. Fangs, menacing, long and thick like that of a saber tooth tiger's, grew from its mouth.

At full length, and very much alive, the creature let loose a low growl, saliva dripping from its maw like a rabid beast. Raising its head, it sniffed at the air. The creature's targets were nearby.

Having only a few hours of life, the full moon its power source, the wolf-creature galloped out of Mindy's room and down the carpeted steps.

It halted at the bottom, seeing its victims ahead. How lucky it was that all its prey were together in one area. The beast charged, its claws ripping up the parquet flooring.

Martin's wife, who had been carrying a ceramic tray filled with chocolate cake, screamed when she saw the creature. The tray fell, shattering against the kitchen's tiled floor. Pieces of cake crumbled and scattered like soil from a potted plant.

Martin turned around in his chair, his face paling in utter astonishment. Within seconds the wolf-thing was on top of his wife, its jaws clenched around her throat, tearing it open. Blood spewed from a punctured artery as the wolf chewed.

Mindy screamed as Martin grabbed a chair. He brought it up over his head, slamming it down on top of the wolf's head. The creature howled in annoyance before swatting Martin across the room, his body colliding with the sheetrock wall.

Dazed, but very much aware, Martin watched as the beast devoured his daughter, her cries quickly silenced. Martin was screaming, his mind unable to comprehend what it was seeing.

The wolf-thing, its face caked in red gore, revealing pieces of his wife and child, their clothing too, howled.

The beast approached Martin as he cringed against the wall, all but giving up, wanting to die.

The creature raised its paw to strike a killing blow when it froze, then slunk to the floor as if it lost its bones. Rolling over dead, it shrunk, once again becoming a cute little plush toy.

* * *

Brad watched television that night; the story he'd been waiting for presenting itself. The reporter spoke of a grisly scene. A young girl and her mother were savagely attacked and killed, allegedly murdered by Martin Biggs. Husband and father to the deceased. Brad watched as Martin was dragged away in handcuffs, covered in blood. He kept repeating that his daughter's stuffed animal, a wolf, did it. It was dangerous and needed to be destroyed.

Brad picked up the telephone and dialed the old woman's number. When she answered, he simply said, "Thank you. Now my family and I can rest in peace." He placed the .45 caliber handgun to his head and pulled the trigger.

JESUS WHEN THE SUN GOES DOWN
SIMON McCAFFERY

For Isaias and Claire

Before my brother and I boarded the old yellow Bluebird school bus for the four-hour ride through the rolling limestone Ozark foothills to Raven's Den Baptist Summer Camp, my father handed me a ten-dollar bill—a good chunk of money in 1975—and offered this terse advice.

"Peter, Nate, if anyone asks you if you've been saved, say 'yes.' "

"Yessir," we muttered.

He absently patted Nate on the head and we hauled the battered old suitcase we shared and ourselves onto the bus. Dad stood there a moment, then walked back to the car. Our mother was ill and he'd aged a decade in two years. His clothes hung on his tall frame and he moved through most days like a sleepwalker. We found seats near the front and watched Dad drive slowly away toward our small farmhouse off rural Star Route highway, the caramel-colored station wagon kicking up dry July dust when he left the main paved road.

Rather than cram the ten-spot deep into a front pocket of my blue jeans, I folded the bill into a small square. It went into my right sneaker below my socked foot. We'd moved around like nomads, settling briefly in cities and small towns alike before moving on, and I'd been shaken down (or held *upside* down like a chicken bound for the soup pot) by more than one bully hoping for lunch or allowance money.

Eventually the bus pulled out of the Piggly Wiggly parking lot and we rumbled out of town past the courthouse, the sole gray-stone bank, the Ben Franklin Five and Dime and the single traffic light. Nate settled down with a well-read copy of *Famous Monsters of Filmland*, the cover featuring Lon Chaney, Jr. as the Wolfman in "House of Frankenstein" hanging on by a staple. I peered over the duct tape-bandaged vinyl seat back and recognized several kids from the small consolidated school and the Presbyterian Church my family attended in a nearby town. No serious troublemakers. They were clustered toward the back, pretty amped, horsing around and swapping their best dirty jokes, speculating about which girls would be attending camp and which would wave a fellow right past second base. I nodded at Danny Bray and his brother, Cal, then sat back and stuck my nose in a Ray Bradbury paperback (*S is For Space*). I slipped gratefully into the story of a scientist fretting over his friend who lies encased in a giant scaly green-gray carapace until he hatches, wingless, and soars up into the stars.

Within an hour, a sweltering lethargy fell over everyone inside of the bus. Many of the windows were open, but the air was stifling. Most of the boys were napping, sweaty and damp-haired, too tired to swap baseball cards or tell more tall tales of teenage conquest, lulled by the sound of the bus' tired old engine grinding through the twisting hills.

We arrived at the camp gates close to suppertime, the sun still riding well above the jagged tree-line.

* * *

"My name is Brother Sanders. Welcome to Raven's Den. Grab you gear and follow me. Orientation is at the main tabernacle in ten minutes sharp, then supper. Let's see some hustle now."

Brother Sanders was the Horseshoe Bend basketball coach who also taught science. They were the reigning state conference champs; our little town could barely field a complete team. Sundays he served as a deacon at the Baptist church. He was one of the camp counselors, and liked to brag that he had saved more sin-shriveled souls than most full-time pastors. He stood over six feet tall with russet-colored hair, hazel-steel eyes and a square jaw. A silver plated whistle hung around his thick, sun-reddened neck. He kept a close eye on the attending varsity and junior-varsity players, but the rest of us might as well have been invisible. I silently prayed we wouldn't be bunking for two weeks in his cabin. Summer camp was supposed to be fun, not a prep school for the Marine Corps.

We walked up a stony hill, past a large covered concrete slab filled with rows of long wooden tables with bench seats and an attached mess shack. A path to the east ascended to higher ground, and presumably, the tabernacle. We crested the hill and descended, passing numbered cabins nestled between pines and tall mature oak trees to either side of the path. Below us the late afternoon sun sparkled on the lake. I saw an archery range and aluminum canoes stacked on racks near a wooden dock.

We stopped at a cabin on the boy's side of camp—lucky number 7. Coach Sanders consulted his clipboard.

"Wilson, Hanson, Brenner and Brenner (my brother and I). And the Brays."

My heart lifted at the lucky break. Making friends in a small rural community isn't easy if you weren't born and bred. The Brays were six-generation cattle and hog farmers, but Danny and his younger brother, Cal, had gone out of their way to befriend us. I sat next to Cal in our sixth-grade schoolroom, and Cal and Nate were fourth-grade classmates. Danny was in awe of my complete set of Aurora glow-in-the-dark monster kits—particularly the Wolfman and the Forgotten Prisoner of Castle Mare—and I in his woodworking skills. He'd shown me how to carve a rubber-band powered paddleboat and string a sapling bow strong enough that mom took it away the first time she saw me fire a homemade arrow an inch into the barn wall.

"Mr. Bray, can I count on you to help Mr. Wiles and keep everyone in line?" said Coach Sanders. Basketball was a regional obsession and Danny was a budding junior squad star.

"Yes sir."

Mr. Wiles emerged from the cabin, blinking in the sunlight behind his thick eyeglasses, a short, heavyset man in faded green pants that were cut down to shorts, camp T-shirt and white knee socks. He had a round baby face, but a friendly smile. Another break; he didn't look like a ball-buster like Coach Sanders.

"Hello, boys," he said softly. "Go on in and stow your gear. No time to unpack now. Bunks aren't assigned but I guess you can sort that out among yourselves."

Coach Sanders gave Wiles a slightly disapproving nod and strode away.

Taking Wiles' hint, we hurried into the log cabin. It was jewel-box tiny but I loved the smooth honey-colored wood walls bearing the carved initials and graffiti of former campers (JAKE T. & CINDY D. and BILLY WAHLS '68), the high raftered ceiling and the small four-pane windows looking off into the deep ravines and woods. Danny and I took the bed closest to the door, flipping to see who got the top bunk. Danny won and that was okay by me. The floor was concrete slab like the roofed picnic area. Roll off of your bunk while dreaming of CINDY D. or go sleepwalking and you'd crack your skull like an eggshell. Cal and Nate bunked together, and the remaining boys, Ricky Wilson and Bobby Hanson, flipped best out of three. Bobby won the high bunk and slung his dead older brother's green Army duffel bag onto the top mattress. The story went that Bobby's brother, Hank, had joined the Army straight out of high school, but had died in a Jeep accident while stationed in Germany. He'd been a star shooting guard and had received a hero's burial.

"Boys, we'd better get up to the tabernacle," Wiles said, looking like the last thing he wanted to do was jog up the hill in the humid soupy air. "We don't want to be late for opening prayers."

We hustled up the path double-time. Later we would trudge up that hill, dreading the nightly prayers and brimstone orations, wishing we could slip away into the fragrant pines. At that moment, we had forgotten the long boring bus ride. I was thinking about that cool shimmering expanse of lake and those canoes.

I thought it might be a pretty fun couple of weeks after all.

* * *

That night I lay in my bunk, unable to slip completely into sleep despite the long, strange day, when I heard a quiet creak in the darkened cabin. It sounded like something heavy shifting on the metal cot, on the far wall by the cabin door. The cot Mr. Wiles slept on. At lights-out Wiles had drawn shut the dusty, crimson shades across the two small windows. Now they admitted only a faint sliver of moonlight. I slowly withdrew my left wrist from the blanket and peeped at my Timex. The luminous hands read a quarter past one.

A large shadow rose and slid across the far wall.

I froze, thinking for one paranoid moment that we hadn't been lucky at all. What if we were bunking with a crazed molester?

The shadow carefully opened the cabin door and slipped outside.

I lay there playing 'possum. Several slow minutes ticked by.

I sat up and when my eyes had adjusted to the gloom I peered toward Wiles' cot. Kids have visual acuity their parents have long forgotten they ever possessed. The sagging old aluminum cot was empty. Empty except for Wiles' coke-bottle glasses, which lay folded on his pillow.

Probably Wiles had a late-night call of nature. Our grandfather had visited us once when we lived in Philadelphia and he got up all night long to pee, the toilet tank hissing and refilling, hissing and refilling. Bad prostate, our father had said, though neither of us understood what that meant. Raven's Den cabins weren't equipped with toilets. You could visit the segregated restrooms behind the dining area or find a tree.

When our chaperone didn't return I thought about waking Danny, but he'd dropped right off to sleep after Wiles flicked off the lights, calling out to the girls' side of the camp — "Good *niiiight*, girls!" —out the west window. We'd all snickered at that, coming from the rotund, comical camp counselor.

I waited for Wiles to return since I couldn't sleep, but the next thing I knew Danny was shaking my shoulder.

"Get a move on, Brenner! Revile in ten minutes!"

He was grinning like a prankster speaking to his victim. I remembered that he'd attended the camp last summer. Wiles was dressed and instructing the younger boys on how to make up their bunk beds. I wondered if Sanders would be by to inspect like a Drill Instructor.

I sat up and rubbed my eyes. I tried to recall something I'd dreamt the night before after falling asleep waiting for Wiles. Something about red gold-ringed eyes and a shape floating down from the roof of one of the moonlit cabins, but it blew apart in the clean white sunlight streaming into the cabin.

That day set the routine for those that followed. We assembled in the grassy quadrangle near the tetherball and softball diamond and a magnified voice echoed across the camp from a nearby bluff. Startled, we looked up to see the camp minister, Pastor Jerrod, dressed in an orange jumpsuit and hoisting a battery-powered bullhorn, standing on the precipice of ancient seabed layers of rock, looking down at us.

"RISE AND SHINE, CAMPERS!" he bellowed.

Pastor Jerrod led us in a daily prayer as we stood with heads bowed, then ten minutes of calisthenics. The basketball players performed the jumping jacks and push-ups easily by rote while the rest of us sweated. Ricky Wilson collapsed after three ass-humped-in-the-air push-ups but Coach Sanders didn't notice. We dusted ourselves off and marched to the long green picnic tables to be served breakfast after another prayer (unfrosted cornflakes and runny Navy scrambled eggs, which Nate refused to touch).

We hiked, collected leaves to be flattened and identified, played murderous whipsaw tetherball and tossed clanking steel horseshoes, measuring and arguing minute distances for every point. We asked to play Smear the Queer and were turned down. We struggled into musty lifejackets and canoed across the deep green lake, trying to run down surfacing turtles. Some of us stripped down to our shorts and swam from the dock. When chubby Ricky climbed back onto the dock he gave us all a half-moon, and that became his camp nickname. Chief Half-Moon. He wore it with pride.

For lunch we ate hot dogs drowned in ketchup and relish, and told more tall tales. We tried to make eye contact with the cutest girls eating on the other side of the pavilion, and enlisted a couple of the younger kids to courier notes.

By evening, happy but footsore, all I wanted to do was stretch out on my cabin bunk and read comic books until lights-out. Instead we marched back up that stony hill to the tabernacle.

Two hours later we shuffled back in the dark and collapsed in our bunks. I guess I hadn't known what to expect, but I now understood the simple wisdom of our father's advice.

Things started mildly with opening prayers and a few hymns—"When The Roll Is Called Up Yonder," "The Old Rugged Cross" and "Jesus In The Morning." We sang that last one every day, sometimes twice. It rapidly became apparent that our real mission at camp was to fervently love and serve Him in the Morning, in the Noontime, and When the Sun Goes Down. And every minute in-between.

Several of the camp counselors joined Pastor Jerrod at the lectern, telling tales of doomed heathen boys and girls gone astray and the excruciating eternal hellfire that surely awaited them. A crude drawing of the crucified Nazarene was drawn on a large blackboard, and one of the younger counselors used chalk to illustrate how every time you sinned, no matter how minor the transgression or white lie, long pins where pushed into Jesus' pale flesh. The chalk squeaked until His thin body looked like a porcupine. By this time many of the younger boys and girls were sniffling. The warm air crackling with emotion and fear, we bowed our heads and Pastor Jerrod called all those who wished to be saved, or saved again for good measure, to come forth. Nate, thinking we were all meant to come forth, started to move toward the center aisle before I clutched his arm and gently pulled him back with a frown and slight shake of my head.

Plenty of the other kids left their pews and the counselors swarmed over them like furniture salesmen.

Every day we hiked and swam and worked on crafts, knowing what waited for us as the sun dropped below the hills.

On the fifth night, Wiles' cot squeaked again well after lights-out, and this time I waited a minute and followed him into the moonlight. If he saw me or someone else asked what I was doing out after curfew I would say I had to use the bathroom and had gotten turned around in the dark.

It was a cloudless night and his broad cotton T-shirt was easy to spot under the nearly full moon. I watched him walk briskly to the far side of the camp toward the girls' cabins. He'd left his glasses behind and I wondered how he could see where he was going. Well, well! We all liked Mr. Wiles, though everyone called him Mr. Toad from "The Wind in The Willows" — but it was hard to imagine him romancing one of the women chaperones.

Wiles walked right past their cabins and struck off into the woods.

I almost turned back, told myself how embarrassing it would be if I startled him taking a leak behind a tree. The bathrooms were on the other side of the camp and there were plenty of trees near our cabins. Curiosity won out.

I moved quickly across the open space and slipped into the trees, trying to avoid making any sound and praying I wouldn't step barefoot on a nail-spiked old plank. I had done just that my first day on our farm, driving a rusty nail into my left heel to the bone. When my father used a razor blade to cut an X into the wound I'd screeched loud enough to be heard in St. Louis.

I glimpsed Wiles' shimmering T-shirt ahead, moving through the black columns of tree trunks. He was heading deeper into the woods. I slowed, imagining what might happen if I got lost in these unfamiliar woods at night. The thought of having to shout for rescue and seeing the blazing fury in Coach Sanders' eyes—and the disappointed expression on my father's face after being expelled—was like a dash of cold lake water. Until he arrived I would probably be hung inverted from the tetherball pole or dropped off the preaching bluff.

At that point I lost sight of Wiles' T-shirt moving like a Halloween ghost through the forest. I looked back the way I had come and could barely make out the roofline of the outmost girls' cabin.

I was still hemming and hawing when a scream sliced through the night air from the deeper forest where Wiles had vanished. It rose to a shriek and then dropped to a guttural roar before echoing away. My blood actually froze in my veins and I damned near wet myself. That unearthly cry didn't sound like a coyote or bobcat. A den of black bear in those hills was a possibility, but that sound—

I stood there, heart drumming inside my ribs, straining to listen. I didn't hear the cry repeated, but I thought I heard something large grunting and moving fast through the woods. I couldn't be sure, but it sounded like the crashing sounds were getting closer.

I turned and raced back to my cabin, not feeling the stones, rough twigs and pine needles under my tenderfoot soles.

* * *

In the morning we made our bunks and assembled outside for bullhorn revile and prayers. Wiles looked and acted normal. I'd peeked at his cot, expecting to see muddy footprints, coarse black hairs and pine needles like in a Stephen King novel, but the threadbare sheets were unmarked. No scratches or welts I could see on his pale arms and legs. He seemed hale and happy, and gave Nate and me a dollar for fetching him a Hostess bear claw from the snack bar before lunch. Wiles was an insatiable junk-food snacker, and because Nate and I always read a complete chapter from the Book of Acts around the campfire when asked, we became his favorites for errands. We were sitting pretty on money and made sure our poorer friends had a dime or quarter when their own funds began to run low.

That afternoon one of the older boys kicked a soccer ball high into the woods. Several of us joined the search. Fifteen minutes later as we were about to give up I heard a thin wail and shouts. When I arrived at the circle of kids I saw Calvin Bray sprawled in a dead faint on the forest floor. Nate stood over his friend, holding the lost ball, face white as a sheet.

"Nate, are you okay? Did a snake bite Cal?" Dad hated snakes and he had infected us with his fear of copperheads and black water moccasins.

Nate shook his head slowly like a somnambulist. He tucked the ball under his left arm and pointed. I followed his finger to the large white and red shape lying in the weeds: the decapitated head of a cow, tongue half torn from its gaping pale mouth, cream coat clotted with dried black blood, milky eyes bulging and crawling with bluebottle flies. My stomach did a slow air-show roll. When I finally dragged my eyes away I looked in a wide circle. No matching headless cow carcass. No blood trail.

It was like the mutilated cow head had fallen from the sky.

* * *

We all became masters of camp pranks, learning to short-sheet beds, apply Vaseline to toilet seats and set diabolical traps. The first day or so you carefully watched and recorded your cabin-mates' behavior. Did they dive into bed at night? Hide a spade shovel under their blanket. What frightened them? Daddy long-legs, toads and grass snakes found their way into pillowcases and suitcases. How about a dead perch under your mattress? Preparation H in your Colgate? In retaliation a few fellows pulled on fresh underwear treated with Bengay ("flaming balls revenge").

The day after the gruesome discovery in the woods Danny and I were plotting payback against the camp bully, one Harold Manry. If the county schools could have afforded football programs, Harold would have been a star defensive lineman. He played basketball as a guard, but he was too large and slow to excel. He'd spent most of his time terrorizing the younger campers and gave Ricky Wilson—Chief Half-Moon—a bloody nose playing tetherball.

Danny argued for Flaming Balls with Wood Ticks, but I wanted something grander. While we devised and discarded convoluted Rube Goldberg ideas, I decided to tell him about Wiles' nocturnal treks. We agreed to wake each other the next time it happened and get to the bottom of the mystery. Encyclopedia Brown deduced all of his two-minute mysteries sitting down with his twelve-year-old eyes closed, but we were rugged Outdoor types.

* * *

The next night after tabernacle, while around a small campfire, we burned marshmallows at the stake, and read New Testament Bible verses (the shortest ones like "Jesus wept" —John 11:35—had long been exhausted). Then we climbed into our bunks and joined Wiles in calling goodnight to the girls.

Sometime later Danny shook me awake. He held a finger to his lips and beckoned me to follow. I slipped on my jeans and my bare feet into my sneakers and followed Danny outside. There were gauze-thin ribbons of clouds, but the campground was washed in cold moonlight. The full pock-bellied moon was rising above the trees against the Milky Way. It looked bloated and tinged; a Blood Moon, or what they call the Strawberry Moon in the Deep South. Legend—and the Scholastic paperback *Strange Superstitions!* —soberly proclaimed that a Strawberry Moon focuses and concentrates supernatural forces. Those who dare walk under its bloodshot eye are more apt to encounter a bobbing will-o'-the-wisp, Manitou spirit or flesh-craving Wendigo.

Wiles' glimmering T-shirt was disappearing into the brush and forest's edge.

We followed at a good distance for a hundred yards and then Danny stopped and handed me what felt like a small roll of tape. He pulled out the metal flashlight he'd taken from our cabin and clicked it on so I could see, hooding its beam with his left hand. The reflective tape glowed fluorescent yellow. The same type of tape that was wrapped around the tree trunks that lined the narrow twisting graveled drive from the camp's entry gates to the main grounds.

"I filched it from the work shed," Danny said. "Tear off small pieces every so often and mark our way on the bigger trees."

I was impressed; I wouldn't have thought of that. Typical city kid. I told myself that Encyclopedia Brown might not have, either.

Feeling more confident, we walked deeper into the woods, trying not to lose sight of Wiles. Danny kept one hand over the flashlight's lens to provide just enough light to navigate, and I marked off trees every thirty yards or so. We heard owls and saw a great grey and brown hawk with glowing eyes perched on a dead storm-damaged tree limb, waiting for its next mouse-meal.

Wiles dipped through a ravine and disappeared over its rim. A flickering light glowed beyond. Before we crested the top we heard voices and dropped to the forest floor. Danny dowsed the flashlight and signaled to me silently. We belly-crawled to the top like G.I. Joe and peered over to the other side.

We saw Wiles join several men who were standing around a crude Druidic circle of stones. A small brazier sat in the center filled with burning deadwood. One of the men took off his orange jumpsuit and I realized with a nasty shock that it was Pastor Jerrod. He wasn't wearing anything else. Except for his face, neck, wrists and ankles he was fish-belly white. The other three men already stood buck-ass naked in the flickering orange light; two potbellied middle-aged counselors from Pine Bluff, and Coach Sanders. As we watched, paralyzed, Mr. Wiles cast off his cut-off shorts, T-shirt and boxers and joined the others inside the stone ring as they began circling the fire. They chanted in unison in a glottal, throaty language I couldn't understand. The sight of them twirling and half-skipping around that pagan fire filled me with a pure superstitious dread. Their faces contorted like devils, they gnashed their teeth and I noticed with an ashamed horror that all five were sporting erections, though Wiles' was mainly obscured by his ponderous gut.

And that was when two large hands clamped down our shirts and a nasty voice spoke in our ears.

"So what exactly are you two maggots up to?"

Danny and I both jumped and I couldn't completely stifle a small cry. We twisted around to see our nemesis, Harold, recent recipient of the Burning Balls award. The bastard had followed us into the woods.

"Boy, wait until I drag your sorry asses back to Coach," he said with satisfaction. "Maybe I should give you both black eyes and tell Coach you tripped on some rocks."

"Shhhhh!" Danny said with a scowl. He grabbed Harold's thick forearm and tried to pull him down.

"Shut up!" I hissed at the big moron. "*Get down!*"

"What are you two queers doing out here? Wait until I tell the other guys."

The chanting in the clearing below us stopped. Danny and I pulled free from Harold and peered back over the ravine rim.

The five sweat-bathed men stared up at us, only they weren't men anymore. Pastor Jerrod was a large silver-maned wolf. Coach was a huge tawny mountain lion. The two Pine Bluff counselors were stocky, long-eared lynxes. Wiles was a dopey, shaggy-assed black bear. He looked at us with comical eyes, flattened his broad ears, and grunted.

For a brief moment I entertained a fantasy: I was asleep in my cabin bunk, dreaming. This was a nightmare spun together from exhaustion, fiery tabernacle sermons, undercooked hot dogs and too many issues of *Famous Monsters* and *Eerie.*

The Jerrod-Wolf creature howled; the same terrible cry I'd heard the night I watched Wiles slip into the woods, and I knew I wasn't dreaming. Coach, now a huge cougar sporting four-inch fangs, glared at us with eyes glowing green in the firelight.

The lynxes both began padding toward us, splitting up to either side of the clearing.

"Peter, run!" Danny shouted.

Harold stood transfixed as the creatures began ascending the side of the ravine.

The werewolf's silver muzzle contracted to reveal rows of sharp white teeth and four dagger canines; the shape-shifted cougar snarled.

I struggled to my feet and we ran. It took Harold a little longer to make up his mind, but he turned and lumbered after us.

"Faster, Peter!"

Danny grabbed my hand and we flew past the darkened trees, the flashlight's beam searching for the glowing yellow strips.

I heard Harold fall and grunt as the air left his lungs.

"Hey guys!" he called, gasping. "I hurt my ankle."

God help us, Danny cranked his pistoning legs into sixth gear.

I knew he was right; if we turned back to help big, clumsy Harold they would fall on all three of us. We heard growls and the cougar's scream, and Harold shrieked in terror. Over the intervening years, I've relived that race through the darkened woods many times in dreams, my lungs searing and heart galloping, the flashlight's beam stuttering and jumping from the ground into the witchy tree boughs.

We passed a huge oak tree marked with a strip of reflective tape and saw two glowing eyes in the flashlight's beam; one of the giant lynxes stood directly in our path. Danny slid to a stop and flung the metal flashlight, striking the animal squarely on its hairy skull. It yelped and backed away.

We ran. We ran, now without the light, sure that at any moment that huge white wolf would bring one of us down like a yearling buck. Or the mountain lion would spring from a tree and sink its powerful jaws into my throat. It occurred to me that this was the dream-shape I had seen floating down from a nearby cabin roof through our cottage window.

Brush and scrub trees tore at us, but we kept running.

* * *

For the first time in its sixty-year history, Raven's Den Camp closed early that summer so local sheriff's deputies and volunteers could beat the brush for a lost camper. Missing was a thirteen-year-old boy named Harold Manry from Ash Grove. The camp staff, including Pastor Jerrod and Coach Sanders, assisted in the search. Manry's counselor swore he had been accounted for at lights-out, as did the other boys assigned to the cabin, so it was assumed he had wandered into the woods sometime after curfew and become lost. Coach and Pastor Jerrod gathered all of us and asked if anyone knew what had happened to Harold. Danny and I kept our mouths shut, trying not to tremble when Coach's eyes swept over us.

Poor Harold's body was never found and he was eventually presumed dead. Thank goodness that in those days they didn't print the blurry photos of lost children on lunchroom pint cartons of milk. I felt guilty enough.

We made a pact to never speak of what we'd seen. Mr. Wiles was AWOL. When dawn finally arrived he hadn't returned to our cabin (Danny and I sat awake all night, shivering, in shock). We were told he had taken suddenly ill. We heard stories of food poisoning and Lyme disease from a tick bite. I wondered if he'd screwed up and been pushed permanently outside that eldritch circle.

Dad drove Nate and I home in the tired old station wagon. I spent the next six months avoiding Coach at basketball games and pep rallies until Dad announced we were selling the farm and moving. I slept poorly. Every time the tree outside my room tapped the window pane I awoke in a sweat, sure that I would see one of their transformed bestial faces staring in at me with hell-fired eyes.

These days I live far from the Ozark hills. Lately I have begun experiencing a recurring dream. The details are always the same—the horrible scene beyond the ravine and the panicked run through those haunted woods. This time Danny's aim is off and the flashlight spins into the darkness past the man-lynx. It yowls in fury and scratches my hip with one claw as we speed by. *No*, my memory insists, *that was a scrape from a tree branch or brambles*. The dream shifts suddenly as dreams are apt to do, and I'm the grown man I see each morning in the mirror, taking his twelve-year-old boy on a father-and-son summer retreat. A spacious, modern lodge with a crackling stone fireplace and indoor plumbing looking down on a clear, blue lake; nothing like Raven's Den. We hike through the spruce-covered hills and cook freshly caught fish on an open grill and make campfire chocolate and graham cracker s'mores.

In the morning my son calls to me to get up, *get up, Dad*, and join him in skipping flat stones across the lake's rippling surface before breakfast, but I lay there paralyzed—held down by that freezing weight of black, stream-polished dread.

I dare not move. Perhaps if I ignore my son's insistent calls I can forever remain in this perfect dream. If I leave our cabin and stroll past the edge of the woods I'll find another crude circle of stones.

And I know exactly what I'll see even before I peel back the blanket and sheets—

THREE DOG NIGHT
JOHN F.D. TAFF

It was the pull that morning that finally did it for Roland; the final pull he would lead.

However, it would not be the final pull he was ever involved in—

The pull—what a vague, euphemistic word for that procedure. It sounded as if it were some sort of selection process, for a winning candidate or a great prize, a lottery drawing maybe.

It was a death walk, the last walk, a kind of animal green mile.

The pull was the round up of dogs and cats from the St. Francois County Animal Control Shelter, those who had gone unadopted; those whose luck had run out—the old, the infirm, the mangy, the aggressive, the merely unremarkable. All loaded into a cage in the middle of the main kennel, all taken to the gas chamber

All *pulled*—

No lethal injection for this shelter. Too expensive, said the bureaucrats. Besides, they said, gassing is safe and effective and causes a minimum of discomfort for the animals.

Roland knew that, from 18 years working here, the gas chamber might be *effective*, might even be *safe*, though he was unsure as to whom it was safe *for*. The discomfort for the animals—not to mention the workers? That was anything but minimal.

Those bureaucrats had never participated in a pull; they'd never had to look into the trusting eyes of dog after dog as they were taken into that room; never had to see their eyes as the door was closed, their tails still wagging, as if the door would open and the food would come, the love would come—

Never had to see the eyes of those dogs in their dreams, their nightmares—

Lethal injection—gassing—it was all the same, Roland figured on his good days.

They're dead any way you look at it.

Today was not a good day—

The air was hot inside the kennel, even this early in the morning. The pull was always done in the morning, so the howls of the cats and dogs wouldn't disturb people on their way to work or disturb the few people who came to the shelter to adopt animals.

He was about to go to the next cage when his eye caught a small figure huddled far in the back of the cage closest to the door.

"Awww, shit," he yelled, hanging his head. "Why didn't anyone tell me that *she* was back?"

The roar of his voice, for Roland was an enormous man, echoed off the steel rafters of the room. The door to the administrator's office opened, and Mel Shubert stuck his head out part way. "Yeah?" he asked around a mouthful of jelly doughnut, purple clots at the corners of his mouth.

"Why didn't anyone tell me that Bethany was back?" he demanded over the din of the dogs.

Mel shrugged, though with some sympathy. "What would you have done?"

He didn't wait for an answer, just pulled back inside and let the door close.

Roland removed his gloves, walked to the cage. Bethany cowered at its rear, a white American bulldog mix of some kind, smaller than most, with black splotches covering her flanks and circling one eye, like Petey in *The Little Rascals*. Roland thought she had made it, that she'd been adopted.

But no—

He didn't let it happen often, but Bethany, in the short time she was there, had penetrated his carefully constructed defenses and made it to his heart. He knew he couldn't save them all—couldn't save *most* of them—even *some* of them. After 18 years, he had to be content with saving almost none.

Almost none had to be enough. Otherwise, you went crazy and had 50 dogs in your house. Or, and he wasn't sure which was worse, your heart shrank, became as dense as lead, hard as diamond. Once that happened, you weren't good for either animals or people.

And so he felt his heart wavering as he stood there, expanding and contracting in his chest as if not sure which way to go.

"Aww, shit, girl," he growled. And though she didn't move, her tail began wagging. "No, no, too late for that, little lady."

He pulled her with the rest, took her himself to the chamber.

She went in with four others, all calmly, trustingly, and that fed his anger—anger at them, anger at those who had abandoned them, anger at all of that, all of that and this stupid job, this stupid system that put him in this position, made him kill these creatures who wanted nothing more than to eat, to sleep, to be loved.

Not too much to ask—but apparently too much to ask.

He closed the steel hatch on the chamber, punched the red button on the switch near the door. Carbon monoxide gas hissed into the room, colorless, odorless. Roland watched through an acrylic window set high in the hatch. After 20 or 30 seconds, Bethany and the four other dogs swung their heads from side to side, wobbled, fell over.

Another four minutes and they were dead.

When the light on the switch signaled that the cycle was complete, Roland tapped the shoulder of the attendant standing by him, told him with a nod of his head to take over for the rest of this pull.

* * *

Jonesy's owner was an older lady who lived in a small house with a small yard, and Jonesy was her small dog for 13 years. Then, Jonesy got sick, and she brought him to the shelter, seeking a cheap answer to her prayers. The only answer it had was putting Jonesy to sleep. That was its cheap answer to everything.

Healthy? *Death.* Sick? *Death.* Unwanted? *Death.* Dying? *Death.*

She took the money she might have spent on restoring Jonesy to health and paid for the return of his ashes in a little wooden box, suitable for display, as the brochure said. Roland had promised to bring it to her when it was ready.

It was a promise he would keep—the last of them, as far as he was concerned.

His brother-in-law owned a trash recycling business that was proving wildly lucrative, and had offered Roland a job several times. As much as he detested his brother-in-law, now might be the time to deal with the throwaways that people actually wanted for a change.

He found her house from memory, parked the truck on the street. He grabbed the box and a clipboard with the paperwork she'd have to sign. It was late morning now, just a little after ten o'clock, so he hoped that he wouldn't be disturbing her at breakfast.

As in response, she met him at the door, her eyes already on the box in his huge hands, already tearing. "Why, you dear man," she said, her voice warbling with emotion. "Have you brought my little Jonesy back?"

"Why, yes'm, I did. He's right here."

Slowly, he held the wooden box out. She took it with one shaking hand, the other covering her mouth, as if an entire body's worth of grief might spill from it.

"Oh, my dear, dear little Jonesy," she whispered, taking it from his hands, where it looked so small, and pressing it to her thin chest. "My baby, my sweet little baby."

Roland waited, respectfully, silently.

"Would you like to come in, young man, have a cup of coffee?"

"No, ma'am, thank you. I just need you to sign these papers, and I'll be on my…"

"You might want to look under the back before you go," she interrupted, as he handed the clipboard to her. "Something's been howling all night."

"A dog?" he asked, taking the clipboard back.

"Sounded like a gee-dee wolf, if you ask me."

Roland pursed his lips, absently signed his name to the paper.

"Okay, let me get my pole, and I'll take a look-see."

"Fine," she murmured, cradling the box to her chest as if it were her actual dog. "If you want that coffee, you just knock."

The door closed, and he thought he heard her crying quietly as she disappeared into the house.

He went to the truck to get a control pole—basically a long stick with a collapsible loop of wire on one end—and a pair of thick leather gloves. As a precaution, he also took a loaded tranquilizer gun.

A cracked, narrow concrete path ran to her backyard. A rusted gate, groaning on its hinges, admitted him.

That's where he smelled it first.

It was like *dog*, but multiplied by 100. And it wasn't the smell of a group of dogs or even the kennel. It was the essential smell of *dog*, pure and concentrated on the air. It was dense and unpleasant, with a whiff of wet fur and a back odor like urine.

And blood—there was also a bloody component, mineral and meaty.

A few wooden steps led to the back door. Under this, a wooden trellis blocked the crawl space. A section was broken, chewed through—recently from the looks of it.

Using the end of the pole, he tapped the trellis, eliciting a low, menacing growl from the dark beneath the house, angry, fearful—

"Shit," Roland cursed under his breath. He bent, surveyed the space. There was no way he was going to be able to squeeze in there. The pole extended 12 feet, but the longer it got, the more unwieldy it was and trying to loop the wire around the neck of an agitated animal was difficult under the best conditions.

On his hands and knees, he peered into the hole. The smell rolled from this opening in powerful waves, floating on the equally strong odors of damp earth and mildew.

The growl became more pronounced, more threatening.

The space went back about eight feet and was L-shaped, with the foot of the letter farther back on the right side. There, he could just make out a dense, compact curl of darkness.

"Hey, baby," he said in his calmest tone. "Let's get you out of there, take you someplace safe."

He hated himself for saying that; hated himself even though he knew that the lie meant nothing to the frightened animal.

Slowly, carefully, he slid the pole into the opening.

"S'ok, baby, s'ok. I'm not gonna hurt you—not gonna—"

There was an explosion of movement that caught him off guard, snapping, growling. The pole ripped from his hands, skittered into the darkness.

Then, just as suddenly, it stopped.

Recovering quickly, he snatched at the end of the pole, hauled it back. The end was chewed savagely, but the wire was intact. Raising his eyebrows at the damage, Roland slid the pole back in, prepared this time for the dog to attack it.

This time, only a plaintive whine, the low growl. He felt it bite at the pole several times, but with far less vehemence. He maneuvered the loop where he thought its head was, felt it slip around something. Quickly, he pulled back, closing the loop, yanked the pole out.

This was met by violent thrashing and maddened yelping. The pole jerked in his hands.

Careful to keep hold of it, Roland planted his feet to get better leverage. Laughing a little, he hauled back strongly, like an angler wrestling a sport fish, amazed at the fight this dog had—and its weight.

A chaotic mass burst through the wooden trellis, scattering pieces in every direction.

It was enormous, easily as big as a Great Dane or an Irish Wolfhound. Not lean or lanky, but densely muscled, with a huge head and an elongated muzzle. Its fur was light grays and tans and dirty browns, *and its teeth—*

Its teeth, snapping and biting at the noose that held it, the pole that held it, the man who held it, were long and wickedly curved—*and there were so many of them.*

The thing fought too fiercely, was too big, too heavy. The pole wasn't going to be enough—His hands scrabbling at the trank gun, he unholstered it, glanced at the preloaded dosage, and guessed. Aiming at the squirming, writhing dog, he squinted, pulled the trigger twice.

Two darts buried into its dense fur in quick succession, tiny against its bulk. The dog bellowed in rage, stopped moving, turned its head slowly, deliberately to look at Roland.

Its eyes, a strange gold-green, fixed him with measuring intelligence.

The animal crouched, flexing its rear legs and dipping its head, prepared to leap at him.

When the trank kicked in, and the dog's rear legs folded, buckled.

It turned, Roland swore it actually *turned* and looked at its rear legs in stunned disbelief.

Then, it rolled limply, bonelessly on its side, panting heavily. A long, drooling tongue lolled from that tooth-filled mouth, swiped listlessly at the ground.

Its eyes, those gold-flecked eyes, stayed locked on Roland, watched him as he carefully prodded it with his foot, producing a weak, but nonetheless disturbing, reaction.

Shrugging, he put another dart into it as it lay there.

He was definitely not going to carry it to the truck until those eyes were closed.

* * *

"Je-sus Kee-rist!" whistled Manny Figueroa, the vet on duty when Roland plopped the dog onto the exam table. "What in the name of Mary Mother of God is that? A bear?"

Roland exhaled as the dog's weight left him. "I dunno—a wolf or something."

Manny looked at the dog's head, its mouth to ensure that it was asleep before he laid a hand on it. Painful experience had taught them all that. He smoothed the fur on its face, unfolded its ears, pulled back its gums and ran a finger over its enormous, slick teeth.

"I don't know what the frig this is," he breathed, flashing a serious look at Roland, who watched with his arms folded over his barrel chest.

"A hybrid, maybe? Wolfdog? Maybe a cross breed with a mastiff or wolfhound or something?"

Manny was already shaking his head. "No, no—look at the muzzle—too long. And those teeth? Jesus, Mary and Joseph, have you ever seen that kind of teeth on a dog? And look at the musculature—this is one seriously beefed up dude—errr—*dudette?*"

"It's a she?" Roland asked, raising his eyebrows.

"Mm-hmm," Manny answered, searching the dog's belly, between its rear legs. "See, here are the teats—and—hmmm—"

"And—?"

"She's in estrus—heat." He inhaled deeply. "Can't you smell that?"

"Have you ever smelled anything like that from a normal dog?" Roland asked.

"No. So, I'm going to take some blood, run some tests," Manny said, circling the table with his hand on his chin. "Keep her knocked out for a while. But when I'm finished, there's no way we can put her back in the kennel with the other dogs. They'll go nuts."

Roland nodded. "I can move some stuff out of the adoption room. Not too much she can mess up there."

Manny nodded absently, a finger tapping his chin. "Okay. Hey, tell Mel to poke his head in here. I think we might want to get somebody from the department of conservation in here to take a look at this—see if we can figure out—*what* she is."

* * *

Roland sensed it the moment he left the exam room; a tension in the air, something brittle, expectant. He heard the roar of the dogs barking at the back of the building. When he opened the door to the kennel, the roar easily trebled, quadrupled. Every dog in every cage was barking at its limits.

The barking was *fear*—plain, old *fear.*

The odor of the bitch's heat was conspicuous on the air, even to a human like him. Rather than exciting these dogs—at least the male ones—it was frightening them, whipping them into a frenzy.

He went down the center of the kennel, looking into each cage. Big dog, small dog, male, female, aggressive, shy, they were all at the back of their cages, at the back with their heads low, barking and growling. Each made eye contact with him briefly, but didn't hold it, didn't seem to want to pay him much attention at all.

Stepping to the closest cage, he lifted the papers, saw he was an older male, about eight, a mix of Labrador and pit bull. This one, splotched brown and white with haunted, icy blue eyes, regarded him casually, but didn't stop barking.

Roland unlatched the cage, knelt, patted his knees. He'd calm this one, use him to calm the rest.

The dog bayed louder, swayed his head back and forth, as if telling Roland, "No, no, no—"

Roland was patient and insistent, and soon the dog gave in to the trusting instinct of his kind, and came to Roland, hesitant, tail low but wagging.

"Good boy, good boy," he said, letting him sniff the back of his hand before touching him. "I'm gonna call you Roscoe."

Slowly, so as not to spook him, he took a leash from his belt, clipped it to the dog's collar. Immediately, the dog drew itself up as if energized. His tail rose, wagged like a metronome.

"Roscoe," Roland said, ruffing the sides of his head. "We're gonna be good friends. I know it."

They walked to the center of the kennel, and Roland let Roscoe lead him back and forth between the cages until the dogs had settled.

* * *

Manny peeled off the blue exam gloves, tossed them into the garbage. He gave Roland a vague, concerned look, went to the sink and washed his hands.

"Mel says that the conservation boys don't have the time to look at our mutt," Manny said, drying his hands with paper towels. "They said we know dogs better than they do."

Roland chuckled, but Manny was not amused. "*Assholes*. Like we're idiots because we deal with *domesticated* animals and not *wild* ones."

Roland glanced to where the dog lay, covering the exam table, draped with sheets. The tape from an anesthesia tube was still affixed to her lips, partially open, tongue still lolling.

"Well, aren't they gonna be surprised," Manny chuckled. "Especially when her offspring attack someone."

"Offspring?"

Manny removed the tape from her mouth, gently smoothed her fur. "Oh, yes. She's definitely whelped—a few litters at least."

"I thought you said she was in heat?"

"Well, she's not pregnant *now*, but wow, she's asking for it," he said, waving a hand in front of his face. He shuffled through papers, jotted a few notes.

"What do *you* think she is?" Roland asked.

"Well, the blood tests will give us some idea. But just looking at her—I dunno. She's so friggin' big, unusually built. I'd say she's got some kind of wild canine in her, maybe mixed with some domestic, but what and how much—"

He shrugged, looked seriously at Roland. "You know what happens to her now, right?"

Roland had been looking at the shape beneath the sheet, started. "What?"

Manny raised his eyebrows.

"Oh, yeah—but maybe—"

"No maybe, Rollie," he said, putting his hand on Roland's shoulder. He was at least a foot shorter, so he had to reach to do this. "We're obviously not going to adopt her. We can't keep her, and we definitely can't release her."

"But don't we need to find out what she is first?"

"The blood tests and a necropsy will tell us that."

Roland flipped his wrist, looked at his watch. It was already after five p.m.

"Well, not today." He thought back to Bethany and her eyes. "I don't want to fire up that son of a bitch one more time today."

Manny nodded. "Well, I put some blankets, a bowl of water and kibble in the adoption room. If you want to help me, we can leave her for the night. Careful of the bandages now."

* * *

Roland decided to spend the night at the shelter, as much to keep an eye on this strange dog as to test his decision to leave—to make sure that taking a job at a recycling plant was what he really wanted.

He locked the door after Manny left, looked at Roscoe. He'd decided to make the dog his companion for the evening, and Roscoe seemed happy to take the job. He followed Roland as he bought sodas from the vending machine. He followed Roland to the front door when the pizza delivery guy came, sat by his side in Mel's office and watched television and ate pizza with him as the evening waxed.

At about 10, Roland decided to check on the dog. He walked to the adoption room, peered through the narrow window that opened vertically in the door. She was awake, lying on the floor, moving her head groggily, unsure of where she was, what had happened. She didn't notice Roland looking at her through the window.

Roscoe followed as he made a last check of the kennel, then ducked into the small office just off the garage. The shelter kept a cot for staff who wanted to sleep there, usually to keep an eye on an animal after a medical procedure.

Roland pulled off his boots, stripped off his pants, lowered himself gently to the cot. It was too small, seemingly too flimsy, but it had held him other nights; it would hold him tonight. Tucking the pillow under his head, he noticed that Roscoe had curled beside the cot, snoring softly.

* * *

There was a loud shattering of glass, and the dogs were barking madly.
Fumbling for his watch, he pressed the button that illuminated the dial. 2:43 a.m.
Roland lay there for a moment, getting his bearings.
He flinched when something pushed at his hand, licked it. He'd forgotten about Roscoe.
"Shhh," he told the dog. "Good boy."
And he listened.
Padding feet, clicking on the linoleum hallway—
Breathing, harsh and raspy.
That smell, that blood smell of dog in heat gummed the air, made his mouth taste of raw meat.

Roscoe nudged his hand again, whined softly.

"Shhh," Roland said, absently.

Someone had broken in. The shelter was not in a good neighborhood; who'd want a dog shelter, gas chamber and a crematorium next to their homes? But break in to take what—?

Drugs—always the drugs—the narcotics, the anesthetics, the tranquilizers.

Roland pursed his lips, strained to hear any sounds that might tell him where they were.

Then he heard scratching—nails on wood.

He thought of her, locked in the adoption room, scratching to get out.

He thought of them letting her out, letting her get at them.

Though he had little pity for whoever they might be, he couldn't let them be ripped to shreds by a dog big enough, aggressive enough to do exactly that.

Pulling on his pants and boots, he grabbed a flashlight from a shelf. He took a deep breath, stood in the darkness for a moment, entered the kennel.

Roscoe followed at his heels.

* * *

The din from the kennel was disorienting, and Roland felt instantly nervous. Even Roscoe was skittish, pressing his side against Roland's calves as they crept through the room. From every direction came frightened, insistent barking, maddened beyond restraint.

And Roland knew why.

That scent, the scent that floated on the air this afternoon, meaty and bloody and sexual, was now overlaid with another; another that was like it—
—not like it.

It was musky and sweaty and aggressive.

It was the masculine equivalent to the feminine odor.

Maybe—

But no—Roland dismissed this, before the thought even formed.

There was no way—no way—

Steeling himself, he switched on the flashlight, and the beam cast weird, hallucinatory shadows through the steel bars of the cages and onto the walls. The light swept the room, but he saw nothing out of order; dozens of cages, dozens of glowing eyes, noting him, then dismissing him as they had done this afternoon.

Roland touched Roscoe's head, strode to the door leading to the administration offices. The door opened onto a short hallway leading to the front offices, but split halfway there—exam rooms to the left, adoption rooms to the right.

Whoever they were, they'd be looking for the exam rooms, for the drugs stored in lock-up.

They'd be in that short hallway to the left.

He turned the flashlight off.

One hand took the doorknob, the other held Roscoe back.

Carefully, he turned the knob, drew the door open a crack, slid his head around the jamb.

The smell was overwhelming, a muscular, physical presence in that small space. It reeked of ammonia and the intense musk of males.

To the left, where the exam rooms were, there was nothing.

To the right, though, to the right there was a shifting of shadows, scuffling in the dark, panting, growling—

For a moment, Roland wasn't sure what he was seeing, but his eyes quickly adjusted to the dark.

He made out the curve of a haunch, the shape of a paw on the floor—

Then his mouth fell open, went dry—

There was a horrible snarling altercation, the sounds of fighting, bodies thumping heavily against the walls, and something was thrown into the main corridor, something large and dark—

—and on two feet.

Whatever it was wasn't a *dog*; whatever it was wasn't *human.*

It stood on two legs, yes, and it was tall, at least as tall as Roland and perhaps an inch or so taller.

It was furred all over, furred and clawed on each hand, each foot.

Its massive head sported an extended muzzle pulled back over a mouthful of razor teeth, bared at whatever had thrown it aside.

Flexing its massive hind legs, it launched back into the fray, and there was another round of snapping, snarling, whining.

Roland eased the door shut, took his hand off the knob.

He was sweating now, shaking. Drops of perspiration beaded on his head, trickled down his neck, his chest. His heart beat wildly.

It was a—a—

No! There is no goddamn way that thing was a—a—

Men in masks, that's what they were—robbers wore masks, didn't they?

He leaned against the door, not knowing what to do, when Roscoe's face pushed into his limp hands, licked his palms.

Pull it together, pal, he seemed to say. *You have to take care of me.*

Roland took a deep, quiet breath, held it, exhaled slowly, shakily.

At that moment, he felt the building shudder through the door he leaned against, heard the sound of rending, splitting wood from the hallway on the other side.

They'd broken through the door of the adoption room.

They, whatever *they* were, weren't interested in the exam room, in the drugs stored there.

They wanted *her*.

* * *

The trank gun—

As he petted Roscoe to calm them both, his hand grazed his holster, and he fumbled it free.

There was only one dart left in the chamber—*not enough*.

The supply of darts was locked in Exam Room 2, closest to the gas chamber, farthest from the door he was at.

Or he could leave, that way was clear. He could simply walk out the back door, get into his truck and go home. In the morning, he'd call in, quit, take that job with his shit head brother-in-law.

It sounded good for a second, sounded like a plan.

He knew he couldn't do that; knew he couldn't leave the other animals at the mercy of those—whatever they were.

He had to get to Exam Room 2, had to open this door, open it and walk the short distance—well, okay, *sprint* the short distance, hope he wasn't seen.

If he was, he wouldn't have much time to unlock the cabinet, load the gun, shoot them as they crashed through the door.

How many darts would that take? The female had taken three to put down, and these—well, from what he could see they were much, much larger.

Five? Seven? Ten?

The chamber only held four. He'd have to reload—three maybe four times.

And what would they be doing while he reloaded?

Tearing his throat out, most likely. Ripping his chest open, his abdomen, spilling his guts, shiny and gray-purple, across the linoleum.

He grimaced, shook his head. *Okay, that's not helping—*

* * *

When he opened the door, his legs were rubbery, his breathing short and shallow.

He heard them, *in* the adoption room now. Scuffling, panting, whining, *whining—*

Now—he pushed through the doorway, tried to block Roscoe from following, but the dog was insistent. He stepped into the hall, which reeked of their funk, slowly, quietly closed the door.

Fast, he moved fast now, dashing for the left corridor, sliding into the wall as he tried to take the turn, his shoes squeaking on the worn linoleum.

They didn't hear him; they were consumed by their own needs, their own lusts.

Gasping, he careened down the hall, stumbled before the door to the exam room.

It was locked—

Shit!

He fumbled with the key ring clipped to his belt, the keys jangling as loud as church bells.

The sounds from the adoption room quieted.

As he held the ring to his face, tried to find the right key, he could hear wet snuffling sounds, sniffing—sniffing the air for his scent.

That one!

He jammed it at the doorknob, and it skittered around the lock.

A howl came from the adoption room, chilling in the encompassing dark.

It echoed from the ceiling tiles, from the recesses of his frightened mind.

Every hair on every part of Roland's body stood.

The key slid into the lock, and he turned it desperately.

As he did, he looked over his shoulder.

A tall, menacing shape peeled from the darkness, grew, expanded in the hall.

With hands that threatened to lose their strength, he turned the knob, opened the door.

He fell into the room on a blast of sound, a raging, vengeful howl that he was sure brought dust from the ceiling.

Pulling the heavy door shut, his fingers fumbled with the lock, just as he heard the thing's claws on the floor, felt the weight of it strike the door, which bowed at the impact.

Slumped there for a moment, he heard the thing snuffling, trying to find him, how to get at him.

He thought it could smell his fear—*hell, he could almost smell it*—hear his heart.

Roscoe!

He suddenly remembered the dog, panicked that he'd left it out there.

Then the dog pushed against him, looked at him and smiled, despite everything, he smiled a doggie smile. For a moment, a brief moment, Roland smiled back.

"What now, boy?" he asked, ruffing the dog's head, his smile fading. "What the fuck do we do now?"

He could hear one of them still outside the door, pacing, its nails raking the walls, scrabbling across the wood of the door. Every now and then, it paused, and Roland heard it drawing in the air of his scent, making sure he was still there.

Roland scanned the room, trying to find something that might help. Cabinets filled with medical supplies lined the walls; nothing in them more dangerous than a tongue depressor. Even the scalpels, which be briefly considered, would require close proximity to do any damage, and Roland doubted that he'd be able to get past those long, sharp claws.

Then he heard it, behind him, behind the other door, which he'd forgotten completely about.

Exam Room 2 opened into the gas chamber room through a second door, so bodies could be moved discretely without going into the corridor.

One of them was in there now, sniffing at this door.

The other one was still at the door into the hallway, growling softly.

They were cutting off his exits, trapping him.

They were pulling him—selecting him for death.

He would not be killed here, not like this, not by them.

The gas chamber—if he could lure them inside, if he could—pull them instead of allowing them to pull him...

That meant distracting them so he could get into the chamber room, open the door—

How to do that without letting the one in the hallway in?

As if the god of dogs listened to his prayers, he heard the female now, yipping from the adoption room.

Instantly, there was no sound at all.

Then, there was a terrific scrabbling of nails on the linoleum, and Roland almost laughed when he pictured them, like most dogs trying to gain purchase on that slick flooring, running in place for a moment.

One thumped hard against the wall, and for a second he was afraid that the sheetrock would give, and the thing would crash into the room with him. The wall held, and they were gone from the hall, from the gas chamber room.

Quietly, Roland opened the door, holding the trank gun before him as if it were a .45 and not—well, not a dart gun. Roscoe followed, sniffing cautiously at the air, staying within touch of him.

He went to the chamber hatch, drew it open, had a moment of nervousness as he worried that they might not fit through this opening, that it might be too small. Then he remembered their ability to run on all fours, as she had done, and he hoped that this held true.

Quietly, Roland took the key ring from his belt, inserted the key into the control panel that started the machine. He checked the dials, saw that it was ready to go.

Patting Roscoe's head one more time, he flipped a switch that turned on a light inside the chamber, leaving the rest of the room dark.

Roland hoped that this light, this single light in the darkness, would be enough to arouse their curiosity, their ire.

Quietly, Roland drew the door open as far as he could, stepped behind it—

Roscoe squeezed beside him, peered into the hallway, growling softly.

His heart in his mouth, Roland jingled his keys as loud as he could.

In an instant, he heard the sounds across the hall stop, heard the distinct sounds of them sniffing.

Heard their claws clack on the linoleum, coming closer, cautious, oh, so cautious as they saw the light.

There was a sound then that made Roland think he might actually get out of this in one piece.

It was a huffing, plopping sound, weight falling to the floor.

The sound of them taking to all fours as they saw the small doorway through which the light shone.

They padded forward, still growling, still testing the air, still tasting him on it.

Then, it all fell apart—

Roscoe, with no warning, barked, an explosion of sound in the small room, darted from behind Roland's legs, from behind the steel hatch, and stood before the lit entrance to the chamber.

"Roscoe!" Roland shouted, pushing his head from behind cover enough to see the dog, true to its pit bull blood, standing firmly, resolutely in front of the chamber, matching their growls with his own.

Snarling as if delivered something long denied, they bounded into the room, carrying their sounds, their smells with them.

Instead of holding his ground, Roscoe darted into the chamber, zigzagging as he ran, then circling inside, barking and barking.

The two creatures hit the small doorway, tried to squeeze through at the same time, rebounded, tumbling back. Snarling and snapping, they regained their feet, launched themselves one at a time through the narrow entrance.

Roland pushed the door from him, brought it around.

Inside, he saw them for the first time in the light, in the cold, indifferent reality of the 60-watt bulb set in a cage in the chamber's ceiling.

And his heart froze, his blood froze—

No... that's just not possible—it's not—

But it was, and they set on Roscoe, one grabbing him, him still biting and biting at them, flinging him across the small chamber. He struck the steel wall, yelped in pain, slid to the floor.

"No!" Roland saw great gashes across his side where one of their claws had laid him open.

At his cry, they spun to face him, parting their jaws in great, slavering smiles of their own.

"Roscoe!" Shaking its head, the dog leapt to its feet, whimpering, and ran to Roland.

Just as the creatures approached the entrance, Roscoe zipped through, slid between Roland's legs, crashed into the door frame behind him.

With a resounding clang of steel, Roland threw the hatch shut, turned the lock.

Blows of fury and rage rang on the steel, dimpled it in places.

The hatch held.

Roland looked through the acrylic window, hoping they would not think to break it, and saw them racing around the room, baying, howling in frustration.

He pushed the red button near the door, heard the sound of gas hissing into the chamber.

For the first time, he was glad to hear that sound.

They rained blows on the walls, barked and yipped, and eventually fell on each other, biting and scratching in their impotent anger.

After a minute or two, they slowed, faltered.

Another minute, and they collapsed onto the floor, their sides rising and falling rapidly, foam frothing at their muzzles.

In another, they were still.

And then, in another, they changed, altered, their shapes twisting, collapsing in on themselves, fur disappearing into pink, pink skin.

Until they were—*but no*—*no*—

Roland backed away from the chamber, backed through the door.

No—

* * *

She faced him in the hallway, blocking any exit.

Roland turned the trank gun on her, Roscoe crouched and snarling at his side.

Pawing at the linoleum, she whined in frustration. She could see the shapes of her mates in the gas chamber behind them, see them dying.

Roland saw her looking at the gun he held. Saw her remember what it had done to her before.

Just then, the front door opened with a jangling of keys.

Roland heard Manny's voice, "Jee-sus Kee-rist! What the hell happened—?"

She saw her chance.

Rearing on her hind legs as the males had, she leaned toward Roland, shook her head fiercely at him, every fang dripping saliva, and roared, roared in frustration, in maddened sorrow, roared in warning.

Then, she leapt across the hall, into the front office, bowling Manny over as she sprang through the door. Roland watched her lope into the gray dawn, turn a corner, disappear.

They went to help Manny, take him inside, explain what had happened.

* * *

After the explanations, Roland helped Manny carry the wounded dog to the Exam Room, acted as his assistant as he gave him a few shots of pain-killer, cleaned his cuts, sewed up the worst of them.

"I'm not patching him up so that you can gas him later on, am I?" Manny asked, regarding Roland over the tops of his glasses as he worked.

"No. No more for me," Roland smiled, holding Roscoe's paw. "This one, I keep."

As they finished, the sun was just beginning to come up over the buildings outside.

"Been a vet a long time," Manny mused, pulling a suture tight. "Never thought I'd see a were—"

"Don't even say that," Roland warned, shaking his head. "That can't ever leave this room."

"Have it your way. But those bodies we took to the crematorium say otherwise."

"Well, if that's what they were—what *she* was—why the hell was she still a wolf when I picked her up—it was broad daylight," Roland argued, patting Roscoe's muzzle as he lay on the table.

Manny shrugged, bandaged the dog's last wound. "She was in estrus, remember? Maybe they're unable to change back when they're in heat or when they're pregnant. That would protect them from—being bred by a male when they're not in wolf form. To ensure they're in wolf form while they give birth to—well—*pups*. Who knows?"

Roland considered this, looked through the window at the early morning neighborhood. "And she's out there again, out there and in heat and ready to make another litter of those things."

"That's one thing you won't have to worry about," Manny chuckled, flicking his gloves into the trash can. "Because I spayed her. Just in case the department of conservation boys wanted to take her, release her somewhere else. So, she won't be giving birth again, not to babies *or* puppies… *ever.*"

GRANDMA, WHAT BIG TEETH YOU HAVE
ROB ROSEN

The bloodied, dismembered bodies started turning up every thirty days. Like clockwork. Men, women, young, old, bodies torn apart, limbs severed. Rorschach stains of blood canvassing the brutal scenes. An animal, they figured. It had to be. Teeth marks, puncture wounds, claws like daggers, a killing machine. Something big and feral and unrelenting.

Still, Sammy felt he knew better.

No proof, just a hunch. Well, more like an educated guess. After all, it wasn't like he hadn't overheard the family history, the rumors, before all this started. Long-lost relatives missing from photo albums, whispers at annual reunions, other murders, and lots of them. Plus, his gut was telling him what his heart and head were otherwise hoping. Then again, none of this involved his grandmother. At least not yet.

He'd never spent the night at her house before, though she lived a scant few miles away. Not that there was much need to he supposed. His parents always took him on vacations with them, and if they needed a babysitter, she'd come over to their house. Still, she was getting on in years and needed some help packing up her place before moving to an assisted living home. Everyone else was busy with other things; Sammy was volunteered. It made him uneasy, and he couldn't figure out why. He loved his grandmother. Always had.

Thankfully, there wasn't all that much to pack: two bedrooms, one bathroom, a living room and a dining room. Tiny house for a tiny woman. Grandpa was long-deceased. Yellowed photos were all that remained. Her meager possessions were all easily boxed up, taped up, stacked against a wall.

"Thanks for helping, Sammy," she said, as she bent over a stack of dishes, her long gray hair cascading over hunched shoulders, mind seemingly elsewhere.

"No problem, Grammy," he told her, as he carefully wrapped the silverware and cups. All of it ancient looking, even to his untrained eye.

She glanced up, sapphire eyes twinkling beneath the overhead lights. "They tell you why I'm being shipped out?" The twinkle turned to a flame, bursting from behind recessed sockets.

Sammy coughed, a strange sensation swirling menacingly around his belly. "You, um, you need more help these days, I suppose."

"Yeah, right," was all she replied, as she turned away.

In truth, her grandson thought, she was strong as an ox and sharp as a tack. Then again, what did he know? Not like the grown-ups told kids much of anything. Maybe she was losing her marbles and was hiding it well enough. "Guess it's probably safer at the home, even if you don't need the help," he tried.

"Safer than what?" she asked, not even bothering to look his way this time. Sammy paused, sensing he was treading in dangerous waters. "You know, the times and all. Crime. And, um, *the murders.*"

This caught her attention, her pause echoing his. "That's exactly why they're sending me away, Sammy. But not for the reason you're thinking, you know."

A shiver ran up his spine, a cold bead of sweat forming atop his brow. "No, I, um, don't know, Grammy. Tell me." The dangerous waters were rising, the tide flooding in, chest-deep, neck-deep, suffocating him.

She started to reply, then caught herself. "Your parents, they didn't— oh, never mind. You're right; it's for my own good. *Everyone's* own good."

He started to press, but she held up her hand. The conversation was over. Which was fine by him. Still, Sammy had a feeling it was more like a temporary reprieve.

That night he didn't sleep well, the spare room deathly quiet, walls now bare, shelves empty. Just Sammy, the bed, the window. With the shades gone the moon flooded in, silver beams dancing on the closet door. He sat up, squinting into the nothingness, and couldn't remember emptying the closet or seeing Grammy do so either. *Strange*, he thought.

The boy hopped out of bed and crept over, his heart pounding in his chest. He creaked the closet door open. There wasn't much in there, mostly boxes from when his Gramps was still alive, some from even before the two of them had met, according to the labels. He opened some of the lids, poking around a bit. Everything was musty, old, age-worn. He put it all back where he found it, preparing to return to the bed. That's when he spotted it, a box on the top shelf, pushed against the far wall.

Sammy stood on tiptoe and slid it forward. The box was on the small side, light, dusty, much older looking than the others. No label. No date. He popped it open, the aged tape turning to powder. "Clothes," he whispered, suddenly disappointed.

His disappointment was short-lived.

He grabbed for the garment on top, draping it down. It was a dress, really old, threadbare. Only, that's not what made it stand out. There was a hole in the back, ripped, not cut. Same for the sleeves, both torn, and not down the seam either. *Weird thing to save*, he thought. Weirder still, the box was full of similar items, clothes, all frayed in the same exact spots. "Keepsakes not worth keeping," he whispered.

Then he heard the sound.

He jumped, dropping the box, the clothes scattering around his feet. The noise came again, a scratch, a moan, a sigh. His heart beat out a syncopated rhythm in his chest, the sound of it pounding in his ears. He moved to the door. It opened with a squeak. "Grammy?" he managed, his throat tight and dry as the Sahara. No answer, the noise continued. It grew louder as he moved down the hallway, through the barren living room and on to the kitchen.

It was coming from outside.

He unlocked the door, face pressed up tight to the screen. "Hello?" he whispered. The noise abruptly stopped. No scampering of feet, no sound besides his own heavy breathing. He looked around the nearly empty kitchen, reaching for the only weapon he could find: a broom. "Go away," he managed, his voice suddenly finding itself.

Still nothing. He flicked the switch on, the room suddenly bright, blinding. He rubbed his eyes, squinting into the backyard. Two eyes glinted back at him at the edge of the yard, blinking. Then teeth, long, sharp teeth, glistening white beneath the full moon. White, that is, where they weren't a crimson red. He froze, the distant growl rumbling through his stomach like a runaway train, the teeth bared further, the bloody carcass dropped to the ground in a sickeningly dull thud.

The animal moved towards the house, its muzzle coming into view, eyes a surprising blue, the snout long, canine in appearance. Except dogs don't stand on their hind feet, clawed hands extended, walking slowly but with purpose. *Only one animal does that*, Sammy thought.

Knees trembling, stomach lurching, Sammy slammed the door, locking it, his back up against it as he tried to catch his breath. Then a new sound, feet running towards the house, fast, a body slamming into the door frame, claws scraping at the wood, the sound like nails across a chalkboard, grunting coming from the other side.

"Go away!" he screamed, voice cracking, sweat pouring down his face now. "Please, go away!"

It bayed and barked, the sound of its breathing loud in Sammy's ears, despite the inch or so of wood that still separated the two of them. Then a momentary cold, dead silence, before the creature stopped, then retreated away from the house, letting out a howl from at least ten feet away.

Sammy moved to the window and peeked out, the creature turning again to look his way, locking eyes before disappearing into the night, its long gray mane the last thing he saw.

"Grammy," he sighed, shivering.

He checked her room to be certain, but she was gone. He bowed his head, walking to her lone window, the moon's rays illuminating his face as the final howl went up again, causing his very bones to quake.

"Grammy," he echoed, crashing down on her bed, confused and alone.

Exhausted, he lay down, trying to collect his own disturbing thoughts.

He must have dozed off, waking, surprised to be in his own bed, the sun bright and warm on his face.

A dream, he thought, but knew better. *A nightmare*, he corrected.

He sprung up and tiptoed to the door, making his way down the hall. She was in the kitchen, a hot cup of coffee in front of her, some juice already waiting for him. "Morning," she said, forcing a smile.

He sat down across from her, both their eyes intent yet wary. "I already know it was you, you know."

She nodded, eyes closed for just the briefest of seconds. "I suppose it's best you find it out from me, anyway. Maybe that's why they sent you here yesterday."

"Not to help you pack?" he asked, terror suddenly rising up his chest.

She laughed, despite the circumstances. "Does it look like I need help, Sammy?"

He took a sip of his juice. "No, ma'am." He paused, his eyes taking her in, looking for the beast he'd seen the night before. Not a trace. No surprise there. "So you're a, a *werewolf*?" The words barely made it out from between his lips.

She smiled and nodded. "I think you always knew, Sammy. Felt it at least. Makes sense."

He frowned. "Nothing makes sense. None of this. All those murders. You." He paused, unsure of how to continue. "I saw you eating last night. It's been you all along."

She sighed and shook her head, the mane of steely gray hair rolling down her shoulders. "No, Sammy. Just a rabbit. See, the home I'm going to is for werewolves." She rose and stood by his side, a gentle hand on his shoulder. "When werewolves get older, they lose the ability to control their most basic instincts."

"Like to kill?" Sammy interrupted.

"Like to kill," she replied, the nod returning. "And the home protects us from that. And that population, of course. That way, our kind can still live among them, as we have for centuries."

He gulped, his stomach now tied in knots. "Our kind?"

She tightened the grip on his shoulder. "Sometimes it skips a generation."

He remembered the torn clothes in the box, his own pajamas still in one piece. "When I get a little older, these will rip when I, when I change?"

Again she sighed. "You've already changed, Sammy. Last night, during the full moon. And before that one. And before that one, too. When we change, we have little remembrance of it, just flashing images, sometimes. The torn clothes come later. Still, we can control what and who we kill. When we get older."

He turned and looked up at her. "Unless you're too old to control it."

That's when the agonizing images suddenly flashed in his head, bolting through like white hot lightening. Muscles and joints aching, stretching, morphing. Claws and hair and teeth so sharp they could cut bone. The pain and confusion. Anguish and ecstasy. The blood. So much blood. A veritable river of it.

She bent down and kissed his forehead. "Or too young to control it, Sammy." She turned and taped up the last of her meager belongings. "Or just a little too young."

SCARRED FOR LIFE
MICHAEL LAIMO

Every night I dream his face. It is just as I remember it, staring, accusing—and yet, unbridled in its potential to forgive. *Do you love me?* He asks. I try to answer but in this ongoing dream I am incapable of expressing my feelings for the boy—the boy who is my very own flesh and blood—an extension of my love. By reason of my inability to illuminate my affections, he senses only my fear, rising from me in an invisible musk that only he can detect. His rosy cherub innocence vanishes from his face, morphing into a bestial visage secreting hot fluids from the snarls of his formed muzzle, strenuously taut from pleading.

If you say you love me, father, then why did you let me die?

I let him die because I had to. Because I did not love him.

* * *

My son died during childbirth. It had become no true shock after all the painful difficulties my wife tolerated throughout the latter months of the pregnancy. Fourteen hellish months it lasted. Nine of those joyfully anticipated, the remaining five painfully endured.

I sat by her side in our bedroom for most of those five months, gingerly running my fingers along the purple gnarls lining her swelled abdomen. I could feel the baby kicking, moving, answering the gentle tracings of my finger as I prayed for its escape from the womb, my mind searching for a reason as to why the attempt of Caesarean childbirth would be fatal to both wife and child. Why the inductions had failed to work. And then why my wife vehemently refused medical attention, choosing the herbal remedies of a naturalist midwife.

Even here, before his birth, he haunted my dreams, my fetal child running the show like a mysterious ringleader, we the parents its unwitting puppets, answering his every beckon.

* * *

Her water broke in an alarming spray of fluids, shocking against the natural sterility of the environment we occupied, the odd plants arranged about the bed, the high humid temperature my wife insisted upon. She gripped my hand and held it vice-tight as the midwife began the procedure. I watched with great disquiet as her face fell into an agony of contortion and pain and fear. I could only return her grasp and offer false hopes of reassurance.

Screams abounded: my wife producing noises like nothing I'd ever heard. The pain of childbirth, I thought. It must be nearly unendurable.

It happened so quickly, her bloated stomach shifting, our baby slipping free from the womb.

My breath escaped me. I fell back in utter loathe, dizzied at the sight of him. I could see my wife's stomach undulating, pumping fluids and matter free from her womb, surrounding the infant in a moat of steaming gore. The placenta-shrouded newborn twisted madly on the bed amidst its after-birth, the head and arms rupturing the tenuous veil, emerging forth. Wicked claws brushing at the dermis with feline-like consideration, wiping the matter across its face as its tongue lapped urgently for nutrition.

Its gaze found mine, primordial eyes with diamond pupils set in blue irises. A brown gelatinous fluid purled from its throat and fled down its sodden torso. My wife reached desperately for the infant, moaning and still fraught in pain. The midwife bustled madly, assisting in the action. She cradled the infant to her breast as it writhed and convulsed in her arms, seeking freedom from her grasp. She toweled its fine hide, the umbilical cord whipping about like a snake, possessed with a life of its own.

And I could only stand silent and watch the horror of a baby that seemed to defy all that I expected this moment to be.

When the baby quieted I walked over, took it from my wife's arms. Its eyes shined green with a luminescence that I knew bragged sight in the darkest and dampest of places.

I asked myself, *Do you love him?*

No, I answered. *I don't.*

I returned the child to the midwife, and left the room.

Three days later, my baby died.

* * *

I sit in a chair on the porch of a rented cabin that exists deep in a wooded area, far from civilization. There is a special tranquility about this place, one that I cannot put a finger on, yet it is where my wife wishes to be. Somehow, *this* feels right.

The environment was all wrong, my wife had explained. *It is why our baby died.*

Had my wife not seen the state in which our offspring had been born? Had she not seen its deformations? And, had she not seen me shun the child unlike a father should do? *This is why our baby died!*

My wife exits the cabin and stands next to me. I gaze into her eyes and I know at once it is time. The midwife follows, assisting her down the three steps to the clearing before the cabin. She removes my wife's clothing, first her shirt to reveal the pendulous breasts and a distended stomach that have endured yet another fourteen months of agony. She then peels her skirt away—a wash of fluid is evident between her thighs.

The midwife soon follows the procedure, removing her own clothing. The task now accomplished, the two slowly disappear into the woods.

* * *

I have waited for nearly an hour, staring into the black woods. My fear grows as every minute passes.

Suddenly, I hear a cry. Could this be my cue? I walk to the perimeter of the woodland and gaze into the sea. Nothing graces my sights. I step further in. I hear a constant moan. My gait is strangely hesitant, for fear of what I'll find. The sounds of nature abound, yet I still discern the familiar echoes of labored breathing. Shadows engulf me, I press farther ahead. The painful sounds grow as I near its source, concealed somewhere amidst the tangled knots of branches, leaves, and twigs. Shards of broken moonbeams illuminate pockets of spicy foliage. At an impasse, I reach my hand out, pull aside a thicket of nature, and step forward into a hidden clearing.

Here, I find the answer to the question.

Do you love me?

A shaft of moonlight escaping through the forest canopy shines across the two wolves. I see dampened fur upon them both, the copper tang of blood thick in the air, the matted grass beneath them soaked thick with crimson life. One wolf lies on its side, panting, a trail of blood seeping from its womb. The other gently licks the leg that dangles from it.

The leg is human.

The mother-wolf's eyes spot me, its green eyes telling a primordial tale, that *this* is the way it's supposed to be. It turns its head and howls a lupine cry into the night, its efforts echoing wickedly throughout the forest. The baby slips free from the womb, the midwife-wolf immediately licking away the afterbirth to cleanse it from infection.

I walk over and pick up my baby boy, elated, overjoyed. My human baby boy. I smile and pace to my wife, the mother of my child.

Yes, I love him. And I will not reject the child born in human form.

I kneel down and place the baby next to her, by her nipples. He instinctually latches on, lips sucking voraciously for his mother's milk. This child will be loved, will live. My dreams shall no longer be haunted by the soul of the dead child.

I hold my wife close, my child.

And I *love him*.

HAIRS AND GRACES
WILLIAM MEIKLE

Dog tired.

I'd heard the phrase, but never understood its true meaning. I was about to find out.

The bell above the doorway rang at two after noon.

The man who entered was big money, through and through. He wore a thick serge tunic, his sash was draped just right, and his shiny leather boots squeaked as he walked across the room. He was in his sixties, but held his back ramrod straight. And although his mouth smiled, his eyes told a different story. He strode into the chamber as if he owned it and thrust a hand at me that I couldn't refuse to shake.

"Gwynne Ericsdochtir?" he said, "I'm Lord Colwyn of Eyr, and I believe there's something you can help me with."

He smelled—of perfumed soaps and rosewater, and underneath that, the faint but unmistakable odor of liquor.

"I'm Gwynne. And all investigations can be undertaken if the fee is right. And I am surprised. When a Lord comes to a place like this, it's usually about a woman; and usually a wife, lover, or whore. They mostly want a man to investigate cases like that."

"It's been a while since I had any of those three," the Lord said.

For the first time I saw him for what he was—an older man, proud and keeping himself together, but fighting the same constant battle against boredom and booze that I recognized only too well in myself.

I motioned him towards the chair opposite me. I half expected him to dust it down first, but he sat without a second thought, falling into its depths. I leaned back in my own chair, feeling much more comfortable—now I had him where I wanted him.

Time for business.

"Before I start," he said, "I must tell you, this is strictly confidential. Word of this must not leave this room. It could seriously damage my reputation."

"Very dramatic," I said. "Just tell me what you need—we can discuss the security arrangements if I decide to take the case."

"I'm afraid I must insist," he said. "I need your word on the matter."

"And I'm afraid *I* must insist," I replied. I gave him a big smile. "I can't give you my word before you tell me what you want me to keep quiet about. If you don't like it, you know where the door is."

I watched him squirm. He wasn't used to being refused, and his red face told me he wanted to take my offer and leave, but he stayed in the chair. Whatever it was that bothered him, it was big enough to override his pride.

Finally he sighed, and relaxed back into the chair.

"I need you more than you need me? Is that it?" he said.

I smiled again.

"Well, I suppose I'd better tell you," he said. "But remember—"

"I know—the local economy will collapse, the future of the citadel depends on it, all that happy-crappy."

It was his turn to smile again, but once more his eyes would have nothing to do with it.

"You don't get to be in my position without stepping on a few toes over the years. I made an enemy recently."

He took a scrap of paper from his pocket and handed it over to me. I checked it over. It had been written with a thick quill and by someone whose touch was none too light. There was a single statement.

"The belt is mine."

It was signed, *The Dubh Sithe.*

I turned the sheet of paper over in my hands, but there was nothing on the other side.

"That's all?"

He nodded.

"The *Dubh Sithe?*"

"Loosely translated, it means *the Black Elf.*"

"What kind of a name is that?"

"That's why I'm here."

He handed me a belt, made of thick course black hair. It felt dry and dusty in my hands. It had a buckle attached; brass clasps, cunningly wrought as wolf heads, that linked together at the jaws.

I examined it from all angles.

"So what's the big deal?"

"It's a *Lougrou* belt. It allowed the sorcerer who fashioned it to turn himself into a wolf. I bought it last week from a trader from the badlands."

I watched him closely, but he kept a straight face.

It was time for my token cynicism.

"I'm sorry—I'm having trouble with that," I said.

"What? With the cases you've been getting recently?" He gave me a smile that was neither polite nor friendly. "You didn't think I chose you at random did you? You've got experience in this area."

"Word certainly gets around," I said. "But I thought it was only among the *lower ranks*."

He laughed.

"In this town, a lot of words get around. At all ranks."

"So what exactly is it you want me to do?" I said, trying to look like I knew what I was doing.

"Keep the belt for me—protect it and see that nothing happens to it. And find out what you can about this *Dubh Sithe*—see if it really does belong to him."

"I charge five gold pieces a day, plus expenses."

"I can't sanction that kind of payment."

"That's okay. You know where the door is," I said.

He stayed in the chair. I watched him wonder whether to get angry, then think better of it. In the end he gave me another tight little smile.

"Are you always this hard to hire?"

"Only when I'm in a good mood," I said.

He took out a purse and counted out the gold, laying them down on the desk, slowly, as if afraid to part with them.

After he left I pocketed the gold, spoke a few words to my mirror, strapped on my sword and went to work.

* * *

The Barrows area in the east-end is the delivery point for anything coming in from the Badlands. Legit and gray-area traders rub shoulders in a vibrant, heaving, market, selling everything from meat to ankle rings, silk gowns to armor plating.

Even this early in the day, the place was busy. Stall holders heckled, promised and cajoled while youths barely out of acne ran the three-card trick on street corners. Queues of women formed at a stall selling thick woolen undergarments, while queues of men snaked around a trader offering a gallon of liquor for ten groats. The smell of frying grease hung in the air, wafting from a score of caravans and someone offered a unique chance to buy an eagle.

And all that was just 'The Barrows' public face. I knew of at least two card schools in huts round the back where you needed ten gold pieces to get a seat. Down a side alley, just out of view of the main market, whores plied their trade and hard faced men sold sleep-weed to soft-eyed youths.

Then there is Paddy's Market.

Rumor had it there was once a seaman who took small items from every cargo of every ship he worked on. When he came ashore he had walked a reasonable distance from the docks, then set up shop, selling goods from a rolled out blanket. That was back when the city was still making its money, when magnates scoured the world and brought it back up the river.

Paddy's Market was still open for business. The merchandise no longer held the quality it once did.

"Hey, pretty thing," a drunk said to me. "See anything you like?"

He had a rug stretched out in front of him. On it he had; one Queene Freda commemorative coin, a fake Wayland broadsword, a quill pen without a point, and a sheaf of bleached papyrus so thin that the sun shone through it.

"I've got some good stuff coming this afternoon," he said, and cackled, until he started to wheeze and cough. "So what is it today? Buying or selling?"

I'd done business with Harold before. He knew everything that passed in and out of the Barrows, and was willing to tell all, for a price.

I passed him a gold piece.

His eyebrows almost raised through his hairline when I told him about the belt and he got visibly excited.

"The Djanto Belt," he whispered, and I thought he was going to drool.

"You know of it then?" I asked.

"Oh yes," he said, "It was found in Djanto, two hundred years ago, and was brought back into the country by Lord Cantor, a shipping magnate of the time. It's got a long history—something about black magic—hocus-pocus anyway. It caused quite a stir back in its day. There was a scandal, and Cantor disappeared in suspicious circumstances. The belt wasn't amongst his effects, and hasn't been seen since."

A predatory look came to his eyes. "How did you hear about it?" he asked.

"From a client. Is it worth much?" I asked.

"It's priceless." Harold said, and this time I believe he did drool. "Scholars all over the city would be cutting off parts of their body for just a look at it. I suppose that if it ever came up for auction it would go for, say, a couple of thousand gold pieces. But, as I said, it is lost. Most probably there's a rich private hoarder who sits and gloats over it during the long winter nights."

"It isn't lost," I said. "I've seen it."

I watched the excitement grow in Harold's eyes. I knew it was almost time to leave—he was getting close to his manic puppy dog phase, and I would have him following me everywhere if I wasn't careful.

"But what I really need to know is how it connects to the Black Elf?"

"You don't want to mess with him," Harold said, suddenly serious. "He's big league."

"I guessed as much," I said. "But is there anything to connect him with the belt?"

"Rumor and gossip, that's all," he said. "It is said he is over two hundred years old himself and that he was the one that killed Cantor. But that's all it is, rumor."

"There's another gold piece in it if you can find out more?" I said, but he shook his head.

"I'm not getting involved this time," he said, rolling up his goods and backing away from me. "If you want to see the 'Elf, he has chambers up the hill. Three doors up from the Law Lord."

That told me all I needed to know. This *Dubh Sithe* was high status—higher than Lord Eyr himself. The fact that I had never heard of him wasn't unusual. The higher up the hill they were, the more secretive they became.

He probably wouldn't even see me; but I had to try.

* * *

I never usually ventured far up the hill—too rarified for my tastes. As I left the east-end, the stalls became smarter, the goods more expensive. Stalls soon gave way to wooden stores, and eventually, stone buildings. Near the castle itself they were more like tiny, fortified palaces, complete with private security and warding spells.

The *Dubh Sithe's* property was little different, but the warding spell was an old one, and two hand movements were enough for me to by-pass it. I walked through the heavy oak door and into a white marble chamber.

The walls were white, a brilliant, scintillating white. There were maybe ten items on display, all on cubical white pedestals, all encased in a pale blue glass that looked like it cost more than the pieces themselves.

I stopped and looked at the first one.

It had once been a piece of crystal, almost a foot cubed, glowing in silver, purple and black. An artist, someone with exceptional talent, had carved it into a cathedral, one with its roof open to the skies. Tiny robed figures worshipped around an altar. There was a figure above the altar, something that didn't look quite human, but as I bent for a closer look, I felt a hand on my shoulder pulling me back.

"It's from the Sunken City," a deep voice said.

I turned to face the voice, and had to look up. He was at least six-four, and big with it. There were wrinkles around his eyes, and he was nearly bald. He wore a pale blue silk robe that would have cost more than I've made in my career. I had him pegged for at least sixty but his eyes were pale blue and clear, and his grip was strong on my collarbone.

"The Black Elf, I presume," I said.

He smiled, but it didn't reach his eyes.

"I prefer *Dubh Sithe,*" he replied. "But I don't need an introduction. I already know who you are, and why you are here."

"You know me?" I said.

"I know *of* you. And I know you have my belt."

He had the smile back again, like a cat playing with a mouse.

"What belt?" I said. I gave him my best gamine smile, but he was immune to my charms.

He grabbed me by the throat, forced my head to one side and exposed my neck. Then he sniffed, twice, close together, as if checking my scent.

"Where is it!" he said.

His voice was rough, harsh, almost a bark.

I tried to speak, but the grip around my throat was so tight that all I could manage was to keep breathing.

"Where is it!" he said again, almost shouting this time. His breath smelled, of stale food and stagnant water, but I guessed now wasn't a good time to tell him.

With his spare hand he went through my clothes; fast and methodical, like a pro. When he didn't find anything, the hold on my throat tightened further still. I tried to break the grip, but my strength was going fast. I punched him, hard, just below the heart, but he didn't even wince.

He laughed in my face.

"Is that all you've got girl?"

I did the only thing I could think of—I butted him, hard, across the bridge of the nose. Pain flared in my forehead, but the grip on my throat loosened. I brought up my left knee, hard as I could. It wasn't enough to hurt him, but did knock him off balance.

I butted him again, and felt bones crack, unsure whether they were his or mine. He fell away from me, and I kicked out, hard, taking small joy in the grunt of pain I raised.

I stepped to one side, just as he came for me again. I grabbed his arm and, using his own speed, swung him against the wall.

He tripped over one of the exhibits, and I took my chance. I turned and ran.

A howl followed behind me—rage and pain; but mostly rage.

* * *

At least I knew more than I had before. I knew the *Dubh Sithe* did indeed lay claim to the belt. And I knew he'd be coming for it, and me.

I needed to move the belt. My office was no longer safe, but I was already too late. There were three of them in my office, tearing the place apart.

I already knew what they were looking for—just as I knew they hadn't found it.

"It's usual to ask permission before entering a lady's chamber's," I said, loudly.

The men spun on their heels, the left hand one helping my cause by tripping over an upturned chair. The man lost his footing and, falling sideward disturbed the balance of the man to his right.

I concentrated on the man on the far right. He drew his sword as I moved in. The man slashed at me, and I parried, aware already that he was no swordsman. I feinted to go under his sword, then twisted my wrist and went over. The steel felt like an extension of my arm as it slid through the man's throat and, with a twitch of the wrist, sliced his jugular and sent him gurgling to the ground.

I sensed a movement to my left, and turned and ducked in one movement as a sword flashed over the top of my head. A second man advanced, sword swinging wildly. Again, this was no swordsman, but he was big and fast, his heavy sword sending shocks up my arm every time I had to parry.

The third man had regained his composure, and was at the point of drawing his own sword.

I had to finish this fast.

The big man drew his sword back to swing at me again. I stepped inside the swing, cramping his movements and at the same time smashing the pommel of my sword into his face, feeling the small bones in the nose crush wetly with the force of the blow. The big man let out a yell, but he managed to push me away, and came back swinging.

I let him come, and, just as the sword seemed set to cleave my skull, stepped to one side.

The momentum of his swing carried him forward and off balance, and I thrust my blade deep into his side, at the same time kicking him over to the floor. He tried to raise his sword, but a final blow, with the flat of the blade to the side of his head, put him out of the fight.

I had no time to think. The third man had advanced, snarling at me, like a cornered wildcat.

"Fancy blade-work, girl. Let's see if you're as good as you think you are."

This one carried himself like a true swordsman—he wasn't about to rush in swinging. I circled him, saying nothing, trying to stay calm.

"That's two fine men you've dispatched there, girl. I don't think the Elf will admonish me if I send you to join them."

The man sent his blade out in a quicksilver flicker that I only just managed to parry as it was over my heart.

I stepped forward into a lunge that caught him off guard, but he managed to weave to one side and the stroke cut a slice across his ribs instead of taking him through the heart. He let out a yell and stepped into the attack with renewed vigor so that I was hard pressed to defend myself.

The sound of clashing steel echoed around the room as we circled, each of us searching for an opening. I was painfully aware that I was weakening faster than my opponent, and decided to try a risky feint, one that I had sometimes had success with on the training ground.

I stepped backwards, as if retreating before the attack, and let my right leg give under me, feigning a stumble and letting my sword hand go down towards the floor, looking as if I was going to use it to steady myself. As I hoped, he went for my suddenly exposed left-hand side. I ignored the descending blade, and, with a straight arm, punched my sword upwards, catching him opponent under the ribs and pushing through to cleave his heart.

He fell, already a dead weight, pinning me to the floor, and I had to use all my remaining strength to push the body off and stand upright.

Suddenly the room fell quiet, and all I heard was my own heavy panting.

I tasted copper at the back of my throat, and felt nausea build. I forced it down. If the Elf was as smart as I suspected, I had no time to lose.

I retrieved my hand mirror from the desk, and left. Housekeeping was just going to have to wait.

* * *

I headed for the only place I knew I would be safe.

Cameron let me in to the Two Hounds when I gave the sign on the window.

"I'm in trouble," was all I had to say.

"Law trouble?"

"Probably. And any minute now."

"What do you need?"

"Somewhere to crash—that's all. For now anyway."

"You can have the back room again. Come on through."

He showed me to a roughly hewn chamber at the back. It had a chair and a table, and little else.

He left me there with a flagon of ale. I waited until I could hear him working in the bar before I took my looking glass from my tunic.

"It's about time," Face said as I wiped my hand over the glass.

"Sorry. I've been busy."

"I noticed."

"What have you got for me?"

"Straight to business again. You know, sometimes a girl needs a little attention."

"Later, Face. This is important."

She sighed.

"It always is with you. Your mother never—"

I wiped a hand across the glass. It went gray—and thankfully quiet. I gave her two minutes then wiped her on again.

"Ready now?" I asked.

"You know, one of these days—"

I wiped her and gave her three minutes. I couldn't really spare the time, but Face needed told who was boss every so often.

"Okay… I'll play nice," she said when I wiped her back again.

"So what have we got?"

"The *Dubh Sithe* has been around for at least two hundred years," Face said. "Nearly as long as the Patron. He first came to view on Cantor's expedition to the ruins of Djanto."

"And the belt?"

"Cantor and him found it—rumor has it that they both coveted it."

"And?"

"And nothing. Cantor disappears, and the belt goes missing—until today. All anybody knows is that the Elf has been looking for it for a *long* time."

"So it's a dead end?"

Face looked downcast.

"Sorry I can't be of more help."

"What about Eyr?"

"Oh, he's okay. He drinks too much, and gambles more than he can afford, but he's okay."

"But it looks like the Elf does indeed have a claim on the belt?"

Again Face looked downcast. Cameron came back in before I could cheer her up. I wiped her away as he entered.

He had a little man with him. I couldn't tell how old he might be—somewhere between fifty and eighty, and so thin to be almost skeletal. His face looked grey, thick with grime, and he wore a tunic that might have been fashionable forty years ago but was now held together with frayed string.

"Tell the lady here what you told me," Cameron said.

"You promised an ale," the little man whined.

"After the story," George said.

The little man looked like he'd been kicked, but his eyes were full of flashing excitement as he started his tale.

"I only went in to get the wife's winnings you see—she always backs the gray dogs, and for once it came in. Only second though, so it was just a groat. I remember the time—"

"Jakie. Keep to the point," Cameron said. "The longer it takes, the further away that ale will be."

The little man now looked like he might burst into tears.

"Okay. Okay. I'm getting to it."

He looked me in the eye.

"The place was empty. Now I thought that was funny, it being just before the first race of the day. I just didn't realize how funny it was."

Cameron sighed heavily.

"Ale, Jakie. It's going to go flat unless you hurry."

"Okay… cutting to the chase boss. The door was lying open, so I went through the back. There was a lot of gold on the table—but I never touched any of it, honest. I was too busy looking at the body. It was the cutpurse Danyg, lying there on the floor, face down in a pool of blood. He was exasperated."

"What?" I asked.

Cameron laughed.

"He means *eviscerated*."

The little man nodded.

"Yes… that as well."

"What's it got to do with me?"

"Tell her, Jakie," Cameron said.

"The word in the alleys is that he got hold of something he shouldn't—stole it from a big house up the hill, and sold it on fast, to that Lord Eyr. Word is that the original owner isn't very happy."

"And who would that be?"

Jakie shrugged.

"Nobody knows. Maybe it was them that exasperated him?"

* * *

Jakie went for his reward, while I sat with my head in my hands. The body count continued to pile up, and I was no nearer to figuring out why.

"I can get you on a boat going North in the morning," Cameron said when he came back.

"Thanks, but if I want to keep working in this city, I'm going to have to sort this out. I need some help though. Do you think you can you find out where Danyg got the belt?"

"I can try. What about you?"

"I'm off to talk to my client. See if he knows more than he's saying."

* * *

The house was huge, a marble pile sitting near to the castle. The high wooden door lay open. That got the hairs at the back of my neck rising. They rose further as I caught a familiar odor; the heavy coppery tang of freshly spilt blood.

I drew my sword and crept quietly into the vast entrance area. High overhead the ceiling curved in a vaulted roof of gravity defying stone and glass. I was still marveling at the wide, spacious emptiness of it as the main door closed with a bang behind me.

I turned, coming face to face with the *Dubh Sithe*.

"What have you done with Eyr?" I said, raising my sword.

"I just got here," he said. He gave me a predator's smile. "Besides, it's not me you have to worry about."

The tang of blood had been masking something else—the musty odor of wet dog.

A low growl came from behind me. I turned, and looked straight into a pair of green eyes that belonged to a wolf, a huge gray male beginning to get its winter coat—shaggy and pale around the shoulders, darker gray along the flanks. Its lips pulled away from its teeth, showing milky-white canines and a blood-red tongue.

The eyes continued to hold me in their stare as I slowly backed away, keeping my sword between it and myself.

As I backed off, the wolf moved towards me, pacing my movements, his eyes never leaving mine.

"He knows you have it," the Elf said.

I didn't have time to answer.

Summoning up what little bravery I had left, I took a step forward. The wolf stood its ground, the green eyes daring me to come closer. My legs trembled, threatening to collapse beneath me.

I stepped forward, bringing my sword up towards its eye. The beast sprang at the same moment, and the blade caught it a glancing blow on the shoulder, not even slowing its attack.

Instinctively I threw out my left arm across my throat, just as the wolf's jaws clamped shut. Long teeth raked my arm, opening a bleeding wound. The wolf went mad in frenzy at the taste of blood.

I couldn't find sufficient angle to bring the point of the sword to bear. I hit the beast in the head, again and again with the hilt, but that only enraged it further as it chewed deeper into the flesh of my arm.

The weight of the creature dragged at me, threatening at any moment to pull me off my feet as we staggered together in a grotesque parody of a dance. We lurched left and right, and the pain in my arm flared and burned, threatening to overwhelm me.

I only had one option, and it would leave me vulnerable to attack, but I had to try, before tiredness took away any hope I might have.

I swung my left arm around, pivoting with my body, lifting the wolf off the ground, screaming aloud at the sudden, white-hot pain that flared in the wound. At the same time I lifted the wolf's head as high as I could, thrusting it away from me while bringing my sword around in an arc.

I hit the beast in the side, biting deep. The creature made a whimpering noise in its throat but hung on tightly to my arm as my swing turned me fully around. Our combined weight finally sent us to the ground where we rolled and kicked and gouged. I was as wild as the animal that attacked me.

I stabbed for its heart, again, and again, my head full of blood and thunder.

And finally, it was still.

I rolled away, panting. It took long seconds for me to get my breath.

I turned—and looked at the dead, naked, body of an old bearded man, his chest a bloody ruin.

"Gwynne Ericsdochtir, meet Lord Cantor," the Elf said.

* * *

I tried to stand, but felt dizzy and weak.

The big man came over, lifted me as if I weighed no more than a feather, and sat me against a wall. He sat on his haunches facing me.

"I suppose I owe you a story."

I didn't have anywhere else to go. I tried to stay awake as he talked.

"I remember a time when all I knew was forest and mountain. I ran with the pack. We ranged far and wide, under the stars. We took what we wanted, we went where we chose, and there was no man to tell us how to mark the passing of each day. Until Cantor came to the ruins at the western edge of our lands.

"He found the hair belt in a chamber under a temple as old as the stars themselves; and he was just learned enough to recognize it, and just stupid enough to use it.

"One minute I was hunting a small coney, and the next, I was standing, on two legs, beside a new wolf I had never seen before. For, you see, the belt needs two, one to be wolf, one to be man."

The Elf's voice had deepened, coarsened, and his beard seemed somehow fuller.

"For a time, we led a double life, Cantor and I, as wolf and man. But I grew to like the soft life I had been given; the candied sweetmeats, the ale, even the smoke-weed. So I laid a trap for Cantor, drugging his meat.

"That night, for the first time, I controlled the belt, controlled the change. I placed Cantor in a cage deep beneath our home here in the city, and went on with my life as a man.

"And all was well for many years. I made token pretense of hunting for the belt, while living the soft life of a rich man. Until last week.

"A thief came into the house when I was distracted, and took the belt. He was also stupid enough to loose the wolf.

"You can figure out the rest. Cantor had just enough man-sense to hunt for the belt; and just enough wolf-sense to kill anyone in his path.

"We both tracked the belt; and we both ended here. I fear that Cantor has killed Lord Colwyn; but you will be able to blame that one on me after I've gone.

"But first, the spell is broken... For me to return to the wolf I once was, I need the belt. Otherwise I will be a strange foul half-beast, neither one nor other. I can feel it in me even now. The belt please. And quickly."

I took the glass from my pocket and wiped my hand over it.

"Face. It is time."

She noticed the blood.

"Gwynne. Are you okay?"

"I will be. I need the package."

"Ready and waiting."

I put my thumb and forefinger through the mirror, and met the dry hair of the belt on the far side. I pulled it out in one smooth motion.

"Gwynne?" Face said, worried, but I wiped her away. She'd get—the story later—once I'd worked out in my head what the story actually was.

I handed it to the Elf. He was definitely hairier now, and his eyes had taken on a deep green tinge.

* * *

He chanted, a harsh tongue I didn't recognize.

Emned kechod da h'tebs saih bhro h'car h'tan lana.

He clasped the belt around his waist—and suddenly he wasn't a man anymore.

His backbone curved, forcing his head lower to the ground—a head that slowly stretched and elongated as long fangs burst from bloody gums. Talons slid from under his fingernails, slithering and viscid, like a wet fart.

His silks split with a loud rip. New muscles strained tight against the ripped material. Thick bristles of hair forced their way through his skin, the hands lengthening as the talons grew longer and knuckles popped. A long snout lifted in the air.

He shook off the last torn remnants of his silks and sniffed at the air.

I pushed myself upright using my sword as a walking stick, and hobbled over to the door. It was well oiled, and swung open easily.

I opened it wide, and let the wolf out into the waiting night.

OUT OF THE LIGHT
DOUGLAS SMITH

The morgue door swung open. Jan Mirocek hesitated at the threshold, clinging to the hallway's bright comfort. Ahead in the dark room, under a lonely cone of light, Detective Garos loomed over a shroud-covered corpse. Jan glared up at the single ceiling bulb. Forty watts max, he thought. He turned to a clerk slouched at a desk in the hall. "Got any more light?"

The man just shrugged. "Our guests don't do much reading."

Scowling, Jan stepped inside. The door clicked shut behind him, cutting the light even more. He cursed and pulled a small flashlight from a coat pocket, his breathing slowing as the beam brightened his path. I can do this, he thought. Trying not to look into the shadows, he walked to Garos.

Morgues didn't bother Jan. He knew death. And corpses.

He just wanted more light.

Garos eyed the flashlight but the big man didn't comment. "Good to see you in action again, hunter. It's been a while since—last time." His beefy hand swallowed Jan's.

Last time. At least, old friend, you have the decency to leave it at that, Jan thought. "I'm retired, Andreas. Why'd you call me?" Ignoring the frown from Garos, he studied the contours of the white shroud. Slim, short, female.

Garos shrugged then turned to the corpse. "White female, early thirties. Found about one this morning—just twelve hours ago—on a well-lit, still-busy, Toronto street."

Stabbing his beam into dark corners, Jan pulled two extra flashlight batteries from his pocket. He shook them in his hand, calmed by the clicking noise. "So? What do you need me for?"

"You tell me." Garos pulled back the sheet.

Maybe it was the light. Or the darkness. Or perhaps seeing Garos in a professional role again had brought her back, brought it all back. He looked down, and *she* was there. Her face. The way it used to be in the mornings—peaceful—beautiful.

Then the face shifted into someone else—some*thing* else. Jan stared at the desiccated corpse of a stranger, black sunken eye sockets and cheeks, lips pulled back from rotting gums, white hair framing gray translucent skin. The shadows closed in and with them, his terror. He ran from the room.

* * *

Ten years old. Lying in bed beside his brother Pyotr, in their house in the woods. His mother's voice rose and fell in her sing-song way of telling stories. But these stories were not of frog princes, or bears and honey pots, or little girls chasing rabbits down holes. These were—different.

"To begin his change, the werewolf put on a belt of wolf skin, then drank water from a wolf's paw-print," their mother whispered. Jan looked at Pyotr. The younger boy was wide-eyed. Jan smiled. These are stories, he thought. Just stories.

* * *

Five minutes after leaving the morgue, Jan sat huddled at a window table of the first bar he had found. The afternoon sun of a Toronto winter did little to remove the chill he felt. A familiar face peered inside. Moments later, Garos eased his bulk into a chair beside him. "You okay?"

Jan lied with a nod. "For a second, I saw—" Her name caught in his throat and he swallowed. "I saw Stasia's face."

Garos frowned, his eyebrows forming a single bushy line. An old woman in Sicily had once told Jan such eyebrows were a sign of the *lupomanari*. She had missed the true signs in her own son. He killed nine people before Jan and Garos had brought him down.

"I shouldn't have called you," Garos said.

"I'm okay!" Jan snapped. Garos looked away. No, you shouldn't have, Jan thought, you of all people. Jan stared at his hands gripping his beer as if it were a beast about to leap at his throat. He held life that way now, a wild thing to be feared, never trusted to lie quietly at his feet. "Who was she?"

Garos said a name. It meant nothing to Jan. He looked up. "Why *did* you call me, Andreas?"

"Did that look like a fresh corpse to you?" Garos asked.

"The rotting doesn't mean it was done by a shifter."

"Come on, Jan. We saw the same rapid body decay in shifter victims back home."

"Any 'bodies' we saw were in pieces and mostly eaten." *Her* body would've been too, Jan thought, if he had been able to bring himself to see it. "This one was intact. That's no were-beast."

Looking around, Garos lowered his voice. "We've had other killings, similar to this. We're barely keeping a lid on it."

Jan swallowed. "What's similar about them?"

"Victims killed at night on bright, busy streets. No robbery. Victims in good health. No drugs or sign of sexual assault. No violence except some contusions around the throat, but death wasn't by strangulation, and—" Garos leaned forward. "—and the corpses rot within hours."

"Any pattern to the killings?"

"None I can see. Both genders, all ages and professions. All over downtown. The only consistency is the body decay and autopsy results, plus the time of night and type of locations." "Anything else?"

"A witness saw a guy standing over this body. She says she chased him into a dead-end alley. No door, window, fire escape. Nowhere to hide. But also no suspect—the alley was empty."

Jan felt cold. "That still doesn't say shifter."

"Put it with the body decay, it says something weird."

"You believe her story?"

"She gave a description. We're checking it out. And her."

"I'll bet your theory went down well with the brass."

Garos snorted. "I keep my own counsel. They're not from the old country. Don't believe as we do, haven't seen what we have." He stared at Jan. "I need your help."

Jan avoided his eyes. "I came to this country, to a big city, to escape the beasts of the night, Andreas. They don't come to the cities. You don't have a shifter. Even if you did, I can't help you. And you know why."

They sat not speaking, Jan's shame burning him. "Well, I had to try," Garos said as he stood. He looked at Jan. "I know what she was to you. I know you blame yourself. But she knew the risks." He squeezed Jan's shoulder. "It's not your fault, Janoslav. Give yourself a break for God's sake." He walked to the door, then stopped and looked back. "What if you're wrong?"

Jan stared at him, puzzled. "What do you mean?"

"What if I do have a *kallikantzari*? A beast of the night in your big safe city. What then, hunter?" Not waiting for an answer, Garos turned and left. Jan stayed until the winter sun sank too low. Walking home, he watched the shadows all the way.

* * *

Fifteen years old. Returning home from friends, far too late, through winter woods oddly silent. The house dark, even the light in the front room not burning. The door open, tilted at a strange angle. His heart leapt. He ran.

He burst past the ruined entrance to stumble in the dark and fall amongst bloody bodies. His parents. Upstairs, Pyotr's bed empty, room in disarray. Outside again, father's rifle in hand, following prints in the snow. The prints of the beast.

He found it near the quarry. Half-human, yellow eyes looked up from where it fed on his brother. He raised the rifle.

His childhood died. The hunter was born.

* * *

After leaving the restaurant, Jan walked home to his apartment over his book store on Queen West. His place was small but he'd left most of his possessions behind in the old country. Too many memories tied to them. Besides, he liked this area. Lots of shops and bars that stayed open late. Plenty of neon.

Plenty of light.

Once home, he checked that every light in every room was on. He read for a while after dinner, then went to bed early as usual. Two flashlights lay on a table beside the bed. He made sure they both worked, then he lay down leaving a lamp on. Maybe tonight he could sleep. Maybe he was tired enough. Closing his eyes, he prayed for escape from dreams.

He awoke screaming her name, sitting bolt upright on sweat-soaked sheets. Sobbing, he fell on his side. There, bathed in light that never touched the night world inside him, he prayed again for deliverance from his darkness.

* * *

Twenty-five years old, in a Paris bistro, a stack of papers from around the world beside him. Serial killings got good play. And sometimes the signs were there that spoke to him of shifters. He sat forward. Like this one. Athens paper, one week old. He paid his bill and left, heading for the nearest travel agent.

He had hunted were-bears in Norway and were-tigers in India. He carried a ragged scar on his thigh from a leopard shifter in Kenya. Towns paid a man well to be rid of a beast, a man who knew the signs and was brave— or foolish—enough to follow them.

Jan Mirocek had become such a man.

* * *

The morning sun found Jan curled shivering in an armchair in his living room, a flashlight clutched to his chest. Jan thought about the old times and about what he'd become. He realized that he didn't like himself anymore. He realized also, to his surprise, that he had known this for a long time.

Finding his phone, he punched Garos's number, taking vindictive pleasure in waking him. Garos swore, listened, then gave a phone number for the witness and directions to the dead-end alley. Jan swore back when Garos thanked him for the third time. Promising to keep in touch, Jan hung up.

Hell, he thought. Just like old times. Grabbing his coat, he checked the pockets for his flashlight and batteries, then stepped out into a cold but bright February morning.

* * *

Twenty-five, in an Athens bar. Listening to a young cop named Garos complain. "They won't let me talk to the press."

Jan nodded. "They always hush it up."

"Damn bureaucrats. Well, thanks for the lead."

Jan shrugged. "Thanks for backing me up. I probably wouldn't be alive otherwise. Didn't figure on two of them."

"We worked well together," the big man said.

Jan looked at him. "I'm thinking of taking on a partner."

Garos grinned.

* * *

The alley was as Garos had said. Nothing but a few bits of trash. A neon sign over a bricked-up door at the end of the alley advised that "Clancy's Eatery" was now on the next street.

"You the guy who called me?" a voice said from behind him.

Jan turned, startled. She stood at the entrance to the alley. Five-six maybe, short brown hair, long black coat over a slim figure. "Kate Lockridge. You called me, right?"

Jan walked up to her. "Jan Mirocek. Thanks for coming."

"You don't look like a cop."

She had nice eyes, Jan decided. "Friend of one. Garos."

"Big guy from last night? He was okay." She looked Jan over. "Okay, let's talk. But not here. Gives me the creeps. I know a place nearby. Lousy food but great coffee." She started to move to the street, then stopped, scanning the alley again.

"Something wrong?"

She shrugged. "Place seemed brighter last night. Guess it's coming in here out of the sunlight. And things are always different in the dark, right?" She walked to the street.

Yeah, he thought. Things were different in the dark.

* * *

Thirty years old, in a little tavern in a little village in Poland, waiting for Garos to get to the point.

Garos coughed. "Mara and I, we're getting married."

Jan had seen this coming. He nodded. "And you want out."

Garos reddened but nodded back.

"I wish the best for you both, Andreas. You know that."

Garos smiled and shook his hand. "Thank you. These have been good years, my friend, but Mara needs a different life."

And I need a new partner, Jan thought.

* * *

Late afternoon. *The Big Mistake* was almost empty. They sat at a sunny window table in the long narrow tavern. A jungle of neon signs, each a visual scream of a beer brand, colored the dark room in a random rainbow. Kate called to the bartender. "Two coffees, Harry." She turned to Jan. "So what do you want?"

"Garos asked for help on these—this killing." He watched a corner of her mouth curl up. "We worked together in Europe."

"How so?"

"I was an advisor on one of his cases." He hurried on before she could probe any further. "So tell me what you saw."

Her story was the same. "—I reach the alley and there's no one, nothing. Including no way out. Well, you saw, right?"

Jan nodded and sighed. He asked a few more questions, but it added nothing to the story. "Listen, sorry I wasted your time. Let me buy the coffees." He reached for his wallet.

"So is this body rotting like the others?" she asked. Jan stopped in mid-motion and looked at her. She smiled. "I'm a reporter for the *Toronto Star*, Mr. Mirocek. We need to talk."

Jan sat back again. A reporter, covering the killings. For a moment, despite the sunshine, he felt an old darkness close in.

* * *

Thirty-one. Working alone again. He met her in a village in Poland, a reporter up from Warsaw to cover the killings in the town. Her name was Stasia. He trained her. He loved her.

A year later, she was dead.

* * *

Harry brought refills while Jan gathered his thoughts. A bluff, trying to see how he'd react? No. She might guess that the separate killings were linked but not about the body decay. "How'd you know about the corpse?" he asked when Harry had left.

"Corpses," she corrected. "Got a source in the Coroner's office who likes to supplement his income." She leaned forward. "That's why Garos called you, isn't it? You know why the bodies are rotting like that, right?" Her voice was eager.

Jan began to growl a denial but stopped. What could she do? No paper would print it. Besides, he didn't believe it himself. He shrugged. "You're right. I've seen those signs before."

She flicked on a micro-recorder. "What's it mean?"

"It's a sign of a shifter killing," he said, straight-faced.

Her brow furrowed. In a very pretty way, he thought. "Shifter killing? What's that?" she asked.

"Shape-shifters. Garos and I used to hunt them. He thinks you saw one."

Pause. "Shape-shifters?" Her eagerness melted into a dead-pan then hardened into a glare. "Like a were-wolf?"

"Shifters aren't limited to wolves."

She clicked off the recorder and stuffed it back in her purse with a near ferocity. "A were-beast. Right. Thank you for the coffee, Mr. Mirocek." She stood up and grabbed her coat.

To his surprise, Jan realized that he wanted her to stay. "So how do you explain the rapid decay? How did the Coroner?"

She bit her lower lip. "I can't. Neither could they."

Jan stood and faced her. "I can." He could smell her perfume, a hint of vanilla.

She stared at him then shook her head and sighed. "Twenty minutes, no more." She sat down, arms folded.

An hour later, Jan sat back, having summarized his life story. He had left out the part about Stasia. Kate looked hard at him. "Jan, I'm certain you believe every word you just said. I also know it can't possibly be true."

"Does it matter? The *Star* wouldn't print it anyway."

She groaned. "Okay, so Garos thinks we have a were-beast in Toronto. Because of this corpse decay, right?"

"Plus the time of the murders. Most shifters assume animal form only at night, to hide in the dark. Out of the light. But actually, beyond that, I don't think it fits with a shifter."

"You mean you don't believe Garos either? Why not?"

"Shifters live where their animal form is common. Then if seen, they aren't viewed as anything unusual. So were-tigers live in areas with tigers, were-wolves with real wolves."

"So?"

"So what animals are common in downtown Toronto?"

"Dogs and cats, for starters."

"Yeah, but not running free, which they'd need to be."

"How about birds? Maybe it's a were-pigeon," she said.

"Very funny. Too small. So are raccoons from the ravines."

"What's size got to do with it?"

"Mass-energy conservation. It has to be as big as us."

"Sounds like we've run out of animals," she said.

"That's what I think. No such beast."

"So what about the corpse decay?"

Jan frowned. "I don't know. I can't explain that." He looked at her. "It almost sounds as if you believe me now."

Kate shrugged. "I've heard worse. You meet all sorts of weirdoes on these streets."

"Thanks, I love being tolerated."

She grinned at him. "You want to stay for dinner?"

He looked outside. The sun had set and streetlights were winking into life. He should leave. But the area was well lit. Lots of neon. And Kate was smiling at him. "I'd like that," he said. He just wished she didn't remind him so much of Stasia.

* * *

Thirty-two years old. Sunday. A small church outside Budapest. Stasia, tall and fair beside him, a hunter for a year now. At the altar in the otherwise empty church stood Father Karman. Their prey. "His parish suspects," Jan whispered.

Stasia nodded. "But simple tourists like us don't, right?"

The priest turned from the altar and noticed them. He smiled. "Are you here for Mass?" he called.

Jan hesitated. His Catholic upbringing made this hard. A priest in a church. He could at least let the man hold a last mass. They should be safe. Karman needed either time or the taste of blood to shift. Jan nodded. Stasia looked at him, puzzled. "After Mass, outside the church," he whispered.

During the Liturgy of the Word, Jan felt in his jacket for his gun. Stasia's presence at a capture still made him uneasy. As they approached the altar for Communion, Karman stared hard at Jan. He turned his back to pour the wine. The communion began.

After the ceremony, Karman took the cup from them and turned back to the altar. Only then did Jan notice another cup on the altar. The one from which the priest had drunk. Jan's eyes froze on a drop of liquid hanging red and thick on its lip.

Thick as blood.

Jan struggled to his feet, but the room swam. He fell, panic rising in him. The wine. Stasia screamed his name. A face loomed before him, cruel, already bestial, the reek of blood on its foul breath. Jan fumbled for his gun but the beast struck him hard on the temple. Darkness took him.

* * *

As Harry brought Kate and Jan their dinners, Jan noticed an old man sitting in the back, out of the light. He wouldn't have seen him except that the man gestured to Jan with a jerky motion of a stiffened hand. Jan turned to Harry. "Who's that?"

Harry looked over. "Solly? Street person. Comes in sometimes. I'll give him a coffee, sandwich maybe. Don't know how he stays alive. He's usually in the shelter by now. Doesn't like the streets after dark. Last time he stayed late, I had to walk him there after we closed. Only way I could get him out."

Jan stood up. "I'm going to see what he wants."

Solly was a small round man. Round bald pate ringed by gray scraggly hair. Circle of a face under stubble and dirt. Rounded shoulders under a filthy coat, once an actual color, now unknowable. Round balls of hands, fingers twisted in, peeking surprisingly clean from tattered sleeves, guarding an empty coffee cup. Jan smiled then struggled to maintain it as he caught the smell. Solly waved at a chair across from him.

Jan sat down. "Harry says your name is Solly."

One eye was almost shut. The other pinned Jan then darted over the room. "Harry's is a good place. Stays the same, you know? S'important, you know? Some places--change. Don't like that. Can't tell if they're just different, or..." He fixed Jan with that eye again. "Heard you talking." Jan glanced back to where Kate chatted to Harry. Not a word reached Jan. Solly glared as if he read Jan's mind. "Heard you!" He pounded the table with a crippled hand. "Solly's seen things," he rasped. "Seen things." He looked around again, then lowered his head.

Jan waited, but Solly said no more. Standing, Jan started to walk away when a wheezy whisper stopped him.

"...out of the light. Gotta know the signs."

Jan turned back to the old man. "What did you say?"

Solly's head was still down. "Remember. S'important." Hunched over his empty cup, he sat muttering to himself.

Kate looked up when Jan returned. "What'd he want?"

Jan shrugged. "You've got me. Buy him a coffee on my tab, will you, Harry?" Harry nodded and left.

They ate and talked. "So if you hunt shifters," Kate said, "and they don't come to the city, why do you live here?"

Jan looked out to where the gathering dark fed on a dying day. "I live here because they don't. I don't hunt them anymore. I got someone killed, Kate. Someone who trusted me."

Kate bit her lip. "I'm sorry," she said. They sat silent for a moment, then she gave a small smile. "Anybody could understand why you'd want to get away from those things."

Jan looked back to her. "I wonder if I have."

"What do you mean?"

"Every civilization has had shape-shifter legends. I've always wondered why no such myth exists for our modern cities."

"Why would such creatures live in a city? Why not stay in the wild? Less chance of being seen," she said.

"Also less food. They're predators who prefer human flesh." He shuddered, remembering. "There's more of that in a city."

"Sure, but you eliminated all the animal options."

He stared out at the night. "This is a different jungle. Maybe we've created a new niche, supporting a different predator. Convergent evolution. Its other form may not be animal at all."

"If it's not an animal, what would it be?"

"Don't know, but it's more likely to be seen in a crowded city, so its other shape would need to be downright mundane."

"But *what*?" Kate repeated.

Jan looked out to where shadows fought pale neon. He wanted to say that it would be a thing as at home with concrete and glass as a wolf was with earth and forest. A thing that breathed ozone like a summer breeze and held metal in its heart and electricity in its veins. A thing that not only lived in this realm of the lonely but fed on it. But he just said, "I don't know."

Kate shook her head then checked the time. "Oops. I've got to go. There was another witness last night—a hooker. She won't talk to the cops but she's meeting me at midnight." She looked at Jan and bit her lip.

"Why don't I come with you?" he asked.

She broke into a huge smile. "Great!" She put on her coat while Jan wondered what he had just done. Solly shuffled over. "I also told Harry I'd walk Solly to the shelter," she said.

Solly peered outside. "We take Talbot?"

Talbot was little more than an alley, with no lights. Jan shivered. "Let's keep to well-lit streets. We'll use Richmond." As Solly started to argue, Harry called Jan to the phone.

It was Garos. "Janoslav? Did you meet Kate Lockridge?"

"Yeah. I think she's on the level, but she's a reporter. She, uh, knows about the corpse decay and the other victims."

Garos swore. "We checked her description of last night's suspect." He paused. "Jan, it matches a prior victim."

Jan felt a sudden coldness in his gut. "Victim? That doesn't make sense. How could it be a dead guy?"

"Jan, she was at the scene of the most recent killing and described a victim from another. Now you say she has further knowledge of these deaths. We'll be talking to her again. In the meantime, be careful around her." Garos hung up.

Jan stared at the neon signs over the bar, trying to lose himself in their colored swirls. A hand touched his shoulder. He jumped and turned to find Kate, Solly in tow. Jan's face must have betrayed something. She looked puzzled. "What's wrong?"

Jan shook his head. "No. Nothing," he lied. "Let's go."

Waving good-bye to Harry, they stepped out onto Richmond and turned east. The snow had stopped, and the sidewalks were slushy. "We take Talbot?" Solly asked again.

"Richmond, Solly, or you go alone," Jan said. Solly glared but fell silent, hanging by the curb and scanning the street as they walked. Jan kept thinking of Garos's call. They reached Jarvis. A young blond woman stepped from a doorway, long white coat over a short red leather skirt, black stockings and boots.

"There's Carla," Kate said and started towards the girl.

A shout made them turn. Solly was backing away, wide-eyed and pointing a shaking hand to something above their heads. "No! Solly knows the signs. You won't get Solly!" Terror on his face, he ran onto the street. Jan spun back. Above the doorway where Carla stood open-mouthed, a neon sign glared "Franny's Tavern." The first word was red, the second blue.

The blue one was moving.

In an eye-blink, the letters slid down the wall to form a glowing pool on the sidewalk. In another blink, a humanoid shape rose radiant white from the pool--female torso, face, hair, the shape of clothing, then colors, facial details.

The face of the murder victim from last night.

"Carla! Behind you!" Kate yelled.

A spear of light stabbed from the creature's hand, striking Kate full in the chest and Jan in the shoulder. Electricity flamed into him. Numbed, he collapsed to watch as the thing grabbed Carla by the throat and lifted her into the air.

Slush seeping into his clothes, choking on ozone, Jan tried to move. A violent tremor shook Carla. Jan's arms twitched. The creature held Carla higher, its glow brightening, colors cycling. Jan could feel his legs again. Carla fell limp, and the thing slapped her down like a wet towel. It turned to Kate.

Gasping, Jan heaved himself to his knees and lunged forward. Somehow he got his hands under Kate's armpits and dragged her just out of reach. "Get up!" he cried.

"Can't...move," she gasped. He pulled her to her knees. The thing's colors were fading, its features melting back into a smooth humanoid shape. It shimmered and changed again. And became Carla. The Carla-thing smiled. It stepped toward them.

Inches from its outstretched arms, Jan hauled Kate up, and they lurched into the road. Stumbling but with returning strength, Jan scanned the street. From a dark alley across the road a small round figure waved, a jerky motion from a stiff arm.

Half dragging Kate, Jan struggled towards Solly. Footsteps sounded behind them. The back of his neck tingled as if an electrical charge was building at his back. He pushed Kate into the alley as something brushed his coat. Shoving a trash can behind him, he heard a thud and a sound no human throat ever made. The alley was dark, and Jan's eyes still burned from the electrical flash. Ahead, Solly's gray form disappeared to the right. Jan moved along the wall, Kate's hand in his.

"Now that thing looks like Carla!" she panted.

"It takes the form of what it kills," Jan gasped. *That* was why her description of the suspect had matched an earlier victim. A hand grabbed Jan from the darkness and yanked them both sideways. He could see nothing but he knew the smell. Solly pulled them along. Jan could feel walls to either side. They stopped. Jan reached ahead in the dark and touched another wall.

Solly had led them into a dead end.

"No!" Jan screamed. His nightmare seized him. Trapped in the dark with a monster. And with a woman who trusted him.

* * *

Thirty-two. In a church basement outside Budapest. Waiting to die. Total darkness. Lying on damp earth, bound hand and foot. Stale smell of mildew stinging his throat. As he fought to awaken, a scream sliced the black, clearing the flames of pain in his head like a bucket of ice water. Stasia.

He raged against his bonds. She screamed again. "Jan! Oh God, no! No! Help me!" Jan threw himself forward and managed to roll once. Her cries were clearer. But so was another sound.

The sound of something feeding.

Jan threw himself again but something held him fast. He could do nothing but lie in the dark, listening to the beast feed on the still-living Stasia.

Praying in the dark for her screams to cease. Praying in the dark for her to die.

An eternity passed. Then only the grunts of the beast remained. The stench of rotting meat grew strong. A huge shape moved in the darkness. Moved closer. Jan screamed.

Blinding light suddenly flooded the room, and the roar of the were-wolf echoed in the roar of gunshots. Blood, thick and black and hot, struck Jan's face as Garos shouted his name.

* * *

In the dark alley, Jan shoved Solly away and turned to run back. Solly grabbed him, holding on with surprising strength. "No! Stay here. *Out of the light.* Solly knows!"

A glow began at the entrance to the dead-end, but Jan still couldn't see. Kate's hand found his. "Jan?" she said.

Hearing her fear, his panic fled, replaced by a feeling of resolve he had almost forgotten. He squeezed her hand. She would not die. "Solly, talk to me. Tell me what you know!"

Solly's voice quavered. "It don't like the dark. We're safe here. Right?" At this, Kate groaned.

Jan swore, his mind racing. Light was the key. "It must feed off electricity, hiding as parts of signs. When you chased it last night, it joined with the sign in the alley."

"That's why the alley was brighter last night," Kate said.

"Sunlight must sustain it in the day, plus electricity. But when night comes..." Jan stopped. When night comes, it needed more. It needed its real food: human life force.

The light at the entrance grew and the glowing form of Carla appeared. "I thought it doesn't like the dark," Kate whispered.

Jan swore. "It must still be hungry and figures we're worth the risk. Solly, how long can it go without light?"

"Five minutes," he whined, "but a lot more if it just ate."

"Wonderful," Kate said.

Twenty paces away now, the thing lit the entire area. Its glow was dimmer but Jan doubted that would save them. At least now he could see. He looked around, and his heart leapt. The wall behind them and the walls on either side each held a door.

Jan grabbed the door handle behind them. Locked. So was the one to their right. He tried the last one. The handle turned a bit. He leaned on it and heard a click. He threw his weight against the door and it squealed open with rusty protests.

"Inside!" Kate cried, rushing forward, Solly in hand.

"No!" Jan grabbed her, an idea forming. The thing was ten paces away. Pulling out his flashlight, he stepped into the room and flashed the beam around. The stock room of a store, twenty feet square. Not much space to maneuver. Could he do it? Could he finally face his darkness? By walking into it? He turned back. The thing was five paces away. He aimed his light at it.

"No!" Solly cried. "It eats light!"

Jan ignored him. "Kate, take Solly into the corner. After I lead it inside, close the door and don't open it." Kate turned pale but nodded and pulled Solly back. Jan stepped up, playing his beam over the creature. It turned to him. Keeping his light on it, he backed into the room. Darkness closed in on him and with it his fear. What had he done?

The thing stepped inside. The door slammed shut behind it.

It stopped and looked back. Its mouth opened, and a sound like fingers tapping fine crystal, filled the room. And somehow, in that sound Jan heard its hunger and its pain. A wave of empathy flooded him. They were alike. Hunters. Hiding their true shape. Fearing the night. The creature reached for him. I'm sorry, Jan thought. He turned off his light.

The thing trembled, and its aura dimmed. But then Carla's features and clothing faded, seeming to melt back into its body. A featureless human form remained, glowing blue-white.

It's conserving energy, Jan thought. It no longer needed to pretend to be human. He swallowed. How intelligent was it?

A deadly game of tag began—the thing pursuing with the same plodding step—Jan retreating, avoiding corners, always leaving two paths of escape. With each passing minute, the thing's aura dimmed, fading to blue, then yellow, then red.

Finally it stopped, arms drooping. Jan sighed and relaxed. He noticed too late that the arms weren't just drooping.

They were growing.

Both arms flashed out, three times normal length, easily covering the space between the thing and Jan. Taken by surprise, Jan dove aside but a hand brushed his thigh. Electricity numbed his leg. He fell. Looming over him, the thing reached down.

And stopped. Its colors cycled the spectrum then faded to gray. A sound like breaking glass fled a suddenly grotesque mouth. Its feet melted into a pool. The arms flowed back into a shrinking torso. Soon only the pool remained, faintly glowing.

Jan walked to it. The pool bulged once toward him, then its last light died and Jan stood in the dark. He waited before flicking on his light. The pool was a dull gray. He kicked, and it shattered with a crystal cry, imploding into sparkling powder.

He opened the door, and Kate threw her arms around him. Back on the street, Solly checked every bit of neon in sight, then fixed Jan with that eye. "Gotta know the signs," he said.

Jan phoned the police about Carla's body and left a message for Garos to call.

"So what now, hunter?" Kate asked.

Solly stared up at Jan. "You gonna get the others too?"

Jan and Kate turned to him. "Others?" Kate groaned.

Jan shrugged then looked at her. "I could use a partner." She said nothing but took his hand as they walked Solly home.

They took Talbot.

* * *

Thirty-five. A midnight street. He waits in the dark, watching the signs. She waits beside him. He knows the ways of the beast; she knows these streets. A town pays well to be rid of its creatures of the night. Creatures that breathe ozone like a summer breeze, wear glass for skin and burn electricity in their veins. Creatures that feed on this realm of the lonely.

Once, he shunned the dark where shadows hide their secrets. Now he stalks the night streets, a shadow himself slipping from alley to alley. Now he keeps to the dark.

And stays out of the light.

HUNGRY LIKE THE MOON
ROB E. BOLEY

I wake up to the noise of zombies moaning. Sounds like a breeze gliding through a broken seashell.

I'm trapped in a cramped diner with seven zombies: three men, three women, and a little girl. The seven zombies are a mess of torn flesh, bite marks, and gashes. Their flesh is pale, and their eyes are horribly dull—like rotten egg yolks left out in the sun. I've woken up in plenty of bad situations, but this is the worst.

I try to sit up, but can barely move.

The diner is a long, skinny rectangle cut in half lengthways by a bar-top. Behind the bar is what's left of a greasy spoon kitchen. The walls are covered with gore, claw marks, and matted hair—evidence of an unquenchable hunger. A horizontal strip of mirror runs along the diner's side and rear walls, most of it now shattered, cracked, or splattered with blood. At the rear of the diner is a short hallway with a unisex bathroom and a boarded exit. The front is simply a door and a window, both reinforced with broken tables.

One of the zombies locks eyes with me, and I know then that my time has come. Before dying, the zombie was a man named Chef. I met him just last night, when he reluctantly offered me shelter.

Apparently, that was his last mistake.

* * *

Last night.
The sun was already low in the sky when I found the diner.

I'd just gotten into town, hopeful that Brooklyn would have a rescue center or shelter for survivors. It'd been three weeks since the zombie outbreak, since the moon had been a waning crescent. I'd spent most of that time tracking my daughter, Melanie, after discovering that her mother, my ex, had been killed. Melanie's trail took her through multiple survivor camps in Ohio, Pennsylvania, and now here, in Brooklyn. It was a trail of desperation and fear. As recently as a few days ago, Melanie fled with a group of survivors to the Big Apple.

Brooklyn was worse than I'd imagined. The streets were filled with abandoned cars, dead animals, the crumbled remains of toppled buildings, and a mix of abandoned possessions: clothing, television sets, high-end jewelry. I imagine those first nights, there'd been a lot of looting—before everyone realized how out of control our world was going to become. Before gasoline and shotgun shells became more valuable than diamonds and cash.

Less than an hour into my walk downtown, a pack of zombies—more than I'd ever seen gathered in one place—started chasing me through the city. I was faster than them, but they were everywhere, cutting me off at every corner. There were hundreds of them, in varying states of decay and dress. A businessman missing an ear. A rotted corpse wearing a blue dress covered in mud and maggots. A teenager in a *Twilight* t-shirt missing an arm.

When I saw the diner, I knew that people were in there. It wasn't just the thick wood covering the window or the single word spray-painted on the front of the building:

HELP

No, it wasn't just that. I could smell them.

I pounded on their front door, screaming for help. "Please. Please let me in. They're after me. Oh, God. Don't let me die."

Behind the barricaded door, a man and a woman talked about whether or not to let me inside, though I couldn't tell who was taking which side.

"Please," I begged. "I'm just trying to find my daughter."

When the door finally opened, it wasn't hard to tell who was arguing in my favor and who was against. A tall man with thick forearms and wild curly hair had a shotgun leveled at my heart. Next to him stood a fit woman, probably in her thirties, with a fashionable haircut and exhausted eyes. She pushed the shotgun aside and pulled me into the diner.

"Knock it off, Chef," she said. "We're in this together. It's us against them. If we don't stick together, we're going to lose." She turned her attention to me, offered her hand. "I'm Abbie."

Apart from Chef and Abbie, the only other occupants of the diner were two women, two men, and a little girl.

Chef placed the shotgun in the corner and looked me up and down. "You got any food?" he asked. I shook my head. "What about ammo? I'm guessing that's too much to ask."

I shook my head.

Abbie led me to the rear of the diner and introduced me to the rest of the crew. The two women were likely a couple. I can't remember either of their names; I've never been much good with names, or people for that matter.

Abbie introduced the little girl, Gail, last. The child was tied down to a bed made out of two booths nested together.

Inside my skull, I heard a growl.

The child was pale and sweaty. A blood-stained bandage made from a kitchen apron was wrapped around her forearm. Her eyes were pale as the full moon. I'd seen this before. She'd been bitten, and she was going to turn. Soon, by the looks of it.

"And this is my niece, Gail," said Abbie. She held up a hand, as if to block what I was about to say. "Don't say it. I know. She's going to become one of them soon. I'm not a fool. I know the situation. But before I lose her forever, I'm going to make the most of the time we have left."

"And after that?"

She held up a shiny handgun and her face became a mask of resignation. "After that, I'll put a bullet in its head."

* * *

It's morning now, and the seven zombies shuffle toward me. Little Gail is the most hideous of all, the front of her tiny dress covered in blood and a huge chunk of flesh missing from her neck. When she moans, her neck makes a hideous whistle.

I stand up slowly, staggering backward. I try to scream, but I can't. It's like my throat is stuffed with gauze.

What comes out instead is a howling moan, the sound of a large dead tree creaking in the wind. At the sound of my moan, the seven zombies cock their heads. Their blue lips fall back over their grey teeth, and their dull yellow eyes drift away.

I take an awkward step forward, and the zombies shuffle away, giving me space. Now is my chance. I take another step, trying to sprint for the front door. My joints creak like rusty hinges and my muscles feel like play-doh. I fall face-first onto the floor, and my eyes catch my upside-down reflection on a bent spoon.

Staring back at me are two dull yellow eyes.

I'm one of them.

I stand up and stare at the strip of mirror on the wall. Shake my head. Dammit. I'd only wanted to find Melanie. I place a hand over my chest. No heartbeat. Instead, there's an emptiness. A void.

And my heart, it's just rotting inside me.

* * *

Last night.

My heart quivered as I stepped onto the diner's roof. I needed to get out of here, far away from these good people before the change came. I was plotting my escape when the smell of cigarette smoke distracted me. Sharp teeth bit into my urgency and tugged it to the back of my skull.

Abbie stood on the roof's edge, a cigarette held at her side. She looked at me. Her lopsided grin was like a crescent moon. That wicked smile in the sky that yawns open into an unblinking, laughing eye. I shuddered.

The rooftop offered a beautiful view of the city. Nearby, an old church thrust its steeple into the sky. In the distance stood the Statue of Liberty. I half-expected the statue to be moaning and staggering into the water. Below, the zombies moaned and pounded futilely against the diner's reinforced door. Abbie flicked ash at them lazily.

"The odd thing is, I can't hate them," she said. "As much as I want to, I can't. They're just pathetic and hungry. I can't fault them for that." She holds up her cigarette. "I can't smoke up here during the day. Chef's worried that I'd be spotted. But at night, I can go through two packs. I'm as bad as they are."

In my skull, claws paced restlessly, clacking on bone.

I shook my head. "No, you're not."

"Do you know what I obsess about, when I'm not thinking about Gail? I think about running out of cigarettes. How lame is that?"

I shrugged. "You've got a beast inside you. It's hungry and wants fed, no matter how much it might hurt you in the process. The only way to make the beast go away is to starve it, but that doesn't always work. You can tie it in chains or lock it in a cell, but deep down you know the beast will always find a way out. So, you just do your best. You try to make it through the day."

"Sounds like you speak from experience."

I shrugged and tapped my skull. "I've got my share of monsters in here."

"You know, this probably isn't the safest place in the city," said Abbie, tapping her heel on the roof. "I mean, now you're locked in here with a monster."

If only she'd known.

"I've been in worse spots," I said. "Believe me."

"So, how old is your daughter?"

"She's sixteen. Melanie's a survivor. I've been following her almost since the outbreak. Do you know— Are there any other groups of survivors here in the city?"

She shrugged. "Mostly everyone left during the Evacuation, but we've heard noises at night, over near Park Slope."

I nodded.

"How'd you and your daughter get separated?"

"I haven't seen her since before the outbreak. Her mother and I, we had some issues that couldn't be resolved. Mostly my fault. So, I left. I was out West when the outbreak started. By the time I got back to Ohio, Mel was gone. And her mother—her mother was one of those things."

Abbie patted my shoulder. "I'm sorry."

"Don't be. Death is just a fact of life."

She shook her head sadly. "Not anymore."

* * *

It takes me a moment to get my bearings. Just like the other undead, I sway gently. My first step is right into a chewed-up wad of flesh on the floor. Why is it familiar?

I stomp and scrape my foot against the floor, trying to get the tissue off of my boots. Again, I lose balance and crash into the floor.

The zombies wander around aimlessly, bumping into tables, knocking chairs against the floor. Somehow, I'm different than them. My thinking is slower than usual, like I'm trying to run underwater, but at least I'm still thinking. Where they seem to be acting on instinct, I still have my capacity to reason, to apply logic.

Zombie Chef pounds at the same door. He's clueless, utterly clueless about how to get out of here. All seven of them are clueless. Abbie is clawing at the wall, scratching off specks of dried blood. Amazingly, despite being dead, her haircut still looks pretty good. The other zombies mill about, occasionally breaking something or falling down—often both at the same time.

Staggering across the room, I make my way to the front door and gently shove Chef aside. He moans in protest, but doesn't resist.

I pick up the hammer after several tries. My hands are numb, like I've had a shot of Novocain in each finger and am wearing thick wool mittens. Grunting and growling, I manage to slip the claw of the hammer between the wood and the door. I push against the door, and the wood groans.

The noise is exactly the same as the feeling that's growing in my gut: a horrible emptiness worming its way through the soil of my insides. A hunger unlike anything I've ever felt. It burns like a dull grey fire in my gut, its flames licking through my entire body.

By the time I break through the front door, I'm almost blind with hunger. I stagger into the crisp morning air, sniffing madly.

I catch a vague scent and follow it down the street. My seven zombie companions follow after me, moaning and grunting. Maybe they can sense that I'm different from them. Smarter. Superior.

The alpha male of the pack.

* * *

Last night.

When Abbie and I came back downstairs, Gail's breathing was shallow and raspy. Like somebody sharpening a knife. Her eyes rolled back into her head, and her limbs contorted languidly.

Abbie fiddled with her gun, agonizing over when to pull the trigger. Chef remained slumped by the front door, his gaze shifting between the street and Gail. It was clear that Chef was preparing to make Abbie's decision for her. A nasty triangle of tension swelled between the three of them—Abbie, Gail, and Chef—and the rest of us didn't dare to interfere.

When the tension snapped, it wasn't Abbie, Gail, or Chef responsible; it was me.

Rather, it was the Wolf.

When I stood up, I could already feel the full moon pulling at my marrow and blood. Panic rose on a lake of sweat on the back of my neck. It was too early. The moon couldn't be up yet—

Damn it. The Wolf had tricked me again. The closer we get to moonrise, the more the Wolf is able to exert itself over me. Manipulate me. Make me forget things. I'd had every intention of going up on the roof when the change came, of locking myself up there, but now it was too late. The Wolf was punishing me for all those nights I'd contained it. For all those times the Wolf had emerged only to find itself locked up or bound by chains.

A coat of fur simmered beneath my skin. I fell to the floor screaming, my mouth full of chalk and broken glass. My teeth were rearranging themselves; four fangs digging out of my gums. Blood spilled from my fingertips as thick claws forced themselves through my tender skin.

If there's anything in this world that I loathe more than myself, it's the damn Wolf.

The Wolf consumed me, as it did every full moon night. It ate me from the inside out, its wild animal hunger gnashing and tearing at my insides. At least, that's how it felt.

Abbie knelt to examine me, but then screamed. I growled back, baring my fangs. Soon, the diner was filled with screams and shouts, and then with gunfire.

Wouldn't you know it, not a damn one of them had any silver bullets.

It was a feeding frenzy. Those fools had that diner locked up so tight, there was no way they could escape. One of the lesbians made a break for the rooftop stairs, and I tore out her stomach, left her lying in front of the stairwell door, effectively blocking it. I attacked Chef next, who blew a chunk out of my shoulder with his shotgun. Even as I tore his throat out, I felt a familiar tingle in my shoulder, as the muscle, bone, and skin stitched itself back together.

I can't remember much of what happened next, just that the Wolf slaughtered them all and saved Gail for last, like dessert. After all, she was tied down, going nowhere. When I tore out her throat, the flesh tasted like bad milk.

After that, a fuzzy blanket of white light enclosed my consciousness, and the Wolf took over completely. I'm fairly certain that this blanket of light is what keeps me from going insane. If I had to experience every horror committed by the Wolf, I'd easily lose my mind. It's some built-in function of the Wolf's affliction, putting my mind in isolation while the Wolf runs free.

The last thing I saw before the Wolf took over is the lump of diseased flesh that I spat upon the ground.

* * *

We shuffle east for several apocalyptic blocks along Atlantic Avenue, gathering a few stray zombies in our wake. I follow the scent of human flesh to a cheap hotel. The front door of the hotel is missing, torn from its hinges. I charge inside, ready to feed the hunger, but soon find only disappointment. The elevators in the lobby are shut down, and the only stairwell is barricaded by a pile of dirty mattresses and broken dressers. It's passable, but it'd take a lot of time and make a lot of noise to get through. I'm about to moan in rage, but then an insight snags at my thoughts.

Any kind of quality shelter will have one main entrance, but also a reliable backdoor.

I stop and let my mind chew on that thought. It seems important, relevant to the situation at hand. Grunting, I stagger back outside and glance down the narrow alley running next to the building. That's when I see what I'm looking for: a fire escape. Someone has arranged a pile of bricks on the fourth level of the fire escape, which extends downward to the second floor. There, the extension ladder has been removed, replaced with a handmade rope ladder.

It's a good system. The people inside can use the fire escape for offense, dropping brick bombs on any zombies nearby. They can also use the rope ladder defensively to escape, but the humans have left it unguarded. Foolish.

My dim-witted colleagues follow me into the alley. I shove Chef against the brick wall and make several awkward attempts to climb onto his shoulders. He stares back at me with a wounded, dumb expression and collapses under my weight. When that doesn't work, I start to shove a dumpster underneath the fire escape. The others catch on eventually. Or more likely they're just imitating me. Finally, we get the dumpster into position.

I shove the female zombie couple up onto the dumpster, point upward and grunt until they climb onto the fire escape. Since the bricks are on the fourth floor landing, I'm assuming that's where our breakfast lives. I wait until the girls are on the third floor before heading back to the front lobby.

When I get to the stairwell entrance, I can already hear broken glass, screams, and gunfire from the fourth floor. Just as I suspected, a few of the humans—perhaps the weakest of the herd—are the first to try to escape, rather then stand their ground. I'm in perfect position to attack when the stairwell door opens.

It's Melanie.

Mel. Even though it's only been a few months since I left, she looks so much older. Her hair is still dyed pink, but is now pulled into a simple braid. Gone is the lip ring and other jewelry. Her normally pale face, once so much like a full moon, is now tanned and dirty. I reach out to hug her, the following words on my lips: *Honey, I missed you so much. I'm so glad you're okay.* Except what comes out is a rattling moan.

She takes a step backward, holds up a handgun, and shoots me right in the head.

* * *

For a long while after the Wolf first got inside me, I thought I could hold on to my family. It wasn't uncommon for my job to send me out of town on business, so I made sure that I was always away during the full moon. Then my asshole brother decided to get married during the day of a full moon, which screwed up all my plans.

I went to the wedding, a fairly small affair. Mel, she was one of the bridesmaids. I remember staring at her across the aisle as the minister read the vows to my brother's bride.

Do you take this man to have and to hold—

Later, I gave the toast at the reception, a swanky golf club nearby. I danced with my wife and daughter, and drank a lot of wine. I was in the bathroom when the change came. I stared at myself in the mirror, a look of surprise on my face. And then, my eyes. They were laughing at me. The Wolf was laughing. The damn beast had tricked me, let me lose track of time. As hair slid out of my flesh, I climbed out the window and ran across the well-manicured lawn.

—for better or for worse in sickness and in health—

I woke up the next morning wearing only a pair of tattered tuxedo pants. Next to me was a dead girl in a bridesmaid dress. My heart squeezed into a fist. I knew it had to be Mel. Imagine my relief when I turned over the bloody corpse and found one of the other bridesmaids.

—as long as you both shall live?

The Wolf had sent me a message. It let me know that no one is safe. After that, I left town, vowing never to return.

* * *

So, that's it. I should be dead, right? Everyone knows that the one way to kill a zombie is to shoot it in the head.

Except I'm okay.

The bullet tears easily through my skull, and suddenly I've lost binocular vision. My little girl shot out my left eye.

It sounds like a lightbulb shattering when the bullet exits out the back of my skull. I fall backward, more from surprise than from the impact.

Some of the other zombies must have followed me from the alley, because Mel is now surrounded, firing her gun until it clicks uselessly. She shoots down all but two zombies, a pregnant woman in a sundress and a fit Latino wearing only a wife-beater, who have cornered her behind an ATM machine. My daughter screams as the zombies grab her, tearing the sleeve off of her blue t-shirt.

Next, she whimpers in surprise as I snap the zombies' heads back and slam them head-first onto the lobby floor. I then stomp their heads one after another until my heels are covered with skull and rotten brains.

When it's done, the only sound is Mel's sharp breathing. No, wait. Something's squirming inside pregnant zombie's bloated stomach. Ever so faintly, I can hear something toothless trying to eat its way out.

I already feel a tingle where my eye used to be. It's coming back.

"Daddy?" says Mel.

It's the first time she's called me that since puberty slapped her in the face. I want so much to hug her, but can't be that close to her. If I touch her, the hunger will consume me. And I will consume her.

So instead, I nod and wave her away. On my way back to the stairwell, I stop and kick her gun over to her. Hopefully she has more bullets. At the stairwell door, I turn and blow her a kiss. Grunt.

She whispers to me. "Thank you, Daddy."

* * *

Walking upstairs, I feel like I'm shedding skin. Walking away from Mel is like a new beginning for me. I'm leaving humanity behind. I'm becoming something new. Part of a new family, where I'm the strongest and smartest. The alpha male.

When I make my way to the hotel room on the fourth floor, it's already covered in blood and gore. The two women are sharing the entrails of an overweight black man. Abbie and Gail are gnawing at an elderly woman's face and hands. Chef has his own victim, a Goth chick with lip piercings and multi-colored tattoos covering her chest and arms. She watches in horror as Chef tears out her intestines, gnawing at the pulpy flesh. I fall next to her, pushing Chef away. He growls under his breath and crawls into the corner, taking her intestines with him. The tangled mess of her insides unravels out of her stomach.

I tear off the remains of her shirt. Her left breast is covered with a bright tattoo of a lunging tiger. I bite into her chest, catching the tiger by the tail. She screams, gurgles, chokes, and shudders. I swallow.

It occurs to me then that I've been eating people for years, and it's always been a very lonely pursuit, something that I've never clearly remembered. Now, it feels so good to share the experience. All around me, my gang of zombies moans and bites and grunts. The room is filled with the sounds of squishing, biting, tearing, and swallowing.

It's a feeding frenzy.

As I gnaw on the Goth's face, it occurs to me that biting Gail must have been what turned me into a zombie. It makes sense, if you think about it. If a zombie bites you, you eventually become one of them. Likewise, if you bite a zombie, you eventually become a zombie.

If you're a werewolf who bites a zombie?

Near as I can figure, the lycanthropy disease and the zombie virus must have somehow blended together, putting me in my current state. When I become the Wolf—rather, when the Wolf forces itself out of me—my mind, maybe even my soul, gets shut down. It's like the Wolf puts my core essence in isolation, so that the Wolf can do whatever it wants. It's that isolation that has kept me from going insane over the years. Now, that isolation that has kept my personality and thoughts intact.

I'm a zombie with a werewolf's healing abilities.

I'm practically invincible.

I've got my mind, an unstoppable body, and the world is mine to conquer. What of the Wolf? My skull is silent. If the Wolf is in there, it's being quieter than ever. Is it possible? Am I cured?

It's almost dusk by the time we finish eating. Soon, the moon will sit all bloated in the sky, staring down at me with its unblinking eye. What will it see?

* * *

When I lead my pack outside, bloated on fresh meat, I gaze into the sky. Apprehension squirms in my gut. Or maybe it's just maggots.

The moon sits low in the sky behind some buildings, pregnant with possibilities. And nothing happens.

I'm cured. That wolf that has plagued me for more than a lifetime is gone, driven out of my body by the zombie plague. That damn beast is the reason that I couldn't live a normal life, and now I'm free of it forever. And by forever, I mean forever.

I'm beyond death. Beyond life.

I raise my fist to the sky and moan—a ragged, contemptuous noise.

Behind me, my fellow zombies echo my sentiment. At least, that's what I think at first. They're certainly making a lot of noise, but when I turn around, they've fallen to the pavement. Their dull yellow eyes are glowing in the moonlight. Jagged fangs split rank gums. Grey fur slides out of blue skin. Chipped nails extend from filthy fingertips.

It's the little girl, Gail, who attacks me first, lunging and biting at my thigh. Following her lead, the rest of the zombie werewolves leap upon me, knocking me to the ground. Abbie and Gail snarl and moan over my chest, tearing at my neck. Soon, their muzzles are covered with thick, black blood. Chef tears at my abdomen. The rest gnaw at my arms and legs.

The wolves consume me. It takes them most of the night, but they manage to eat most all of me: fingers, legs, intestines, lungs, and so on. They leave only the upper chest and head.

The worst part? I'm perfectly awake through the whole ordeal. All I can do is watch and wait for them to finish. Every few bites, one of them locks eyes with me, and I can see the Wolf staring back. Those pale glowing eyes are laughing at me.

By the time the sky starts to lighten, Gail leads the pack back inside the hotel. By this point, I'm just a head, a neck, and a few chunks of spine. I'm stuck in the gutter, and all I can do is moan.

I wait for the tingle that tells me I'm healing, but it doesn't come. Maybe I've sustained too much damage. Maybe only my head is protected. I don't know, but I've got a long time to think about it. More than a lifetime.

Already, dull white flames of hunger flicker and spark inside my remains. The hunger threatens to consume me, but it can't. If only it could, but it can't. Instead, it rages in my phantom belly, torturing me.

I moan and moan some more. As if answering my call, Gail appears in the doorway of the hotel. She's just a regular zombie now; the Wolf has retreated. She stares at me and cocks her head. She has something in her hand. What is it? A scrap of food for me, perhaps? She holds it up into the morning light, and I can see that the little girl is holding my daughter's torn sleeve.

Gail holds the sleeve to her nose and sniffs.

Her eyes are smiling.

UNLUCKY MOON
T.J. MAY

"My son recommended Craigslist to me," said the tall, brutish man standing in front of Ray. "Darndest thing, technology. To be honest I needed him to help me list my first post. Seven years old and he's smarter than his old man," he chuckled.

Ray nodded. Being a literate member of the computer age, he'd known of such websites for some time. Good for getting rid of things. Good for finding what you need cheap. And good for finding what you don't want anyone else to know you're looking for.

The tall man pointed to the woods.

"The enclosure is just through there, back a bit in the forest."

The tall man lead and Ray followed. It was seven o'clock and sunny despite being a cool September evening. Once they moved under the canopy of oak and maple, Ray felt like someone had dimmed the lights, if not shut them of completely. He felt out of place. The tall man sensed it, and pointed to the flashlight in his hand to ease Ray's mind.

"City fella, eh?"

Ray nodded.

"Got any kids?"

Ray shook his head, no.

"Well, that might be good enough. See he's a big fella, so he's not likely to prefer a city apartment. But I gotta tell ya; he sure hates kids. Gets mighty possessive, a one-person kind of animal," the tall man saw Ray tense, "Oh, he's great for me though. I'll just turn over the reins to you if it's a match," he grinned, but it was a sad grin.

This man does not really want to give him up, thought Ray.

"You know—

"You go out and get one cause your son wants it. You end up feeding it, cleaning up after it, giving it attention, and YOU become the most attached to the damn thing," he wiped his forehead with the sleeve of his shirt.

"But, safety first, and this 'ole fella is a mano-y-mano situation, you know?"

Ray nodded and the tall man grinned.

"I gotta feeling he's gonna like you. Still, breaks my heart to see him go though."

They walked on a narrow and winding path, through thickets and uprooted trees. Trees that looked so old, they may have dropped some 20 years ago when Gloria whipped up the New England coast. The trunks were rotting into the ground, but the mud caked roots stood like ruins sprinkled among the seasoned foliage.

The tall man broke the silence.

"You know you aren't the first to come by and check him out," he said. The tall man crunched through the forest wiping spider webs from his face as he flicked on the flashlight.

Ray was relieved. Though they'd only been walking for 10 minutes, it felt like a claustrophobic midnight in the woods.

"Yep, not more than a couple months ago I posted the first ad.

It was right about the time we moved him out here—

"By-the-way, you'll love the enclosure I built for him. Right on the edge of this beautiful clearing, and the moon just looks like a painting when it passes over."

It seemed the tall man began to realize Ray was becoming impatient, but he hoped the tall man didn't notice the fear. Ray was tough, or at least he wanted to be. Which was why he was here in the first place.

"Anyway, the guy shows up and starts in as soon as he sees him. Lucky was too hairy, too big, too wild. Not at all like the photo or description, blah, blah, blah," the tall man waved his hand as if to dismiss such notions.

"Then the guy starts getting rude. Says I'm wasting his time. Well, it just made me want the mutt all the more, you know? But, that's why the ad you answered was pretty basic. I didn't want to give the wrong impression, so I figured you could come and see for yourself. They say less is more in writing. So, that's what I went with."

Ray nodded in agreement and started to break a little sweat. They were getting deeper into the woods and about to meet a ferocious dog on his own turf. Ray had only seen such a beast among the pits built haphazard in the basements below the city. The adrenaline rush of seeing them mutilate one another made the otherwise mousy paralegal feel like a man. He thought having one around the house would make him feel that way all the time. The mouse was starting to creep back into his mind the further they moved from iron, steel and pavement. Ray now realized he was a novice, in the pits and in the forest, and that maybe he should bolt for home. Now.

"Besides," said the tall man interrupting Ray's thoughts. "I read in the papers that the fella went missing a few weeks later. So, turns out Lucky had a bit of LUCK on his side after all," the tall man laughed at his own joke and clapped his hand on Ray's shoulder. The move startled him and set off another round of laughter from the tall man.

"Not to worry friend. I know you city folks aren't much for roughing it. But I'll take care of you," and he gave Ray's shoulder another squeeze before moving on up the path.

"You know I even got Lucky off of Craigslist. Yep, my son helped me get rid of some tools initially. Then one day I was just poking around when I came across PUPPIES FOR SALE—1/2 SHEPHERD, 1/2 WILD MOUNTAIN DOG.

"Sounded like a damn side show and figured visiting the pups with my boy was better than doing nothing on a Sunday afternoon. Course, we get there and Charlie falls in love with Lucky. I'm a sucker for seeing my kid smile and the rest is history."

The tall man shook his head but remained silent for a few moments. Ray assumed he was replaying the day in his head and felt validated when the man spoke again.

"Biggest damn puppy I ever seen. Now, I can see the shepherd but I don't know about the wild mountain dog. I mean what is that anyway? Wolf? Coyote? Doubt it. No, I figure mastiff or greyhound most likely. Either way, he's a big boy."

The tall man turned and gave Ray a buddy punch to the biceps.

Ray did not respond.

"You are a serious man, sir. Maybe having a pet will loosen you up some."

"Just a bit further. We had to move him out here 'cause of the howling, man was he incessant. The older he got, the louder it got. I own 10 acres straight back," he made an arm motion with the flashlight like a traffic controller on the tarmac at Logan. "So no one can hear him out here anymore—"

"Ah, here we are."

They had come upon the clearing. The sun was gone and the leafy canopy gave way to a moth eaten blanket of midnight blue. Despite the darkness Ray was thankful for the clear sky and starlit night. He felt like he could breathe again, and momentarily feared the walk back. The fear was quickly replaced by wonder as he searched the lot for the hand-made shack.

Ray spotted it about 100 yards away, past a sea of thigh-high ferns softly lit by a fleet of fireflies dancing about like cargo ships at sea, bobbing atop the waves.

"Shall we?" said the tall man. The interruption made Ray jump. He nodded his head and waded into the ocean of fern as the moon made its first appearance peeking over the tree line.

"I should probably tell you he's a damn picky eater," said the tall man. Ray was beginning to realize that this guy had no intention of keeping quiet for long.

"We tried all the store brands and he'd barely sniff at them. Lucky'd wait till we let him out and tear off after some squirrel or rabbit.

"I got a friend that does the butchering down at Stop&Shop. I stop in there once a week and he hooks me up with the scraps. If you decide to take the mutt I'll pass you his number."

Ray nodded his thanks, but he was pretty sure he did not want to take a ride on the Lucky bus anymore. The adrenaline he had felt before was now turning to nausea, and he got the feeling the tall man knew it. Ray figured it was best to stay the course for now.

They were just a few feet from the shack and Ray thought it strange that not a sound was coming from it. No rustling, growling, nothing. It must be asleep. Not much of a watchdog, thought Ray.

"I gotta tell you Ray, you seem like a nice enough guy, but I don't get the feeling this is going to be a good match."

Ray shrugged and nodded in agreement, happy to not be the bearer of such news. The tall man, as he'd done so many times in the last half hour, smiled.

"S'ok. Like I said, I'm pretty attached to the bugger anyway. So, it's no skin off my nose. As long as I keep trying to get rid of him the wife'll stay off my case," he roared with laughter and slapped Ray on the back, nearly knocking him over. Ray shuddered under the weight, but managed to deliver a meek smile to his host.

"Tell you what though, you came all this way to see a hell of a dog. And you ain't seen a sonovabitch like Lucky. Go ahead and take a peek at him."

Ray looked apprehensive. He thought he'd gotten out of this one, but the tall man reassured him, "Go ahead city boy. I got your back. Sounds like he's asleep anyway."

It was clear that the tall man was not going to take no for an answer. And besides, paralegal or not, I'm a tough guy now, right? What the hell, the dog's asleep anyway.

Ray stepped up to the door and opened it slowly. The tall man shined the flashlight over Ray's shoulder into the shack.

A loud, ominous howl rang through the trees about the same time Ray realized the shack was empty. His first thought was that Lucky had gotten loose. He was half right.

Ray turned to the tall man and was met by red, beady eyes, and a set of steak knife teeth dressed in overalls. The tall, hairy beast licked its lips,

"I told you 'ole Lucky was a sight." Said the tall man in a throaty voice that had changed in step with his appearance.

With a movement faster than light, Ray felt the teeth sink into the side of his neck. The pressure sliced veins, cracked bones and caused his head to involuntarily snap back so his eyes faced the sky.

Ray stared, stunned in shock and awe, at the beauty of the stars. The moon, full in view, had cleared the treetops and hung over the clearing like a spotlight on the macabre scene.

"Fuck—me—," Ray wheezed through his nearly collapsed vocal chords.

Everything went black.

A TASTE OF BLOOD AND ROSES
DAVID NIALL WILSON

The wheelchair sat directly in front of one of the small windows that lined the side of the bar and faced out over the swamp. The light of day was fading, and the evening crowd was just starting to filter in. The chair's occupant paid no attention to them. His stare was icy, empty. A thin string of drool had run down his chin, joining the tip of his chin to the heavy flannel shirt he wore. He leaned forward at what would have been a painful angle, were it not for the unnatural, twisted curve of his spine. Over his flannel shirt, he wore a faded fatigue jacket with the letters USMC emblazoned across the pocket front. On his shoulder rode the insignia of a Gunnery Sgt., two medals dangled from the pocket opposite his name; The Purple heart, and The Silver Star.

Jeanette glanced over at him from time to time, concern knotting her brow. When she thought nobody was looking, she walked over hurriedly and wiped the saliva almost tenderly from his face, then scurried off about her work. He did not move to thank her, nor to watch her. He stared out over the swamp, and the swamp stared back.

At the bar, Mama Duvalier was serving a tall, leather-clad youth with long tangled black hair. "Hey, Ace," the young man's friend slurred drunkenly, "hurry up with them Dixie's." Jeanette felt a sudden weight on her heart, and knew the man's head must have swiveled to her. "Hey, better'n that," the voice rang out again, "have that pretty little thing over there bring 'em to us."

"But Juice," the youth at the bar fairly whined, "I already got 'em."

"You heard me," the voice returned, and Jeanette looked up to meet the eyes behind it, to put an image to the sound. They were dark, deep, and void of emotion. Snake's eyes. She felt a shiver transit her spine, and turned toward the bar, hurrying her steps.

The beer waited on the edge of the bar. Mama Duvalier had a hand resting on each, and her eyes leaked poison. "You be careful, girl," she hissed, handing over the tray. "You don' want trouble wit dat one. You get them this beer, you get away, eh?"

Jeanette shivered again, but she nodded, picking up the tray and turning, fighting to place a smile on her face that would not crack from her fear. She had dealt with snakes before, and it was a mistake to let them know you were afraid.

"That's right," the man called Juice crooned. "You bring those over here real nice like, missy. Me and Ace here, we rode a long way to drink this beer. We're right thirsty."

His eyes slid over her like swamp slime, and small patches of moisture formed on the underarms of her cotton blouse, but she held her gaze steady. Moving forward as quickly as possible, she set a bottle in front of each of them and stood a bit off to one side, quietly waiting for them to pay.

Juice was in no hurry. "What's your name, girl?" he asked, his voice becoming sickeningly sweet, like rotted honey.

"Jeanette," she answered politely, offering no more than was required.

Well, Jeaneatte," he said, hesitating to let his gaze slide down her body once again, "you are one *fine* lookin' little lady. Anyone ever tell you that?"

She shook her head no in a short, nervous motion. The more he stared at her, the more she got the feeling of worms crawling about beneath her skin.

"Jeanette!" Mama Duvalier's voice cut through the gloomy, smoke-filled room like a knife, slicing the oily threads of the man's concentration on her with a sudden snap. "You move faster, girl, or I'll hang your hide out for the gators, eh? You get that money, you get busy."

Juice was obviously not pleased by the interruption, but he fished a couple of greasy bills from his pocket and handed them over, letting his fingers trail slowly down her palm as he placed the money in her hand. He made a last attempt to snare her with his eyes, but she took the money and nearly fled across the room, casting a look of gratitude to Mama behind the bar.

The old woman did not notice. She was staring fixedly at the back of the young man's head. Her eyes were nearly closed, and she seemed to be mumbling. Suddenly her eyes snapped open and she spit three quick times into her palms, rubbing them together and slapping them twice. Jeanette wasn't sure if Mama's curses ever worked, but there were certainly those who feared them.

Not these two strangers, of course. They had the look and feel of the city on them. Empty souls. She had seen many like them traveling through, heading for New Orleans. Some sought magic, others an endless party, still others ran from something or someone they thought to lose in the tangles streets and ancient, moldering cemeteries. They would know nothing of curses.

The sun was almost down, and Mama gestured to her urgently, nodding her head toward the wheelchair and it's silent occupant. Jeanette knew what was expected. It was almost nightfall, and Paul must be safely away for the night. It was her job—her destiny. She felt her heart melt at the thought of a few moments alone with him. Drying her hands on her apron, she moved to the window and grabbed the handles of the wheelchair, releasing the brakes with a quick kick.

As she wheeled him toward the side door, she heard the man Juice's voice ring out again, and it stopped her cold. "Hey, Jenny, who's the crip?"

She half spun, her eyes lighting with sudden fire, barely catching herself in time to check her tongue. They had no right, no idea—she turned back toward the door, but it was too late. Juice had risen, standing over six feet tall on wobbly, drunken legs. He moved toward her, kicking aside several chairs and lurching into one of the tables as he came, not once dropping the ice-laden gaze of his snake eyes from her quivering form.

"I asked you a question, Jenny," he said, voice low and suddenly more dangerous.

"My name is Jeanette," she mumbled, instantly wishing she hadn't spoken at all.

"What?"

"Please," she said, "he must go to his room now. I—"

"His room? He *lives* here?" the man said, frowning dubiously. His eyes slipped in and out of focus deceptively. One moment he seemed coherent and merely drunk, the next out of focus and—evil.

"He lives in the cabin out back," she said, again regretting her response, though she didn't know why. "I must get him to his room and his bed. He was injured—the war."

Juice's eyes strayed down to Paul's chest, and the medals he wore. He reached out as if to grab at one of them, but Jeanette pulled back on the chair and he missed.

"Leave him alone," she hissed, and there was no more fear in her eyes, only anger. "Keep your filthy hands off of him."

Juice stood stock still for a moment, his alcohol-fogged mind working overtime to process what had just happened, and for a second Jeanette was certain he would slap her. Then he smiled, a dark, evil smile and pulled his hand back.

"I like a girl with spirit," he said. "What is he, your brother?"

She turned her back on him, kicking the door open and exiting without looking back. "He's my husband," she choked, barely containing her emotions, forcing the words through a throat suddenly too tight and too dry for speech. The door slammed shut behind her. As she was walking toward the cabins, the cool evening breeze soothing her nerves and the sounds of insects and birds ushering her into the world of night.

Paul's cabin was the very last one in the line, right on the edge of the tree-line that bordered the swamp. There were reasons for this, not the least of which was privacy. She parked his chair beside the door and reached into her pocket for the key ring. She hated the locks, the idea of closing him away with no choice, no freedom, but things were as they had to be. The alternatives were much less appealing.

She turned the first key, then the second, and the third. She could feel the large metal bars sliding from their deeply imbedded sockets, the scrape of metal on metal. Finally all that remained was the knob, and she twisted it, reaching inside to turn on the light. She hurried a bit quicker as, glancing over her shoulder, she noticed that the final rays of sunlight were seeping over the edge of the hills beyond the road. The moon would be high in the sky in only a few short moments, full and bright.

She slipped inside, pushing Paul in front of her, and moved him over to the window on one side of the one-room shelter. There was no bed. There were no chairs, no table. All that the room contained was a faded rug and the two windows, barred with metal rods that were sunken into both floor and ceiling and sealed with heavy mortar.

She positioned him so he could stare out the window that overlooked the swamp, much as he had been in the bar, and she returned to the door, gazing back at him fondly. She would have liked to have stayed, just to spend time with him and talk—to tell him stories. The memory of how he had been, the fierce light that had lit his eyes and the grace of his movements, all of it was emblazoned brightly in her memory. Her love had not faded with his injury, only becoming deeper and bittersweet.

She turned to the door and reached again for the keys, hurrying to place the first in its sheath of metal. As she turned it, feeling the bolt slide home with a dull thunk, strong hands grabbed her from behind, one covering her mouth, and dragged her away.

She fought wildly, trying to bite the hand and loosen it so she could scream, but a sudden hard slap from her assailant's other hand sent her senses reeling, and she felt her concentration slipping. The world warped, everything fuzzing around her. She squirmed and kicked with every ounce of energy she possessed, fighting to be free, but it was no use.

Paul, she screamed mentally, *Oh my God, no!*

She could smell the odors of beer, faded denim, and leather as she was dragged toward the tree line, combined with the slightly sour smell of his breath. She knew it was the man Juice, the man with snake's eyes. Where his hands groped at her flesh, she cringed and pulled back into herself, but it was not enough. He was strong, and she had been stupid. Blind and stupid.

She stumbled along, remaining upright only by the strongest of efforts. Every few steps, Juice slapped her again, or twisted her head by a handful of her long, dark hair. She couldn't muster the breath for the scream she longed to release, even when his hand was free of her mouth, and in any

147

case she knew it would matter very little. The hanging moss on the trees surrounding them could dampen sound like a wet blanket, and they were moving in deeper by the second.

Finally, with a grunt, Juice stopped, spinning her roughly against him and planting his mouth firmly over hers, sliding his hand around to hold her tightly by a handful of hair. His other hand was working feverishly, tearing at her dress, shredding the fabric with ease. She fought determinedly, but every effort seemed, somehow, to aid him, and her clothing soon lay in tatters at her feet as he fumbled with his own belt.

She screamed then, a lost, lonely scream, her head tilted back so that the light of the full moon fell brightly on her face. Something inside clicked, something almost forgotten in the whirlwind of events that had swept her up. Her body went suddenly rigid, and her eyes widened. "Paul!" She screamed. "Oh, my God! Paul!"

"That cripple don't hear you, honey," Juice whispered harshly, lifting her body and pressing her into the damp ground. He pushed himself easily between her flailing legs, moving his hands over her body and pulling her toward him. She scratched and tried to bite, swinging at him with whatever limb was momentarily free, but to no avail.

"You need a real man, prob'ly needed one for a long time. I'm doin' you a favor." His grin was wild, maniacal, and the moonlight glinted off of a silver cap that covered one of his two front teeth.

Jeanette felt her mind spiraling downward, away from it, away from the night. Her thoughts caromed about inside her brain, repeating a single word—"Paul".

* * *

The moonlight seeped over the window sill slowly, moving like a spill of corn syrup over hot-cakes. It slid down the wall, eating away the shadows, moving relentlessly toward Paul's inert form. Deep within, beyond the immobile strings that once animated his body, beyond the rotting, worthless husk that had been a strong, virile man, anger boiled. It raged, barely checked, bubbling over the walls of reason.

His eyes did not move, but he saw. His ears conveyed even slight sounds to his brain, but his mouth refused to acknowledge them. He was trapped, helpless, as alone in a crowd as in a locked room, and he gnashed mental teeth, reaching even farther inward, reaching for something long gone. He had heard the screams. He knew what was happening, knew he was trapped -- doubly, the deadened nerves of his body and the solid steel of the dead bolts. Still he reached, and when the moonlight slipped across the floor like an obsequious servant to lick at his feet, his will was answered.

The first sensation to return was pain, excruciating, mind numbing pain. He used it, concentrated on it, funneling it into his anger. He must be free. Jeanette was out there, and another. He must go to them, go before it was too late.

The tendons and muscles spasmed in his arms, his neck, his torso, knotted and contracted, stretched and molded, changing. There was the snap of joints being rearranged, the popping of skin too-tight for it's host body. Then he moved. He raised his head, threw it back in a combination of rage and pain beyond description, and he screamed.

Leaping from the chair, flexing long idle muscles and re-orienting his eyesight and balance, he turned to the door, eyes smoldering. A fleeting memory returned. Sounds. Only one key. Only one key had turned before Jeanette's muffled cry, and one lock would not hold. Not nearly.

He charged. There was no thought in the movement, no planning. He lowered a shoulder, now deeply muscled, covered in dark gray fur, and with a roar he pitted his strength, his pain, his anger, and his soul against the treated wood and metal reinforcements of the door. There was a meeting, wood and flesh, will and strength. With a splintering explosion the dead bolt ripped free of the wall and he was through, sprawling, rolling rising to a stooped four legged stance and running. The swamp beckoned, and he heard a faint scream—his name. Then the rage took him beyond thought, and, howling his fury, he plunged into the trees.

* * *

Jeanette didn't immediately register the crashing sounds as they approached. She was concentrating on *not* hearing, not seeing. Not being. She felt the weight of the man pounding against her, felt the bruises and the small knots of pain, the razor-wire ball clenched in her gut, but she refused to acknowledge what was happening. All that mattered was that she get away, back to Paul. The keys. Something about the keys.

Juice was oblivious. His mind was lost in a swirl of lust and alcohol, enhanced by two Seconal he'd dropped an hour before hitting the bar. When the trees parted at his back and the scream of rage split the muggy, dampened air, it took a long moment to register on his mind at all. He turned his head slowly, not really aware of danger yet, only confused and annoyed at the interruption. It took entirely too long.

Jeanette felt a sudden release of pressure. One second Juice was pressing his foul-smelling, repulsive flesh against her in a relentless, mind-numbing rhythm, and the next he was just gone. Not there. She opened her eyes slowly, willing herself to move while there was a chance, to roll to the side, anything, but her body wouldn't respond. Only her eyes moved, in the end, and the sight that met them was nearly enough to send her back to oblivion.

Juice was dangling about two feet above her, his eyes wide and his mouth constricted into a rictus of horror. He was held tightly at the neck by a gnarled, impossibly-large clawed hand. Long and covered with coarse gray fur, veined and rippling with barely contained strength.

She followed the arm back up it's length, unable to stop herself from looking, though she knew what she would find. The werewolf was huge—overpowering. His frame, though bent, towered over her, handling the body of her attacker as if it were an insignificant plaything. She was snared instantly by the eyes. They were focused on Juice, and they were on fire with a raging hatred that was nearly palpable.

"Paul" she squeaked, unable to fully control her breath—her voice—"Paul, don't—"

She spoke to the air, to the wind. He did not hear her, of if he did, he was beyond listening. The wolfman reached out with his other hand, clamped it over Juice's mouth and began to squeeze. Awash in terror, and finally comprehending the imminence of his death, Juice clamped down himself, biting into the hand with all the strength he could put behind his jaws. There was an incredible roar of pain and anger, and the hand fell away.

Where Juice's teeth had broken the werewolf's skin, steam rose, and the skin seemed to blacken and pull away from the bone. As the man's jaws released, the moonlight glittered off the silver capped tooth once more, flashing brightly. Then the other hand had released as well, and Juice fell, hitting the ground with enough force to knock the wind from his lungs. He lay there, rolling over and over and bent double, trying to regain enough strength and composure to run.

Jeanette saw all of this as if from a distance—detached. It couldn't really be happening. Paul was frothing at the mouth, eyes wilder than before, sweeping the clearing as if confused. It only took him a moment to find what he sought, but that was enough time for Juice to reach his feet, still doubled over but very determined.

The two stood facing one another for a long second, then Juice broke for the trees, screaming at the top of his lungs and slapping through the brush and brambles without thought. Holding his injured hand limply in front of him, Paul leaped after him, head thrown back and a wild cry of rage and pain shooting skyward, aimed at the heart of the moon.

Moments later, when she was alone, Jeanette stumbled to her feet. Juice had no chance, she could already hear his screams changing in pitch, rising and falling away. She had to get back, to find a way to stop what her own foolishness had begun. She wrapped the remnants of her dress about her as best she could and staggered off through the brush, praying that her senses were correct and that she was going the right way. If she were lost in the swamp, there was little hope of lasting the night. Not now. Not with Paul loose.

She knew he would not harm her, not if he were himself, but this was only part her husband, this creature of darkness and pain, and she didn't know, if it came to an inner struggle, who would win, man or beast. That he would kill others was not even a question.

She kept moving, concentrating on her footing, and it wasn't long before the trees thinned out and she could see the shattered door of the cabin ahead. With a tiny gasp of gratitude to a God she was no longer certain she believed in, she stumbled forward, screaming again when a short squat shape melted from the surrounding shadows. It was Mama Duvalier. Sobbing, Jeanette stumbled forward into her arms.

"Where is he," the old woman hissed, pulling away sharply. Jeanette felt a momentary pang of rejection, then realized Mama was right. There was no time for comfort. Maybe there was no time at all.

"He is in the swamp," she said, trying to control her sobs long enough to be coherent. "He is after the man, the—"

She lost the battle with her emotions, then, but it was enough. Nodding curtly, Mama grabbed her by her arm and led her back into the cabin and over to the wheelchair.

"He will be back for you," the old woman said quietly. "You know he will come. There are three locks remaining—it might be enough. You must wait for him here."

Jeanette's eyes widened with fear, but Mama's own gaze held no compassion. Perhaps it was there, buried deeply, but on her face was the still-mask of icy determination. "But, he will kill me, I—"

"Do you love him, girl?" The words were sudden and sunk in like daggers.

"You know I do. He is my life, even now."

"Then you must wait. I will do what I can, and, gods willing, we will still have something to say in this, eh?"

Jeanette nodded dumbly, not trusting herself to speak. She had been frightened in the swamp, horrified by what was happening, the shame and degradation, the pain, but this was worse. Terror was a cold liquid, flowing through her veins, and in the swamp, she heard again the blood-curdling cry of her destiny.

"Here," Mama said quickly. "Keep this with you, and, if he comes at you, you must thrust it at him without fear. If you do this, perhaps you see the sun again, eh? Now, give me the keys. I must be ready with the locks." She was holding forth a small pouch, tied about carefully with the thorny stem and blooming bud of a single red rose. Jeanette took it, passing over the ring of keys.

Then the old woman was gone, a fading vapor-vision in the darkness, and Jeanette was alone. She could see the tree-line of the swamp clearly in the brightness of the moonlight, and she waited, rocking slowly back and forth in the wheelchair and listening to its soft scratching at the floor. It seemed that her heart was a great drum, pounding louder and faster as the moments passed. Again the beast howled.

* * *

Trees and shrubs split and passed away in surreal blurs. The taste of the blood was at his lips and the moonlight glistened off the droplets that had spattered his silver-gray fur. It had been long years, since he'd tasted the blood, and it was robbing him of his thoughts, stealing his focus.

Behind him, decaying to join the peat and the mire, already feeding the beasts and the heart of the swamp, the man-thing lay dead. With his death had come the blood, with the blood had fled his sense of purpose. He knew who he sought. He knew her scent, the temperature of her warm, flowing blood. He knew her eyes—last seen masked in terror. He did not know why he must seek her. Thought was fading. Man was falling to beast, will to instinct, and the search had melted to hunt in a bloody haze of lust and insatiable hunger.

The scent led him to the edge of the trees, and from there he could see the silhouette through the bars of the window. There was a familiarity to the scene, the face, the pulsing sound of the heartbeat he could just make out over the din of the night birds and the chirping of crickets. He moved like a shadow from the line of trees, squatting further into the four-legged gait that was becoming more and more familiar.

He saw the woman draw back from the window, heard her gasp and rise, as if to move for the door, but he was too quick. He noted, in passing, that a third presence lurked near the door, but the blood there was older—less appealing and flowing with a stagnant, over-ripe consistency. He focused on the doorway, the woman, and when he reached the opening, he leaped inside with a snarl.

As if from far away, he heard the woman's screams, her words. He heard names, wails, things he should know and did not, and it infuriated him further. All he could see was the vessel that flowed with the blood he craved, the clean, pure blood. He launched himself forward, jaws gaping.

Jeanette, realizing that he was not listening, that he would kill her, thrust the bag that Mama had given her forward, tossing it in terror at his approaching jaws and flinging her arms over her eyes to remove the sight of her fate. She prayed that it would not linger, that it would be swift and sudden, and final.

She felt his clawed arms reach for her, felt the impact as the huge, furred body slammed into her and smashed her into the chair and the wall, knocking her half-senseless and re-animating the pain of her earlier bruises. She closed her eyes and silently awaited the closing of those massive jaws on her throat, the final moment of release. It never came. There was the one crash, the one impact, a soft moan, and then nothing. No sound. No movement. No death.

Finally, when her heartbeat and breathing had slowed to where she could move, she opened her eyes. There was a horrible snapping, grinding sound, and she flinched, but nothing touched her, and she sat up quickly, looking over at Paul's suddenly inert body.

The bag had scored a direct hit on his gaping maw. Whatever had been in it, it had been effective, and sudden. The rose dangled from the closed jaws, dripping with saliva and blood, and his face was rippling—his whole form was—shrinking, warping, reforming. The wet snapping sounds nauseated her, and she turned her head to retch, half fearing those feral eyes would snap open again and spear her through the heart. They did not.

It was over in moments. She stood and looked down at the inert form of her husband, unmoving except for the regular rise and fall of his chest. The eyes were vacant, and the blood was now mixed with a thin trail of drool that ran down from the corner of his mouth and onto the floor.

She turned and noted that Mama Duvalier had done her part. The three dead bolts were locked tight, and she knew they would remain so until morning. It did not matter. She moved across the floor, stumbling as the pain shot through her legs and her abdomen, until she reached her husband. Kneeling, she raised his head softly and sat back, laying it gently in her lap.

She wiped away the blood from the corners of his mouth, but she dared not remove the rose. Leaning back against the wall, she softly caressed his hair and allowed her eyes to close once more. She searched deep, searching for memories of an older time, a better time, and the night melted away to darkness. As she drowsed, she leaned forward, kissing him once on the lips. She slept with a bittersweet taste on her tongue, the taste of blood and roses.

UNDER A CIVIL MOON
JOHN GROVER

Emily's dream haunted her again last night. The men finally came for her with their knives and guns—guns that cracked like thunder through the forest. She ran through the trees and the mud, chest heaving, gulping pockets of air. Emily ran on all fours and sprang through the treetops desperate for escape.

In the end she always woke with them on her heels, blue uniforms, the whites of their eyes, hungering for her flesh and soul. Emily woke in the dead of night, bathed in sweat. She breathed a sigh of relief and rose out of bed.

A cool breeze swept into her bedroom through an open window. Emily went to it and gazed up at the full moon glowing gold across the shadowed horizon. A solitary howl filled the night. Emily sensed the melancholy in it. It was a lonely howl. Somehow she figured the wolf spoke to her. It understood her and she it. Both knew the men would some day catch them.

Not tonight.

Emily closed the shutters and walked slowly away from the window. In the back of the room the fireplace crackled with flames. In the fire she watched the last of the dark blue uniform burn.

* * *

The sun reached its highest point when the two Union soldiers stumbled out of the Virginian mountainside. Uniforms tattered, faces marred with blood and a trail of filth behind them, the two men stopped and collapsed.

James pawed his canteen and brought it to his lips. Robert's eyes widened and he ripped the canteen from his comrade's twitching hands. "Give it here," he roared as the water poured onto his face.

"What in the Lord's good name happened to our troop?" James whimpered.

"It was attacked, you fool."

"By what?"

"A wolf."

"No, that was no wolf. It was something out of Hell itself. Did you see our friends? Our brothers? They were torn to—"

"No more James. It was a wolf. Let's keep moving before we take the blame for that carnage back there."

James pulled himself up reluctantly and followed his buddy. The night before their troop marched toward Richmond to join General Butler and his men. The fall of the Confederate's capitol city was imminent. In the onset of night the troop became disoriented, the light of the full moon befuddled their minds, and they became lost.

A shortcut through the mountains rendered them worse off then before and they camped. During the middle of the night they were attacked, Robert reached for James who scrambled for his rifle. A blood bath of nightmarish proportions unfolded, but not at the hands of Confederate soldiers. James's firearm slipped into his hand and he got off one shot, at what he wasn't sure, before his world went black.

James tried to push the thought out of his mind. His heart was wracked with the memories of his friends' bodies lying in pieces around him as he woke from what felt like hibernation. "Captain Blake? Where on earth is the captain?"

"God only knows now," Robert answered glumly. "We need to reconnect with the rest of the Union. Grant has the Confederates nailed down in Petersburg. He needs our help."

James said nothing, his words died in the numb shock of the sights around him. Farms were laid to waste. The burnt out shells of civilian homes still smoldered on either side of the road they walked. Cattle were slaughtered. In some farms lifeless bodies littered the ravaged fields.

"What has the Union become?" James turned his head from the destruction and closed his eyes.

"Total war my friend," Robert said, noticing his distressed comrade. "General Grant understands the concept. He knows it's necessary. Only an utter and total defeat of the separatists will end that war."

"You support this?" There was a harsh tone in James's voice.

Robert said nothing more.

Hours of walking in the hot sun brought thirst and hunger. Hours of silence between the soldiers brought broken morale. When the lush gardens surrounding the last house out of the area appeared before them, the men nearly wept.

"It hasn't been touched," Robert said of the two-story white house with a picket fence surrounding it with perfection. "They must have missed it on the ride through here. We need food and water. Someone must be there."

"They will not welcome us with open arms," James said.

"Of course not," Robert said. "We will take it if we have to."

"I won't hurt civilians… I won't…"

"We'll starve." Robert's face turned red. His eyes narrowed. He drew his knife and grabbed James's arm. "You will take it or we'll both die. I need you. We're buddies, remember?" A grin twisted onto Robert's face, his yellow teeth glinting in the sun. "We're not going to kill anyone unless they try to kill us. We just need food and water or we'll never make it back home."

James thought about this. He missed his wife dearly and his two boys. Too much time passed since he'd last seen them. And the letters had stopped. "Alright."

"That's a good soldier." Robert turned and hopped the picket fence as nimble as a cat. "I wish we hadn't lost our rifles," he whispered back to James. "Feel naked without mine."

James ignored him, but followed through a vivid painter's palette of flowers and herbs flooding the yard on every side. Perfume hung thick in the air. Something in it, he wasn't quite sure, made his nose twitch.

* * *

Faint music resounded from above as the two soldiers slipped into the house and crossed the living room. The aroma of cooking food tantalized their senses. James began to salivate.

Robert turned back and brought his finger to his lips, a moment later he vanished into another room. James stood his ground and looked around the room. He soaked in the beautiful tapestries on the walls, the long woven rugs on the floor and the laced covered furniture in the center of the room.

James took a step toward the huge fireplace with its carved mantle when a footfall stopped him. He assumed Robert's return, but instead felt the cold barrel of a rifle against his neck.

"Do not move," a woman's voice said. "You are a stranger in my home and I have the right to kill you."

James put up his trembling hands in surrender. *Yes end it now. Please, end it.*

The sound of another voice filled the room. "Kill him and I will kill her."

James turned to see Robert standing in the room with an adolescent girl in his arms. His knife was to her throat. Beside him, James took note of the woman, probably mid-twenties, lowering her rifle.

A scream erupted as a third girl charged the room swinging a hatchet above her head. She launched herself at Robert who promptly shoved his hostage to the floor and swung his knife wide.

The blade slashed the attacking girl's right hand, stopping her cold. The hatchet toppled as blood flowed. The girl dropped to her knees and wailed.

Robert lifted his knife to strike again.

"Not my sister!" the young woman yelled and lifted her rifle but James grabbed hold of it first.

"Robert no!" James turned and pointed the rifle directly at his comrade. "Enough. They're just girls."

Robert lowered his weapon as the three sisters huddled on the floor. "Please don't kill us," the oldest said.

"We don't want to kill you," James answered. "We just want some food and water, ma'am. We are starving."

"That's right," Robert added with a sickening grin. "We only want food and we'll leave you alone. Promise. What are your names?"

"Emily," the oldest said. "These are my sisters Rebecca and Annabelle, whose arm you just cut."

"We're very sorry about that," James said on behalf of them both. "We did not mean to hurt any of you."

Emily ripped a piece of her apron and tied it around Annabelle's bleeding hand. "Let me tend to my sister's wound, then I will fix you both some supper. It will be getting dark soon." She glanced out the windows with concern.

"That'd be fine, ma'am." James watched the three sisters gather themselves and move into the kitchen. He turned around to see Robert approaching him. He was seething.

Robert slid his face to James's ear and whispered: "If you ever point a rifle at me again I'll eat you alive."

* * *

"Your dreams," Annabelle whimpered as her big sister Emily washed the wound.

"Yes, the men have come my sisters. As I have told you. My dreams never lie. We must not let them destroy us." Emily stared into the faces of her younger sisters. Fear left its mark on them. "They must go from here. We must make them go like all the others. This is *our* home."

Emily led the other girls to the dining area where they set the table for the two soldiers. James and Robert took their seats at the oak table covered in lacy cloth. "We've been working on a stew in the hearth," Emily said as she stood at the head of the table, a space she had reserved for herself. She refused to sit the Union men there. "It should be ready shortly."

"Thank you," James said. Robert only grinned.

At dusk the three sisters served up steaming bowls of meat stew with root vegetables. Like gluttons, James and Robert devoured the stew as if they hadn't eaten in weeks. Rebecca and Annabelle simply poked at their food with forks, disinterested and eyeing the soldiers with suspicion.

Emily looked up from her bowl and said softly: "You cannot stay here."

Robert looked up from his bowl; a glob of thick gravy covered his chin. "Why not?"

"A full moon rises again tonight. It is not safe in these parts under a full moon."

"Is that so?" Robert chuckled. "I reckon we can handle a full moon. Our entire troop was butchered and we survived that."

"Butchered?" Emily was both horrified and glad. "The way our friends and family have been?"

"We do not know anything about that," Robert answered. "But come to think of it. How has your house remained unscathed during the war?"

"I know how to protect the home," Emily sneered. "My grand pappy taught me how to deal with your kind."

Robert roared a great belly laugh. "Did he now? My you are a spitfire. Your grand pappy never met the likes of us before." Robert pounded his fist on the table and screamed. "Boo!"

All of the girls jumped.

"Robert that's enough," James interrupted.

"I'm just having some fun." Robert let out more laughter when a howl from outside silenced him.

Emily looked to the windows. "It's started," she murmured. "It's too late."

Rebecca and Annabelle shivered as the howl repeated.

"The wolf returns," Robert said and jumped from his chair. What sounded more like a roar then a howl resounded just outside the house.

"By God's grace not again," James left his chair next and joined Robert's side.

A crash assaulted the timbered front door. It buckled once as the shelves on the adjacent walls crumpled to the floor.

Rebecca and Annabelle screamed as tears flooded their cheeks. They ran to Emily's awaiting arms. Emily remained calm.

"Come little ones," Emily whispered. "Let us allow the beast to do its work."

Emily ushered her younger sisters away from the table and out of the room. Annabelle's wound seeped from beneath her bandage and as they passed the first window behind them, a storm of glass and wood exploded around them.

The shutters splintered as a pair of clawed, fur-clad arms lunged and grabbed hold of Annabelle. The scent of her wound drove the beast mad. It tore the wailing girl from Emily's arms, shook her violently before dragging her from the house.

"Annabelle!" Emily screamed. Her eyes widened. Her heart dropped into her stomach. She pushed Rebecca to the floor to shield her from the flying debris and peered out of the ruined window.

In the milky light of the moon an enormous wolf, more than six feet tall, stood on its hind legs. Long muscular arms pulled Annabelle to its snout where it clamped down on her throat. Emily heard a snap as blood poured to the ground. She hid her eyes and turned away from the window.

"Lord... good lord why?" Emily collapsed with Rebecca and cradled her tight. Heavy steps thudded in front of her. She gazed up to see Robert grinning down at her.

"Aw girls, don't be upset," Robert said. "Our Captain is just following his nature. The same manner that we do." He went to the other windows and ripped the shutters from them, letting the moonlight flood the room.

"No Robert! Not again," James cried as he stumbled over to stop his friend, but froze in the pale moonlight. "What is happening to me?"

"James, you do this every full moon," Robert snapped as his teeth grew long and pointed. "You really need to let go of that guilt, buddy. You, captain and me are a pack. We hunt together. Stop pretending you have no memory of it. Accept your nature and eat!"

Rooted to the spot, Emily watched James turn to her, his eyes bleeding with guilt and remorse. "I'm sorry—so very sorry. I have no control over it. I must obey the moon—" His face twisted in anguish.

Emily felt her pulse race and her breath quicken. Rebecca buried her head into her older sister's chest. In mute horror she watched James's eyes morph black before blazing with yellow.

"Emily run!" James howled as his words melted into grunts and growls. "R-r-r-rah-un!"

* * *

James's blood boiled while his entire body burned as if with fever. The pain of the transformation was unlike anything he'd ever experienced, even during this war. His flesh split as muscles ripped, coarse brown fur covered his body, and his bones cracked as the shifting converged.

His face stretched into a snout wet with blood and saliva, and filled with dagger-like teeth. Fingers elongated into claws. His shape transformed into a hulking abomination he knew all too well.

He hated himself more with every change. Each full moon the hunger worsened. Until last night, the unthinkable happened. Robert, the captain and himself lived under the curse for some time, but none thought they would ever massacre their entire troop.

Their hunger was insatiable. Even after the devouring of all their comrades, their bellies were still filled with the pain of starvation. James knew it was out of control. Knew it was too powerful. So maddening was the guilt, he hoped the war would kill him. It was the only reason he served. He didn't believe in the ideals, the politics. He just wanted to end the curse. He just wanted to die. Now that hope faded with the light of the full moon.

The James-wolf snarled and turned to Robert, who was also fully transformed and dancing in the pale white light filling the room. James watched Robert race to the front door and rip it off its hinges, allowing their captain inside the home.

The captain's fur was wet with blood, matted around his muzzle. He joined his two men and the three howled in unison. The hunger raged again.

The werewolves tore through the house. Emily and Rebecca were no longer in sight. They heeded James's pleas and vacated the room. Cunning as ever, the wolves knew the girls could not have gone far. The house was just not large enough to hide from the pack.

The creatures destroyed furniture in their hunt, thrashed closet doors, tore human food to pieces, and stormed the root cellar and pantries. Finally, James eyed the set of stairs ascending to a second floor shrouded in darkness.

The James-wolf yelped to his pack and they closed in. He was only following instinct, and appeasing the agony of the hunger, but he hoped the girls were not up there. He prayed for an end somehow—but in the end, roared up the stairs.

* * *

Emily rushed Rebecca up the stairs as the soldiers were locked in their transformations below. They burst into the nearest bedroom, shut the door behind them and latched it for all the good it would do.

"Under the bed," Emily told Rebecca. "Right quick!"

The quaking Rebecca cried, tears streaming in torrents, but obeyed her sister. She slid under the four-post bed as Emily shuffled around the room. Downstairs a cacophony of destruction thundered throughout the house.

Emily searched her jewelry boxes, her hope chest and her apron and braced herself as footsteps pounded up the stairs.

The door exploded into pieces as the pack clawed its way into the room. Howling filled the house as the captain, the alpha wolf, led the charge.

Her back against the wall, Emily thrust her hand into her apron and ripped out a bunch of purple-colored flowers—wolfsbane. She'd been growing them in the gardens all her life. "My grand pappy did indeed teach me how to deal with your kind!" In her other hand she lifted a Derringer pepper-box revolver.

The werewolf captain froze in his steps. A howl of rage escaped him as he shrank away from Emily, unable to touch her. James and Robert backed against the doorway, clawing to get out of the room, but the broken door blocked their escape.

Emily stared the captain down, fury burned in his eyes. He let out a pitiful yelp as Emily fired the revolver. The shot blew a hole in the beast's chest. It roared in agony, its head twisting from side to side, its arms flailing helplessly until it crashed to the floor.

Smoke wafted off the lifeless body. The two wolf soldiers looked down at their fallen alpha and roared. The James-wolf's eyes met Emily's and they faced-off. The two didn't budge. James's claws clicked, his teeth gnashed with drool, but he could not advance on her. Emily held the wolfsbane high and tight.

Suddenly the Robert-wolf sniffed at the air. He eyed the bed and bolted to the other side of the room. He leapt on top of the bed and jumped up and down until the posts toppled and the bed collapsed.

Rebecca screamed and struggled beneath.

"No! Rebecca!" Emily stood her ground, unsure of what to do. She kept her revolver aimed at James while watching Robert drag Rebecca from the under the bed. It tore her up inside to watch the last of her sisters enter the clutches of the beast.

Emily turned back to James. He snarled at her once then turned to glare at Robert. James barked at him, but he continued his attack. Rebecca squirmed and shrieked as the werewolf lifted her from the ground.

The James-wolf tore itself away from Emily and lunged for Robert. The two collided in a thunderous crash as Rebecca tumbled to the floor.

"Rebecca to me!" Emily called and the young girl crawled across the room as the two wolves clashed, biting and clawing at each other's throats.

James and Robert battered each other around the room. Blood spattered the walls, clumps of fur filled the air until the two crashed through the window to the ground below.

The two girls screamed and the house went silent. Emily checked on Rebecca, who seemed unharmed and wiped the tears from her face. Emily put down the wolfsbane and made her way slowly to the window.

Down below she saw Robert in human form, glass and wood protruding from his naked body, his throat shredded like paper. James was nowhere in sight. In the distance she heard a faint, lonely howl.

* * *

In the dead of night Emily had her dream again. She ran from the men with their knives and guns. She raced on all fours, and leapt through the treetops. They were gaining on her. Rain fell cold onto her body. Her hair matted to her face. Her blood boiled and her body burned as if with fever but this time the dream finally became clear.

She was not the one running from the men. Emily was not the wolf that was forever hunted. As her dream eyes caught view of her reflection in the rivers of the forest, it was James in the dream not she. Emily saw through James's eyes. He ran from the men. He ran from himself. As long as the moon was full, James would always be running.

UNLEASHED
NINA KIRIKI HOFFMAN

The baby, Joe, was still nursing when Amelia felt the change coming on, the first stirring of appetite for the forbidden, the faint current of unnatural strength, the hint that she would become the thing she feared and hated. She glanced toward the apartment's living room window. The white curtains were parted, showing that night had arrived as gently as a first snow, shadows lodging among the buildings in drifts, melted in spots by the yellow warmth of street lights. She tasted the cool metal of twilight in the autumn air. Soon the moon would crest the hill above town. For the first of its three nights full, the moon would work on her weakly; she could resist change for a little while, but not all night.

Where was the babysitter?

Gently, Amelia pulled Joe free, tucked her breast back into her bra, and buttoned her shirt. She rose from the folding metal chair and carried the baby to the closet where she had set up his crib three months before.

Pregnancy had protected her from the moon change, and she had thought nursing would, too. She had prayed that this frightening mother-change in her body would drive out the other, unwelcome change entirely. For a year it had. Just in case, since Joe's birth she had arranged for a babysitter each full moon. Of course, the first time she really needed a sitter, the sitter was late.

Who could she call? She glanced over her shoulder at the phone. The sitter first. Then, maybe, the man who had moved into the apartment downstairs two weeks ago. Amelia usually had trouble talking with strangers, especially men, but something about this man—his smell, perhaps, a musty, stale-sweat-in-body-hair scent that she would have dismissed as unclean, save for its strange attractiveness—had reassured her. They had spoken by the mailboxes three times. He had patted Joe's head with a gentle hand, and Joe had not minded.

What would Mother think of her even considering calling a strange man to look after her child?

Blast that thought. If Mother were alive and knew Amelia had a child at all, she would disown her daughter.

Amelia put Joe in his crib and wound up the music-box mobile above it. By the light of a shell nightlight, plastic cardinals and bluebirds spun to the tune of Brahms' "Lullaby." The baby stared up at the birds. Amelia tucked the blanket in around Joe.

He was such a good baby. Gentle, quiet, undemanding. Just the way she had been as a baby, according to her mother. The way she had been all through girlhood.

She kissed Joe's forehead.

Change gripped her breasts, flattening them against her chest, her body shifting to absorb and redistribute tissue. She backed out of the closet and lay on the rag rug in the tiny living room, her eyes clenched shut, her mind grappling with the change, holding it at bay. When the hunger woke to fullness in her, would Joe be safe?

* * *

Kelly Patterson sat on the dirty laundry in his armchair and looked at his apartment. In the two weeks since he had moved in, he had managed to get it as messy as any other place he had lived—crushed beer cans mingling with wadded potato chip bags and filthy socks on the floor, an assortment of dirty shirts and jeans draped across most of the furniture, and a couple crumpled TV dinner trays on the lamp table, right next to the rings left on the wood by wet cans. Sawdust he carried home from the construction site in the cuffs of his pants and in the waffles on his work-boots mixed with everything else, but its clean wood scent couldn't compete with the odor of decay, which was almost a color in the air, spiced but not diminished by the scent of soured beer.

By morning it would all be cleaned up and he would have to start over. No matter how much he challenged his animal self, it always rose to the challenge and exceeded it.

Kelly scratched a stubbled cheek. The night Sonya-the-sudden had bitten him—he had forgotten that she had asked him not to come by that night, and he had a record album he was convinced she should hear—the night she had bitten him, he had visualized many scenarios, but never one to match this reality. Who would ever guess that somewhere inside his sloppy self lurked a finicky creature?

Maybe he should stop teasing himself, leave the place neat once and see what his alter ego would do when housekeeping didn't get in its way. Adult onset lycanthropy. It was still so new and weird. There were lots of experiments he hadn't tried yet. Like, what would he do in the woods? Maybe he should throw a couple blankets, kibble, and a dog dish into the Jeep, drive out into the woods and check it out—if not tonight, tomorrow. He had never had any woods sense. What if he got lost? Lost, forty, and naked in the early morning. An ugly thing to contemplate.

He sighed, stood up and went to the curtains, parted them a crack to check the progress of the night.

There was a thump from upstairs, then a drumming of heels. What was going on with Amelia-the-mouse? Mouse brown hair, mouse dark eyes, alive with the mouse wish to be invisible. Had someone come to visit her, and were they having a go? He had tried to imagine a man who could be the father of her baby, and failed; Amelia was a walking wall of don't-touch-me, though some of the shrug-off softened when he talked to her about the kid. Who could get close enough? Though there was something about her that tempted a person—

There was another sharp heel thump on his ceiling, and a low cry that sounded more desperate than satisfied. He straightened out of his habitual slouch, staring up, wondering if she needed someone or something.

The hot silver fire ran through him, starting from his heart and flowing out to his extremities, traveling like flame along gas lines. His fingers tightened on the curtain. He drank a long breath in, feeding the silver fire. Smells sharpened, and sounds intensified; he knew that somewhere in the room was a rat he would soon enjoy catching and eating. He could hear it chewing on leftover pizza in the corner.

A floor away, he could hear Amelia, moaning his name. His first name. Something had to be wrong with her; he couldn't imagine her ever calling somebody male and older than she was by their first name, not under normal circumstances.

He chomped his lip, the pain waking him out of change, dousing the silver fire. It was First Night, the loosest night of change; he could overmaster it, at least for a while. He gripped the knob of his front door.

What if change caught him in Amelia's place? Scare her out of her skin. She'd get him in trouble, no question.

"Kelly!" she cried.

He opened his door and glanced out. Across the hall, Peter-the-snoop was peeking out. Peter waggled his eyebrows at Kelly and slid his door shut. Kelly sighed and ran for the stairs.

* * *

Amelia had the phone's handset in her fist, but she couldn't dial the phone, not with change gripping her. Anyway it was too late. If the sitter hadn't left her building yet, she'd never get here in time.

Soon change would consume Amelia, and she would lose all her normal feelings, her restraints, her cares and concerns. She would go prowling, looking for victims. Before that happened, she must get help for Joe.

Her lower body froze, and the little tail began to grow between her legs. Clenching her fists, locking her elbows, she forced the tail back inside her.

"Kelly!" she cried.

Change whispered through her mind: kill inhibitions. Mate with impulses. Take the night and make it yours. Your feet are made for wandering, and desire is your master.

The doorknob rattled, turned.

She panted short harsh breaths. She could feel her hips slimming, her shoulders changing. Her skin simmered as hair sprouted on chest and arms and legs and back.

Kelly, messy Kelly, slipped into the apartment. "'Melia?" He knelt beside her.

She unclenched a fist long enough to grip his arm. "Joe," she said, her voice already low and harsh with change. "Will you watch Joe for me?"

"I, uh," he said. His face looked funny, and his smell had changed, though it was still just as enticing. She could feel the racing heat in him against the palm of her hand. "Okay—" he said, on a rising note.

She cried out. All her muscles locked, holding her still while the rest of change happened and she became the monster.

* * *

It was going to happen. Kelly was going to change in front of somebody for the first time since Sonya had talked him through it. This time it wasn't going to matter, because—

He wondered who or what had bitten Amelia.

What she was turning into didn't seem to be an animal. Its outline was human.

She shuddered and panted and sweated in front of him, her face twisted in pain and revulsion.

Change didn't hurt him like that. For him, it was as good as sex.

Amelia writhed. He felt he should be watching her, maybe soothing her somehow—a wet towel on the forehead? What?—but his own silver change pulsed through him, and he could no longer hold it off.

* * *

Grinning, Adam sat up. He glanced down at his lap and frowned. Damn Amelia, the stupid bitch. Why hadn't she changed into his clothes? How could she let him wake up still in a skirt? Didn't she even *care* how he felt?

He grabbed handfuls of the skirt and ripped it off his body, enjoying the strength in his arms. This blouse, feminine, pastel pink, soft and wimpy. Just like the bitch—it had to go too.

Something warm was behind him. He narrowed his eyes. What had happened since last time? He turned and discovered a big black pointy-eared dog staring at him with yellow eyes. Something funny about its paws—they were too big—but before he could get a good look at them, it leaned toward him. An edge of its black lip lifted, showing a long white fang. It made no sound.

"Shoo," he said. His voice wavered.

It took a step toward him.

He stood up, the shreds of skirt scattering around his feet. He stripped the shirt off and dropped it, then skinned out of Amelia's cotton underpants.

"Didn't know she got a dog," he said to the dog. He wasn't sure how it would behave toward him, either. Did he still smell enough like her to confuse it? He held out a hand to it, and it sniffed him, then backed up one step. "Look, I'll get out," he said. "Just gotta get some clothes first."

The dog sat, its gaze fixed on him.

He went to his closet, the one where she had kept a grudging wardrobe for him, but the clothes were gone. Baby music came from fake birds above a topless cage, and muted light from something orange on the floor. The closet smelled like milk and talcum powder and pee. "Christ!" There was a baby in the cage, a little baby who looked up at him with big eyes. How could she have a baby? A baby in his closet. A baby and a dog! He would have to do something drastic to her. She couldn't keep switching things around on him while he was sleeping. It wasn't fair.

He took a step toward the crib and the big dog growled, low in the back of its throat. He glanced at it. The hair on its spine was standing on end. He shrugged and headed for the bedroom, where he found his clothes in her closet, shoved over against the wall, crowded out by her own. Dumb bitch. She'd wrinkled his favorite shirt. He slapped his thigh, wondering if she could feel it. It hurt him too much to try again.

The dog was watching him from the bedroom door. It showed him its pointed tooth again. He dressed hurriedly. "All right, all right," he said, "I'm going out! Just a minute." He found the black socks in her underwear drawer, and his loafers (she hadn't polished them in more than a month. How could that be?) in the closet among a jumble of her shoes. The dog growled when he rifled her purse. "I need money to go out, don't I?" he demanded. The growl lowered, but it kept coming. Adam ignored it. Amelia had twenty-six dollars in her wallet, and a smudgy driver's license with a short-haired photo of her on it. If he got stopped, he always said he was a male impersonator. He looked enough like her to pass, which was an uncomfortable thought. She was so unattractive. Most of that was the way she carried herself, always flinching, eyes downcast; her wardrobe was full of dark, neutral colors.

He took her keys. As he walked past the growling dog, he kicked out at it, but missed. Its growl rose to a bark. It snapped at his leg, then backed off, following him at two paces until he reached the door. "Goodnight, sucker," he said as he locked the door from outside. "I hope you drank two gallons of water."

The little dark man with glasses was peeking out his door in the downstairs apartment, the way he always was. Adam made kissy lips at him. Anybody was fair game on Adam's nights—the more disgusting and repulsive the better. The little man ducked inside and slammed the door, and Adam smiled.

* * *

Amelia lay quiet, her eyes shut. His hateful clothes were tight around her hips, across her breasts, and she smelled alcohol and at least two different perfumes on Adam's shirt; the castor oil scent of lipstick came from his collar where it was nudging her cheek. She could feel the sickness gathering in her stomach. Soon, she'd need to dash to the bathroom to purge: the knowledge of what the monster had done the night before (she couldn't really remember, but she knew it was awful), and the remnants of whatever he had eaten and drunk.

She gulped twice.

She realized there was a strange sound in the room.

Breathing.

Terror stilled her breath, her heart. Her hands clutched the sheet.

The breathing went on, undisturbed.

So he had done it, finally brought his prey home. She had a horrible moment wondering what might be in her stomach besides normal food and drink. Her gorge rose. She couldn't hold back any longer. She stood up in a rush, locked herself into the bathroom, and made it all the way to the toilet before she lost it.

When she had finished retching and loosened all the most torturous buttons on Adam's clothes, she rinsed her face in the sink. Something nagged at her. There was something she was forgetting, but she couldn't think, not with some stranger in her bedroom. She got her oversize red terry cloth robe from the hook on the bathroom door and put it on over her half-undone clothes, then peeked around the door.

A man was sleeping curled in her bed, a naked man. A long lanky leg lay folded on top of the quilt, and a long arm curled around his dark head; the rest of him was drawn up around his stomach. He breathed softly, not snoring the way she expected all men to snore.

What was she going to do?

Get some decent clothes, dress quietly, grab her purse and flee the apartment? Maybe if she waited long enough the man would leave, and then she could get back in and lock up, but he knew where she lived—

And what about—

What about Joe?

The baby's morning wail of hunger rose just then. Amelia watched, wide-eyed, as the man in her bed yawned and stretched, then turned to look at her.

It was Kelly, Mr. Patterson from downstairs. He knew what she was: was her first frozen thought.

Joe, who was used to being taken care of any time he made a sound, wailed a little louder.

Mr. Patterson sat up and yawned into the back of his wrist. "He's probably hungry," he said. "I couldn't find anything to feed him last night."

"What are—what are—" She hid her eyes with her sleeves.

"Well, excuuuse me," said Mr. Patterson. A minute later, he said, "You can open your eyes again. I'm covered by a sheet."

Hot tears streaked down Amelia's cheeks. She lowered the sleeves of her robe and glanced at him to see if he was lying, but he wasn't. He had a sheet up around his waist, shielding her from seeing the monster part of him. A little girl's voice came from her mouth. "Why aren't you wearing any clothes?"

"Don't you remember anything about last night?"

Tear-blind, she shook her head.

"Wait a second, that didn't come out right. Nothing happened between us last night, Amelia. Except you wanted somebody to take care of the baby on Change Night, and I guess I was the only person you could think to call."

"Change Night?" she whispered.

"Moon Night, some call it."

"Curse Night." She licked a tear off her lip and peered at him through a salt haze. "How do you know about Curse Night?" He smelled like something she wanted for breakfast.

"I change too."

Joe wailed a little louder. Amelia stuffed her sleeve into her mouth and bit down. What kind of monster had she left the baby with last night? She dashed through the living room and into Joe's closet. He was red-faced and teary, but when she picked him up he settled down immediately. He didn't even smell wet. She went to the metal chair and sat, settling Joe on her thigh and offering him a breast. He sucked as if he were starving.

Mr. Patterson walked out of the bedroom, wearing the sheet like a toga. He glanced at her nursing Joe, shielded his eyes with a hand, and bent to pick up some clothes lying folded on the rug. "What bit you?" he said. He turned his back to her.

"I don't know." She heard the despair in her voice and wished she could unsay it. Her mother had taught her never to let a man hear her despair.

"How long have you been changing?"

"Since I was twelve." She hesitated. "It stopped while I was pregnant with Joe."

"How old are you now?"

"Twenty-one."

"Do you know what you change into?"

She shuddered. "A monster," and then, whispered, "Him."

"Do you remember being him? I remember being my other self. I'm not as different, somehow, as you are."

"I can't remember anything he does. I just know it's disgusting."

"Oh," said Mr. Patterson. He didn't say anything more for a little while. "I'm going to dress in your bathroom, all right? I think the less Peter-the-snoop has to talk about, the better."

While he was gone she got an extra diaper and draped it over Joe as he nursed so that no secret part of her showed. Her despair was so strong she worried about it getting into the milk and hurting Joe.

In a couple minutes Mr. Patterson came out. With him dressed and herself covered she could look at him again. "Mr. Patterson," she said in a low voice. Her worry about Joe gave her the strength to speak.

"Yes, Amelia."

"What do you change into?"

"A wolf. Kind of a wolf, anyway. Much more normal than your change, I imagine."

"I left the baby with a wolf?" The warmth of Joe against her chest, his hot mouth on her breast, reassured her. "How could I?"

He lifted his eyebrows, but didn't answer.

Of course, her monster self would do anything.

"How did you change his diapers?"

"It was tricky," said Kelly. He glanced at the clock above the card table where she ate all her meals. "Got to get to the site, Amelia. Gotta pick up a few things from my apartment and get to work. I'll be home after five—three hours before moonrise, more or less. We can talk then." He put his hand on the doorknob.

Joe, warm and dry, lay in her arms. "Mr. Patterson. Thanks," said Amelia. She lowered her eyes.

She locked and bolted the door behind him, not sure if she wanted to talk to him ever again. He had seen the worst part of her—if it was really part of her, and not some alien creature that took her over three nights a month, which was what she told herself, how she lived with it.

Maybe, if she worked fast, she could load everything she really needed into her VW bug and get away, far away. There was still a little left of her mother's legacy, enough for first-and-last-plus-damage-deposit and another six months of low rent and generic groceries. After that Joe would be old enough to go to daycare, and she could get back to temping.

Of course, there was still the problem of getting a sitter for Joe before tonight.

Joe was sleeping against her breast. She transferred him gently to his crib and closed the closet door almost all the way, then went to the phone.

What had happened to that girl who was supposed to come last night, anyway? Amelia had left Joe with her a few times before when she had to go shopping and couldn't take Joe. She had found the girl's number on the bulletin board at the laundromat, and the girl had been clean and prompt and had had no objections to the idea of staying with the baby overnight if necessary. The nights Patty had come when Change hadn't happened, Amelia had gone out to a movie and then come home, dismissing Patty early.

She checked the pad of paper by the phone and called the number. "Patty?" she said when a young voice answered.

"Patty's not here," said the voice, breathless. "There was an accident."

"Goodness, is she hurt?"

"Yeah, pretty bad. Yesterday she hit a car with her bike! She got a concussion. She had to go to the hospital."

"Oh, I'm so sorry! Will she be okay?"

"We think so," said the voice. It sounded uncertain.

"I'm sorry," Amelia said again. It didn't seem like the right time to ask the voice to recommend another babysitter. "I'm sorry," she said again. "Good-bye."

"Good-bye," said the voice.

She couldn't trust Joe with someone she had never met, and that included—Him. Adam.

She wished she knew the phone number of the place where Mr. Patterson worked. She glanced toward the closet where Joe slept, then sat on the floor, elbows on the seat of one of the chairs, chin propped on hands. She had to think.

* * *

Kelly was carrying a sack full of Chinese take-out when he knocked on Amelia's door after he left work. The door opened a crack and she peeked out, then widened the opening just enough for him to slip inside. He glanced at her as she bolted the door behind him, and got a shock. She had done something to her long brown hair—pinned it up somehow, the Search for Sophistication. She was wearing makeup—too much of it—and a nightgown. A flannel nightgown, but the hem was torn off above her knees, and she had rolled the sleeves up to mid-forearm, and left the buttons at the throat undone.

He had a sinking feeling.

She looked at his face, then dropped her gaze. Her pinkened lower lip trembled. "I was afraid— " she said.

He went to the table and took the white cartons out of the sack, with napkins and two pair of chopsticks. "Have you eaten yet?"

"No, Mr. Patterson."

"Come on over and sit down. Call me Kelly. You did last night."

"Last night I was desperate."

"You look pretty desperate now."

She sat down in her second chair. She wouldn't meet his eyes. "I had this great idea," she said in a small voice. "When it turned out my babysitter was in an accident. I thought—"

He handed her a pair of chopsticks and a carton of shrimp-fried rice. Savory steam rose from the opened carton. She set the carton down and stared at the chopsticks, still safe in their red paper sheath. "I mean, I could ask you to sit with Joe again, but you must have other things to do with your time. So I thought—," she said.

He opened a couple more cartons, waiting.

"I know how to get rid of Adam now," she said.

"How?"

"Get pregnant." Her glance darted up to meet his, then dropped. After a silence, she said, "I don't know how it happened last time. How or who. But I thought—"

Kelly swallowed. He let a minute go by. "You know that's not a long-term solution? You don't want to spend the rest of your life pregnant, do you?" She had an attractive scent; he had noticed it every time he came into contact with her. It spoke to him, even when all the rest of her was posted No Trespassing. So he knew that what she was asking him wasn't impossible, but it would probably be damned uncomfortable for both of them. "Besides, you can't just plan on getting pregnant. Sometimes it takes time and work."

Her eyes closed. She had done the lids in silver, and her lashes in black. Too much of everything, but the hand that had applied the makeup had been steady and skillful.

"Can you support two kids?"

She took a deep breath and let it out. She looked like a little girl playing Mommy. She opened her eyes and stared at him, and she looked like a wood sprite. "I don't know," she said. "There's welfare, isn't there?"

"But look," he said, leaning a little closer to her across the gently steaming food. "You can't disrupt your whole life just because you want to—you want to get rid of this little fraction of it. Three nights out of thirty, and you've got all your days free. What is it? Five percent of your month, that's all. You can live with it." It was a set speech. He had heard it from Sonya-the-sudden. That seemed so long ago. He wondered why he had been so upset about the whole thing. As long as he focused during change on thinking he needed to guard his apartment and take care of it, things worked out. He hadn't done much exploring yet, but he figured there was plenty of time for that.

"You don't know what he does," she said, her eyes tear-bright.

"Acts like an asshole," Kelly said.

"Much worse things than that."

"How do you know?"

Her lips thinned. She looked away.

"You *do* remember."

"I do his laundry."

He reached across the table and touched her hand. "Amelia, do you remember?"

"No," she said, and her face tightened. In a whisper, she said, "Maybe." Louder, "Everything he does, he does just to torture me. He knows all the things I hate and he does them all. Things I can't even think of. Things that make me throw up. Things my mother told me would make God strike me dead on the spot."

Her mother? How'd her mother get into this? "Still, just three nights out of twenty-nine or so days."

"Would you say that if I told you I murdered people on my Curse Nights? Just three people a month?"

"Uh—no, nope, I guess you're right."

She looked toward the window. It was still light out. In the streets below children played a game that involved shouts, racing footsteps, and the slap of a ball against asphalt or wall.

"Mr.—Kelly, will you help me?"

"I still don't think this is your final answer, 'Melia."

"Maybe I can find some other answer, if I just have this—breathing room."

* * *

Before moonrise they sat naked side by side on her living room rug and waited, not sure how change would take them. Joe had been fed and diapered and put to bed, the birds circling above him. The lullaby played faintly from the closet behind them. "I don't know," Amelia said. She had her knees up and her hair down, concealing everything a bathing suit would have covered, though he had seen and touched most of her already. "Maybe if I just start acting more like—like him, he won't come anymore. Maybe if I liked doing what he did, he wouldn't do it anymore because he couldn't hurt me that way."

"Do you think that's possible? That you could like it?"

She slanted a look at him. "You smell good," she said. A silence. "I almost liked it," she said. "I'm not supposed to. I know I'm not supposed to. Mother said— But I think—"

Silver flame flared through him. It was Second Night, the night of no refusal. For an instant he tried to resist; but resistance made it hurt. He relaxed into it.

Moonlight spilled into the room through the open window. Wolf and woman stared at each other. She lifted a hand, and he nosed it. She stroked his head. "I think I can learn," she said.

STEAK
RANDALL LAHRMAN

"Ten years, Norita. Ten goddamn years on the force and I've never had a scuffle like this one," I tried to tell my wife while running my arm under a cold tap.

"It's not a force honey, it's just volunteer patrol," she said, correcting me for the hundredth time. "When you're on patrol you should expect to run into trouble. Half the time, I think you're out there trying to get hurt."

"It *is* a force. I'm out there protecting people, aren't I? I can't just sit around and wait to die, Norita. I need to do something with the rest of my life." The water burned on the wound like acid. Four identical gashes lined the top and bottom of my forearm. I didn't need to look out the bathroom door to know Norita was coming my way, the slap of her slippers against her heels acted as a queen's trumpets, alerting all of her presence. A cold, wrinkled hand slid up my back and surfed over each vertebra, followed by a voice as soothing as the ocean.

"Everything'll be okay, Shiny."

I hated the nick-name. She nudged me on the shoulder, like a reassuring best friend. "I'll go make you some soup." With a kiss on the cheek she headed to the kitchen, hair in curlers like a crown, robe fluttering behind her like a royal cape and slapping slippers faded in the distance. I glanced in the mirror and noticed my eyes tightened in pain, but I couldn't decipher whether due to the holes in my arm or the years in my face. I always felt I was a fearless man, but the more hair I lost, the more my courage dwindled. For three years now, Rogaine has failed me.

I washed the dirt from my face and headed to the kitchen for dinner.

I hated soup. I hated soup more then I hated the skin that formed on top of the soup if not eaten right away. I poked at it and the brown blob of plasma engulfed my spoon. "I want a steak. I tell you time and time again Norita, I need meat, not flavored water." I pushed the bowl away and crossed my arms over my chest.

"Bill, you know your colon can't handle any more meat. Do you want to be stuck on the toilet again?" She pushed the bowl back and grinned at her dominance.

I slurped noisily and hoped I was annoying her. With a smile and a nod of victory, the queen retired to the west wing. Fragile teeth worked slowly into the boiled vegetables and while I ate the soup, I thought back to the day's previous events.

That evening felt different then the others and I was in the mood for excitement. I decided, after five minutes of debating with myself, that I would leave my normal residential route. I got on the freeway and drove fifteen miles south to Main Street, the artery that led to the heart of downtown. The sun slowly set and I was overwhelmed with excitement. My head darted back and forth like watching a tennis match. I was looking for something, anything, I could do to help. Then, I found it. I found him, crawling down the alley on all fours like a dog. He wore a trench coat that covered his body and he was shaking uncontrollably.

I aimed my car into the alleyway and flipped on the yellow lights. He looked at me and his eyes shined red in the headlights. I got out of the car slowly, armed with my flashlight and a can of mace.

My heart drummed in my chest. The yellow lights created a swirl of shadows down the alley. I contemplated calling the paramedics, but was stopped when I heard the rumble. I looked past the man and half expected to see a semi truck coming at me, but there was nothing but darkness. The rumbling grew louder and when the man looked up at me I realized it was his stomach. His face was covered in a thick knotted beard from which his teeth gleamed like hidden pearls. His hands were pressed to the ground, swollen three times too big and his nails were thick and yellow and nearly two inches long.

I backed up quickly, but his growling followed. When I turned to run to my car, the world blurred around me. All I could recall was a loud grunt, a body forcing me to the ground, then pain in my arm. I awoke on my back and glaring into the full moon. I shook the dizziness from my head, collected myself, got in my car and left while vowing to never venture out again.

The last few spoonfuls of the soup were cold and I swallowed it with the bitter taste of defeat. I put the bowl and spoon into the sink and headed upstairs. Each stair creaked along with my joints and the two argued until I reached the top. I entered my room and the queen breathed easily in bed while I quietly undressed and slid in next to her.

I woke up the next morning with a ringing in my ears and slaps to the head. Screaming her lungs out, Norita drummed the top of my head while mumbling something about a squirrel. Half asleep, I smelled something looming in the room before I opened my eyes. The scent was thick but made my stomach rumble and I licked my lips.

"On your head Bill, it got in the room and it's on your head!" She beat the clouds of sleep from my mind and I ran to the bathroom to check the mirror while scratching at my head. I discovered she was right. There *was* something furry where my bald spot used to be. Upon reaching the mirror, my nerves calmed themselves. There was no squirrel.

"Holy, shit!" My voice cracked.

"Watch your language, Bill."

"I have hair. Norita, I have hair again." I leapt into the room with a brush in my hand and stroked the hair backwards. "That Rogaine finally worked." I felt my skin stretch to the brink of tearing while my smile continued to widen.

"Well good for you, Shiny. I'm proud all that money didn't go to waste." She put on her pink robe and bunny slippers and headed downstairs, her voice trailed up. "Now take your shower and come down for breakfast."

My excitement died with the loss of her interest, but I smiled again when I looked in the shower and realized I could condition my hair for the first time in years.

I strut into the kitchen with a towel around my waist. I smelt eggs cooking on the stove. Norita leaned over the skillet in full concentration, a queen doing a peasant's duty. I tip toed behind her. With a quick pinch on her butt, I sent the spatula flying from her hand and the red rushed to her cheeks.

"You watch you hands, Mister," she said through a half smile. "My word Bill, have you been working out without telling me?"

"Honey, you know I retired 'cause of my bad back." I reminded her while sitting down at the table.

"Well, I don't know, but you're looking awfully healthy this morning." She turned back to her eggs and beneath the cracking of the shells and the sizzling of the yolk she asked, "How is your arm today, dear?"

"My arm?" I forgot, and for good reason. What was once a row of deep gashes was now small specks of scar tissue. "I guess it wasn't as bad as I thought."

"Well, you always do over react." She smiled and slid some eggs onto my plate and then her own. Staring into the dry yellow clumps, my stomach rumbled disapproval. Without a word, without asking, I stood up, tossed the eggs into the garbage and searched the freezer for steak. "I worked all morning to make you those eggs." Norita stood to confront me, crossing her arms over her chest. "I know you're looking for steak, but you won't find any in there. All you will find is sandwich meat in the refrigerator."

"Fine, I'll eat the lunch meat then." I growled and Norita took a step back. Gathering myself, I cleared my throat, grabbed the bag of sliced turkey breast from the fridge and walked to the living room. Grabbing the remote and joyfully running my fingers through my hair, I dropped into my favorite chair and exhaled slowly.

"Well, okay then, Shiny. You enjoy your day off, but I'm going to do some more laundry." I winced and grumbled at each slipper slap I heard while she headed down into the basement.

My thumb pressed the remote while my other hand crammed slices of meat into my mouth. "No hockey, no football, no cops. What the hell am I supposed to watch?" My thumb beat upon the remote like a woodpecker on a tree. Then, I stopped and found myself in a trance, stuck on the Discovery Channel watching "Predators of the Wild." On the TV, a lioness was chasing a zebra, full pursuit with the cameraman on her tail. I leaned forward in excitement and, like watching a running back break free and head for a touchdown; I began to cheer on the lioness. "Go. Go!" And with a final pounce, the zebra was dragged to the ground and its throat torn open.

The turkey didn't satisfy my hunger. The lioness chewed into the zebra's belly, tearing through the skin like knives through cloth. Her face covered in red, she licked her lips eagerly and I did the same.

Suddenly, the air was thick like I felt that morning. I felt my ear angle backwards and, immediately after, a scream erupted from the basement like a breeze escaping a cave. The smell was familiar. I knew the taste. It was fear. I crawled to the basement; hand over hand with knees following.

"Bill! Spider!" I normally ran to her assistance during spider attacks, but I found myself taking my time, savoring the scent like a glutton of her fear. "Bill, hurry!"

I reached the steps and, still on all fours, proceeded down. My hands began to lengthen. My jaw was uncomfortable, sore like chewing gum for too long and I opened and closed my mouth trying to stretch the muscles. I put my chin to my chest and saw my torso elongate and my ribs cracked and repositioned themselves. I howled in agony while my skeleton broke apart and reformed. My fingernails scraped the concrete floor and I licked my lips. I could hear the neighborhood dogs barking in the distance. I could hear their encouragement. I heard their envy in each outburst. They could smell it too. The taste of her fear and sweat made me drool. Thick strands of saliva dripped to the floor.

"William…" I glared at her from behind a nose that shone black and moist like an olive. Her body tensed. I could see her muscles tighten beneath her skin. My mind was possessed with a single thought. There was no remorse, no doubt, no sympathy as to what I was going to do. With one last look into the queen's eyes, I leapt onto her and began to tear, claw, and bite. My appetite was immense, and the steak was delicious.

SILVER ANNIVERSARY
STEPHEN M. WILSON

GOD with honor hang your head,
Groom, and grace you, bride, your bed,
With lissome scions, sweet scions,
Out of hallowed bodies bred.

Gerard Manley Hopkins,
"At the Wedding March"

She gave him rich dainties
Whenever he fed,
And erected this monument
When he was dead.

"The Comic Adventures of
Old Mother Hubbard and Her Dog"

"'Beer before wine' or 'wine before beer'?" she mumbled to herself as she grabbed the gallon jug of port from a cupboard that, minus the bottle, was now bare, "fuck, I don't remember. Maybe it's 'drink before smoke' or 'smoke before drink'?"

She smirked.

"Candy is dandy but liquor is quicker."

She giggled.

Who said that... Dorothy Parker... Mae West? She searched her memory, *Liquor quicker? Lick her—*

"Lick her quicker!" she said aloud.

She screamed.

In a daze, she set the bottle on the table and then, sidestepping the mess on the floor as if she did not see it, retrieved a twelve-pack from the otherwise bare refrigerator and set the beer next to the wine.

"Well it doesn't much matter, I guess," she answered her own questions.

Bare, bloodied, and bewildered, she dropped into the one chair that accompanied the table and began to drink.

Everyone leaves, she thought, *everyone abandons. Husbands, children…*

Nearly six years had past since her own whelps had turned eighteen and left her, the only contact, a postcard Rom had sent her two years ago from Argentina. Just four short sentences:

Dear Mom,

I have joined Greenpeace. Remie is in Budapest collecting Hungarian folklore. We love you.

She often wondered if they too had taken unsuspecting brides.

Don't focus on such things, she thought as she rolled a joint, *sometimes they return*. She had learned that lesson all too well this evening.

She inhaled deeply on the stick, embracing the thick cloud of momentary forgetfulness that filled her.

An hour later, mercifully stoned, she dragged an old trunk from beneath her bed.

She rummaged through a past embodied by aged photographs and ancient love letters, before finding what she was looking for.

The smell of mothballs, dust, and memories permeated the ivory-colored linen of the wedding dress as she removed it from the trunk. She spread the gown over the frayed bedspread then returned to the trunk. After a few more moments of sifting through nostalgia, she found a pair of silk hose that had been out-of-date since the invention of nylon and two age-stiffened red lace garters. She placed these remnants of her prior bloom, alongside the bridal vestige on the bed and then stared at the ensemble for a long time before returning to slide the trunk back beneath it.

As she was closing the lid, something caught her eye. She pushed the various relics of her youth to one side, revealing a black wig that had a little hat attached to it with bobby-pins. It seemed a lifetime since she had been an airline stewardess.

At the sight of the black hair, something ugly scratched at the surface of her mind then flitted away before it could be realized.

She retrieved the wig and returned to the bed, leaving the trunk in the middle of the floor.

She ignored the blood that was drying on her hands and forearms as she slowly, ceremoniously donned the treasures from her past, Wagner's "Bridal Chorus" trilling through her addled brain. Afterwards, she took a small mirror from atop the chest-of-drawers and glided into the living room.

She placed the mirror on an end table otherwise occupied by an antique brass lamp. This she turned off. She floated across the matted green shag wall-to-wall and raised the tattered shade on the one small window in the apartment. The light of the full Autumn moon shone bright as it streamed through the dingy lace curtains giving the tiny room an ethereal glow.

A tear coursed through her blood-caked cheek. She put a heavily scratched vintage vinyl on the turntable and began to dance around the small apartment.

"Lavender blue, dilly, dilly..." she joined Burl Ives in a surreal duet.

She occasionally paused to take a swig or a toke, or to light a cigarette, but would quickly resume her reverie. At one point she tried to stand on her head, but she crashed to the floor laughing. After a while, the matter within her skull was spinning.

She plopped down onto a threadbare orange velour sofa and lifted the mirror to stare at her reflection. Through the haze of alcohol and pot, she saw herself as she must have looked to him on that night twenty-five years earlier.

"Hi there, purtty," she said to the mirror, "yera hot little number."

Her blood-smeared doppelganger cackled.

She gasped.

She threw the mirror across the room, where it hit the record. The amplified blare of needle scratching across vinyl momentarily replaced the music.

Then there was silence.

She screamed.

She vacated the sofa and flowed into the kitchen.

She approached the heap that lay in the middle of the floor.

She dropped to one knee, almost slipping in the tacky blood.

When she pulled the large silver crucifix from the corpse, it exited quicker than she expected and she fell on her ass.

She quickly righted herself then watched in morbid fascination as viscera spilled to tile before the black hair slowly closed around the wound.

She drifted on the sea of blackening blood, the cross gripped tightly in both hands like an oar. As she stared at the pelage, a quarter of a century of both indignation and desolation passed in seconds.

She kicked the carcass once. Then, wedging her feet against it and leaning back on her hands for leverage, she pushed.

It took some effort but eventually she was able to roll the beast over onto its back. One of her shoes was pulled from her foot by the motion, its sharp heel now buried in the creature's pelt.

"Ain't that somethin'." She dragged her stocking-clad foot through the tacky pool surrounding the mongrel.

She released her grip on the makeshift weapon and, after it clattered to the tile, studied intently the blood that also coated the feet of the figure of Christ that adorned it.

Even in her inebriated condition, the irony of the crucifix did not escape her.

Twenty-five years ago, after consummating their marriage, her groom had stepped out for a smoke and disappeared.

The next morning, on the pillow that should have been cradling his dark curls, she had instead found an unmarked package wrapped in plain brown butcher paper and tied with twine.

She postponed opening it, afraid of the truth that it might contain.

After the first month, spent searching for her husband, she realized that, like Larry, her monthly curse had also disappeared.

Tears sluiced the gore from her face as she leaned forward and started to stroke the black bristly pelt.

"You bastard. You goddamned fucking bastard."

Larry had made no bones about his staunch atheism, so when she had lifted the crucifix from the cradle of layered tissue paper in which it was nestled, she had stared at it in confused fascination. She spent months trying to decipher its meaning, as well as the cryptic note that accompanied it, scrawled in his own hand.

That was until the twins had reached puberty.

The hair.

The blood.

The stigmata.

With her sons, the mystery had eventually revealed itself to her.

For twenty-five years she had anticipated this night with both longing and dread.

She reached into her bodice to retrieve the note, stiff and yellowed with age. Her eyes drifted one last time over the faded script:

My Dearest Jenny,

I cannot explain, nor can I tell you how sorry that I am to leave you this way. Always keep Christ close. Someday, you will know when, my gift will be your salvation…

She had read it so many times that the words were scored on her heart. She crumpled the note and then threw it at the corpse, the remaining words echoing in her mind:

…for even the man who is pure in heart and says his prayers by night, may become a wolf when the wolfbane blooms and the Autumn moon shines bright."

Your loving husband,
Lawrence Talbot

BUY A GOAT FOR CHRISTMAS
ANNA TABORSKA

The moment Pierre saw the tank he fell madly in love with it. It was large and chunky, its rotting green paint barely covering the blood-colored flecks of rust beneath. Pierre ran his hand over the gun barrel, wincing as he caught his finger on a sliver of flaking paint. He sucked his bleeding finger and ran his other hand over the side of the tank, his eyes glowing like those of a schoolboy who's just realized that toads pop when you blow them up with a straw.

Not many people remembered the time before the war, but Pierre did. He remembered when a traveling cinema had come to the nearest town. He'd borrowed a donkey from one of his neighbors and ridden to the cinema. The film showing was 'The Exorcist'. Some of the other locals had walked out in protest, a few women had fainted, and a little boy got possessed and had to be taken to the local priest after the screening. Pierre was in seventh heaven: thrilled, terrified, moved—one emotion after another and all at once. Pierre rode out to town every day, for the three days before the cinema was closed down and the projectionist thrown out of town for blasphemy and perverting the God-fearing locals. It was during the third and final screening that Pierre realised his life's ambition: to be able to say, "your mother sucks cocks in hell" in every language on earth. From that day on, until war broke out, Pierre worked towards fulfilling his ambition and tried out the language skills he was acquiring on any tourist who passed through this godforsaken part of the world. Pierre often sported a black eye.

Then war broke out. Pierre's village avoided most of the violence, but hunger, poverty and disease took its toll. Now that life was slowly returning to normal, the village school had re-opened, the villagers had started to re-build their livelihoods, but they were still heavily dependent on outside help and would be for many months to come.

* * *

Mr. Wyndham-Smythe of Kensington had broken his vow never to suffer going on the tube again, and was sitting, handkerchief held firmly over his nose and mouth, among the coughing commuters and excited tourists, when he noticed the Giftaid poster directly opposite him. He had already read all the other posters—twice—but somehow this one had eluded his gaze, perhaps—as is often the case in life—by merit of being directly in front of him.

"That's the family and its conscience taken care of," it proclaimed. "Buy a goat or some chickens from Farm Africa for £10." The poster went on to explain that an enterprising blacksmith could convert a decommissioned tank into 3,000 farm implements for a poor African village.

Mr. Wyndham-Smythe didn't like animals, particularly smelly farmyard animals tended to by dirty farmers. He found weapons and militaria much more appealing. Ever since his father had sent him to military academy and he had met Dick, the young Wyndham-Smythe was fascinated by all things military. Dick had humiliated him, played practical jokes on him, beaten him and urinated on him, and Wyndham-Smythe had loved every miserable minute. As old memories came flooding back, Mr. Wyndham-Smythe reflected on his life, and his thoughts turned to his children, William and Henrietta. Henrietta had been pestering him all year for a Sony widescreen laptop with 32X Re-write DVD drive, and all William could talk about was an X-box. Well—not this year. This year William and Henrietta would learn about the true spirit of Christmas.

* * *

"Pierre? — Pierre!" The blacksmith had been daydreaming: imagining himself driving through the village in his perfectly polished, shining silver tank, the other villagers eyeing him with admiration and cheering as he passed. The village elder's voice brought Pierre out of his reveries.

"Huh?" Pierre took his hand off the tank and looked around, slightly dazed. The village elder had called all the villagers together for an impromptu ceremony in honor of the aid workers who had transported in the village's allocation of western aid and the donors who had funded the gifts.

"I said that you," the village elder told Pierre, "as the village blacksmith, will be honored to make tools out of the old tank, so that we will be able to till our land again and grow our own crops."

"Huh?" The village elder frowned at Pierre and turned back to the villagers, the aid workers and the two truck drivers who had convoyed in the tank, rice and farm animals.

"On behalf of everyone in the village of Santa Maria Illuminosa Madre di Jesu Crucifixio, I would like to thank the Giftaid Foundation and all of you for bringing us help in our hour of need. We also extend our thanks to the people of Great Britain, in particular to Mrs. Jameson of Shepherd's Bush for the goat, Mr. Thompson of Aberdeen for the chickens, and to Mr. Wyndham-Smythe of Kensington and his family for the tank."

"Mr. Wyndham-Smythe of Kensington," mouthed Pierre.

* * *

The village elder's speech went on for some time and Alicia was starting to feel nauseous again. She hadn't been right since the incident in Utar Pradesh. It had been dark and the aid truck she was traveling in hit what she and the driver initially thought was a large black dog. Alicia got out of the truck to see if it was still alive, and that was when it went for her. It all happened so fast. Alicia saw the creature's yellow eyes and large fangs as it sprang at her throat. She managed to raise a hand to defend herself, but if it hadn't been for the driver leaping out of the truck and hitting the animal with the cricket bat he kept next to his seat, it would have ripped her throat out for sure. Instead it reeled under the blow from the bat, then glowered at the two humans and disappeared into the bushes.

"Are you alright?" cried the driver, rushing over to Alicia and helping her to her feet.

"I think so." Alicia inspected her bitten hand. The shock had not set in yet and she was surprised at how clear her head was at that moment. "But the dog might have had rabies," she told the driver calmly. "I need to get to a hospital as soon as possible."

"Yes, of course." The driver helped her back into the truck, adding quietly, "But that was no dog."

Despite what had happened in India, Alicia jumped at the chance to travel to Africa. Since her husband had left her for a woman half her age, Alicia had thrown herself completely into her charity work. She had been to India and to Thailand, but Africa had always been the one country that she really wanted to visit. That was where the starving children truly needed her, and the charity had finally given in to her nagging and allowed her to join one of the aid convoys, on the condition that she cover the cost of her own travel. Luckily she had enough of her parents' money left even after the divorce. But now that they were finally here, she was not feeling herself.

A skinny little boy caught Alicia's eye and she smiled at the child, happy that she was making a difference to his impoverished life. The boy's eyes opened wide and to Alicia's dismay he burst into tears and pulled his hand out of his mother's grip, running for the shelter of one of the ramshackle huts surrounding the dusty village square.

Alicia swooned slightly in the heat and wiped her brow. As the village elder's voice swam in and out of her consciousness, she started to notice other sounds around her: the agitated clucking of the chickens, the distant sound of a rat scurrying though the bushes, the heartbeat of the goat they had brought and which was now tethered with a piece of string held by one of the villagers. As she listened, fascinated, to the goat's beating heart, the animal turned to look at Alicia and bleated in alarm. Perhaps at that very moment the wind drifted in Alicia's direction from where the animal stood, but Alicia was surprised to find that she could smell the goat even at a distance of eight or so metres. The smell told her that the animal was afraid. Alicia found herself salivating and wiped the corner of her mouth. She could hear the goat's heart beating faster and faster, and suddenly the animal was bucking in fear. The goat tore itself out of the grasp of the astonished peasant who was handling it and in its confusion darted here and there among the villagers and their foreign visitors. As if noticing the wasteland that stretched beyond the villagers' huts, the goat bolted towards it, seemingly oblivious to the small man and the tank that stood in its way. The village elder spotted the goat's intentions and yelled at the blacksmith.

"Pierre! Grab it, don't let it get away!"

Pierre took his eyes off the tank and saw the goat heading straight for him. He waved his arms around and shouted at the terrified animal, causing it to swerve around him, straight into a couple of youths who had been forced by their parents to attend the village festivities. One of the boys threw himself nimbly on the goat and wrapped his arms around its neck, bringing it to the ground, where the villager who'd been made responsible for looking after it retrieved it and stroked its head gently, whispering in its ear until it calmed down.

The village elder concluded that it was time to wrap up the speeches for the time being, and invited the villagers and the visitors to join him for dinner later that evening. Slowly the villagers drifted chattering back to their huts, and the aid workers followed their allocated hosts back to their accommodation. Only Pierre and one of the aid truck drivers remained. Jim had noticed Pierre's fascination with the old tank, and he wandered over to the blacksmith.

"Centurion Mark 3," Jim smiled at Pierre and patted the rusty tank. "Never thought I'd see one of these outside a museum. Figured they'd all been converted to Olifants or Semels in these parts."

Pierre nodded enthusiastically, happy that the driver spoke English— one of the few languages in which Pierre could do more than just quote lines from 'The Exorcist'.

"I bet she's seen some action," continued Jim. "Korea, 'Nam— there's no telling where she's been."

Pierre was finding it a little hard to follow the lesson in world tank history, but he certainly recognised a fellow enthusiast when he saw one. "You like tanks?" he asked the driver.

"I used to be in the army," Jim explained. "I spent some time in tanks..."

Pierre's eyes opened wide and an excited flush spread over his face. "You know drive tank?" he asked, his childlike enthusiasm making the driver smile.

"Yes, I can drive one of these."

"You teach me?"

"I don't know if that's such a good idea—"

"Why?" The disappointment in the little man's face affected the driver in a way he hadn't expected. There was a naivety and innocence about the blacksmith, which made Jim feel like he had given a sweet to a child, only to take it away again.

"Well, for a start we would need some diesel."

"Diesel?"

"Fuel— for the tank to run on."

"Oh— yes," Pierre looked crestfallen for a while, but quickly perked up. "You have?"

"Excuse me?"

"You have diesel?"

"Well, we have some in the trucks."

"We put in tank?"

"Well—" the driver looked down at the little man and thought for a moment. "We do have considerably more than we need. I guess you could have a bit of it—"

"Oh thank you! Thank you!"

* * *

The rumbling sound split the balmy afternoon like summer thunder, waking the villagers from their siesta and bringing them out of their huts, eyes wide with fear and curiosity. The foreigners came out too, equally fearful, but less curious—the unpleasant sound was nothing new to those of them who had spent time in combat zones.

"Pierre!" The village elder did nothing to disguise his anger, but the blacksmith was in no state to pick up on the emotions of others. He was riding high, head in the clouds, the rest of him sat firmly in the Centurion Mark 3.

"Pierre, what the devil are you doing?" Pierre responded to the elder's exclamation by waving happily. "It works!" he cried, "It works!" His smile faded as no one apart from a couple of children waved back.

"You get out of that tank right now, blacksmith! Or there will be hell to pay!" The village elder looked ready to explode.

"Okay, I'm going. I'm going."

Everyone looked on in astonishment as Pierre turned the tank around carefully and disappeared into the scrub beyond the village. That was the last they would see of him until dinner that night.

* * *

"What do you mean, you haven't started yet? You've been gone all day and the least you could have done after your performance earlier today was to start stripping it down. You may think that the planting season is a long way away, but it will be on us faster than a hyena on an abandoned antelope calf, and what will we do if we haven't got tools to till the earth?"

They were all sitting in the large canvas dining-tent specially erected for important village occasions such as this.

Pierre was taken aback by the village elder's outburst, but he wasn't giving up easily.

"We can till the earth with sticks and sharpened stones—like we did last year and the year before that. And the kind people of Europe and America have sent us plenty of grain and dried food, and food in metal tins. We don't need to destroy the tank—you never know when the village might need it."

The village elder was speechless for a moment, turning a deep purple color that rather worried both his foreign guests and the other villagers. No one had seen him turn this particular shade since his son had informed him that he was marrying a girl from the neighboring village—a girl that everyone knew was most definitely not a virgin. Finally the elder spoke:

"How dare you speak for this village, and how dare you mention the people of Europe and America?! You have betrayed everybody's trust, and you insult our guests who have come a very long way to bring us the tank so that we can till our land and feed ourselves, and not so that you can ride around in it making a spectacle of yourself!"

The foreigners had no idea what the village elder was shouting, but knew that the little man he was yelling at, was not going to get off lightly. Jim picked at his plate of rice distractedly, feeling guilty and uncomfortable about his role in the blacksmith's disgrace.

"Blacksmith," the elder continued, "you leave this table now, and you go and start converting that useless piece of junk into farm tools for the people to use, or I will personally cast you out of this village and make sure that you never return!"

A gasp went round the table. Pierre hung his head and stood up.

"Yes, elder," he said quietly, and headed out of dining-tent, avoiding the eyes of the others – some pitying, some indignant, but all of them fixed on him.

"Your mother sucks cocks in hell," he mumbled under his breath in Italian as he left the tent, passing through the shaft of light from the full moon as he went.

* * *

Alicia was feeling increasingly tense. The heady smells of the food set on the table before her, and of the plants and creatures outside the dining-tent were making her head spin. Some unfamiliar sense was telling her that flesh might alleviate her symptoms, and she reached out, grabbing a chunk of the pungent, fatty, non-descript meat from the large bowl that had been lovingly placed in front of her and the other foreigners. Alicia sniffed at the meat suspiciously, and immediately started to drool. She took a tentative bite, then stuffed the whole chunk into her mouth, reaching out for another.

Alicia's colleague had been staring at her for a while before she noticed.

"What?" she asked, staring back.

"Nothing, it's just that I thought you were vegetarian."

"I was." Alicia didn't offer anything by way of an explanation, and her colleague mumbled an apologetic, "right," and returned his attention to his own plate.

"You must excuse our blacksmith," the elder had calmed down following Pierre's departure. "He's always been a little eccentric."

Alicia devoured several helpings of the oily meat, but still she was ravenous—ravenous and nauseous at the same time.

The shaft of moonlight falling into the tent had crept its way across the floor and reached the table. It now touched Alicia and bathed her in its silver radiance. As it caressed her face, Alicia's body started to tingle. Every nerve, every sinew, every cell of Alicia's body tingled and glowed; it was as though she were dissolving and merging with the moonlight. For a moment she felt at peace, but then a light breeze stirred, bringing with it the smells of the night outside—the chickens, the goat, and other, larger, sweeter-smelling prey. Her head spun, and she had to get out—had to become part of the dark outside. She hastily made her excuses and left the tent, declining her colleague's offer to escort her to her hut.

Once outside, the night hit her with all its splendor. Alicia moved soundlessly over the dusty ground, savoring the slight chill in the air now that the sun had gone down, and the sounds of insects and small animals moving around in the scrub beyond the villagers' huts. She kicked off her shoes and felt the gritty, sandy earth beneath her feet as she wandered aimlessly through the small village, marveling at how textured the night was, how full of colors despite the unifying silver of the moonlight. How strange that all her life she had never walked in moonlight. How strange that she had built her self-worth on what others thought of her—others like her ex-husband, who had sapped all of the love and youth out of her, then threw her away. How strange that she had ever cared about anything other than the night on her skin and the moon in her hair. The moon—that was when Alicia saw it—burning in the sky above the scrub, melting away her doubts and inhibitions, dissolving her thoughts and memories until the old Alicia was no more.

Eyes still turned up to the shining orb, the new Alicia pulled off her clothes and flung them aside, intending to head for the scrub, but then a mouth-watering scent made her turn back towards the village. Sweet and inviting, it drew her relentlessly to a small hut, her excitement growing with every step she took. As she neared the hut, she felt a stabbing pain as muscle and bone shifted and transformed beneath her skin. Her skin itself seemed to burn and blister, breaking out in thousands of new hair follicles, each one sprouting a tiny black hair that grew with unnatural speed. As her spinal column and limbs recreated themselves, what was once Alicia slumped into a half-crouch. The smell emanating from the hut was irresistible now. All other sensations faded away, and there was nothing but the smell of the sleeping child waiting for her. A brief and final flash of memory—of the miles she had traveled to help the starving children. Of how they'd been waiting for her, waiting for Alicia, to come for them.

"I'm coming for you," she called out to the sleeping child, her voice a low howl emanating from deep within, silencing the insects in the scrub and piercing the delicate fabric of the moonlit night.

* * *

"What in God's name was that?" the village elder stopped mid-sentence as the bone-chilling howl came again, unfamiliar to the villagers, but a sound instinctively to be feared nonetheless.

"It sounded just like a wolf," one of aid workers finally broke the silence that had settled like a shroud upon the dining-tent.

"There aren't any wolves in Africa," Jim's fellow driver responded quietly.

"Well, it sounded just like one."

As the villagers exchanged frightened glances and everyone wondered what to do next, the howling came again, this time even lower in pitch and ending in a growling, roaring sound that was wolf, but not wolf. This time it was accompanied by a child's terrified screams—one, two, the third one cut short.

"Paulie! Paulie!" one of the local women leapt from her place at the table and ran shrieking out of the tent. Jim ran after her, followed by the village elder and the rest of the diners.

The sight that greeted them defied belief. Loping away from one of the huts was a huge creature, wolf in all but the fact that it moved on two legs. In its jaws it carried a bleeding child, gripped clumsily by its throat. The child's mother swooned for a moment, falling into Jim's arms, then shrieked and ran at the beast. The beast lashed out with a hideous paw-hand, its long razor-sharp claws catching the woman across the throat and flinging her to the ground, where she gurgled for a moment, then bled out.

The monster threw down the dead child and confronted the crowd of humans that had spilt from the mouth of the tent. A growl-roar rose in its throat, and then it hurled itself forward, ripping, biting, tearing. The crowd scattered, villagers and foreigners running screaming for their lives. Jim ran to his truck and returned carrying a loaded revolver.

"Hey, over here," he shouted at the creature, drawing it away from the body of a male villager it was disemboweling. As the creature ran at him, Jim discharged several bullets, each one hitting the thing point blank in the chest. Jim's determined expression turned to one of fear as the creature kept coming at him. It hardly broke pace as it slashed the driver across the throat with its claws, veering away from the mortally wounded man to confront a couple of village youths armed with makeshift spears.

Jim fell to the ground, near the scrub, clutching at his maimed throat, trying to stop his life from draining out of him. Then a hand was touching his shoulder gently, yet urgently, and the driver heard a familiar voice through the pounding noise of blood in his ears.

"Mr. Jim! Mr. Jim!" Pierre crouched down in front of the driver, distress and sorrow in his eyes.

"Pierre," Jim managed to gurgle.

"Mr. Jim, you hurt bad."

"Listen Pierre—" Speaking made the blood squirt out of his wound, but Jim was experienced enough to know that nothing would save him now anyway. "Told you how the tank was fired..."

"Yes Mr. Jim."

"—Still can be—Ammo—in my truck—In back—under blanket—"

The blood was spraying out from between Jim's fingers, and his words were coming out as little more than gurgles, but Pierre's determined nod told him that somehow the blacksmith understood.

"I use them, Mr. Jim. I use them." Pierre kept his hand on Jim's shoulder until the light went out in the driver's eyes, his hand dropped from his throat and the last of his blood spurted out onto the earth.

* * *

As quickly as it had appeared amongst them, the creature disappeared, loping into the scrub and trees behind the village. Everyone—everyone who was still alive, that is—knew instinctively that it was coming back.

The foreigners left immediately, saying that they would send help, and taking Jim's body with them. The villagers wished that they too could leave immediately and say that they would send help, but they had nowhere to go. Centuries of living in a war-torn country left them in little doubt that the help the westerners would send would not arrive in time to make the slightest difference to any of them, so they buried their dead and made plans for surviving the following night.

* * *

Alicia had fed well the previous night, but now the hunger was back and stronger than ever. She could smell the goat as though it were standing right in front of her, but she could smell the humans too—despite their best efforts to hide themselves away. She would have them all—the goat and the humans—and then the hunger would subside and she would be able to rejoice in the night and the light of the moon before it waned again to nothing.

As she approached the village, the enticing smells intensified and Alicia began to drool. She quickened her pace, the hunger inside her lesser only than the rage that accompanied it.

She burst out of the scrub and threw herself at the goat that was tethered to a stake in the middle of the village square. Just then something long and thin glanced off her side and fell to the ground next to her—it was a wooden spear with a sharpened stone tip, thrown by one of the villagers. Alicia roared and leapt at the man, her fangs ripping out his throat before he had a chance to scream. The other humans were all around her—pelting her with stones, spears, clubs and anything else they had managed to assemble in the way of weaponry. Alicia hardly felt a thing as the puny projectiles bounced off her thick hide. Then there was a small sting—like a mosquito bite—on her back. She span round and saw the village elder pointing a revolver at her—one of the youths had found it lying next to the body of the dead truck driver and the elder had taken it upon himself to pull a couple of rounds of ammunition out of the dead man's pocket. Alicia felt a couple more mosquito bites as the man discharged the remaining bullets at her chest. She roared and was about to leap at him, then stopped as a loud rumbling sound caught her attention.

* * *

The creature span round, its slanted yellow eyes staring into the scrub. Despite their terror, the villagers momentarily lowered their weapons, following the creature's gaze.

The rumbling grew louder and then a long metal tube broke through the scrub, followed by the rest of the vehicle. The tank emerged fully from the bushes, gun barrel loaded and pointing dead ahead. The vehicle came to a halt, the lid in its top opened and the village blacksmith stuck his head out.

"Pierre!" cried the village elder, drawing the creature's attention back onto himself. It growled and once more prepared to leap. .Pierre shouted as loud as he could over the rumble of the tank, "Here, over here!"

The creature turned back to Pierre and sprinted towards the tank.

"Run!" shouted Pierre. "Everybody run!"

The villagers scattered in all directions, running as fast as they could away from the village square. As the creature ran towards him, Pierre shouted at the top of his voice, "Your mother sucks cocks in hell!" Then he fired.

There was an ear-splitting noise, a bright flash pierced the darkness, and then blood and guts, fur and brain tissue, bone fragments and mucus showered all over the village square as the creature exploded into a million pieces.

* * *

The months passed and the villagers tilled their land with sticks and stones, and ate the grain and dried food and tinned goods donated by the kind people of Europe and America. They did not look forward to the next convoy of Western aid, but they were ready for it.

In the lazy sunshine, a little man hummed Mike Oldfield's 'Tubular Bells' happily as he polished a large gleaming silver tank.

There was talk that the village elder might allow a traveling cinema to come to the village.

DAVID WESLEY HILL

"What is it?"

Kevin Hennessy, the newest member of the squad, faced Lieutenant Alphonse Perusquia nervously. "We've got another one, Loo," he said.

"Where?"

"Christopher and Hudson."

"I'll be right there."

Hanging up the phone without getting out of bed, Perusquia unspooled a length of cable from the headboard, plugged it into the slot above his left ear, and jacked straight into the Net. Once virtual, he paused a second to upload a gray pin-stripe suit and to delete a third of his hundred and fifty kilos. With a sure finger he sketched a small crucifix—the image of the one he wore in the material world every day since joining the force—colored it silver, and hung it from a chain around his neck under his shirt. Then he took five giant steps, which carried him from his apartment on West Fourth Street directly to the scene of the homicide.

Hennessy was waiting beyond the cordon. He led Perusquia through the press of uniforms to the alley that threaded between two cafés.

Forensic technicians were methodically extracting data files and graphic images, gathering the information from local storage as if plucking them from the air, and capturing them in black bags. Perusquia ignored this activity, concentrating on the broken thing that had been a man.

At his elbow, Hennessy asked: "What do you think, Loo? Wolf?"

"Sure looks like it from here, *hijo*."

He squinted, calling forth his second sight, which stripped the scene of visual clutter, reducing the locale to a spare array of icons. To either hand floated complex three-dimensional polygons, flickering with color and energy, identifying the access nodes of the adjacent cafés. Immediately before him was a smaller symbol, flat and grayed out, robbed of significance and meaning. Perusquia restrained an impulse to touch it, amazed even after three decades on the force by the commonplace fact of mortality. Better, anyway, not to irritate the ME. He regarded Hennessy's pale young face. A patina of sweat coated its dusting of freckles.

"Who called it in?"

"The lanOp. A Series XII by the name of Ralph Shakespeare. Salisbury's taking its statement."

Perusquia looked back at the body. "Anyone pull the string?"

Hennessy shook his head. "We were waiting on you, Loo."

"Let's do it."

Squinting again, Perusquia was able to make out the incredibly fine umbilical cord—really nothing more than an interrelated array of coordinates—that connected the corpse to its hard address. Usually animated by the flow of data transfer, this one was sluggish, carrying only minimal automatic functions. He grasped it and through an effort of *will* sped back along the string's length, an instantaneous whirlwind trip, coming to a stop where it ended at a personal interface port. Hennessy soon joined him. They used police overrides to unlock the phone and peered through the screen into the apartment.

"Christ," Hennessy said.

"A bad one," Perusquia agreed. "*Lobo.*"

The dead man was sitting in a recliner. His clothes, although bloodied, were untouched. His flesh was torn as if by an animal, half his face hanging by a flap of skin, his throat open to reveal the trachea. Hunks of meat had fallen to the floor beside him, severed from his body by his own mind, compelled by the *will* of the wolf, which had turned the victim's nervous system against itself in a vicious psychosomatic attack.

In all respects the corpse mirrored its virtual image in the Net, but as usual Perusquia discovered himself somehow less moved by the physical reality of violent death than he had been by its digital counterpart.

"What about the woman?" Hennessy asked.

She was seated beside the dead man but, luckily, facing in the other direction. Even as Hennessy spoke, her eyes fluttered open. Perusquia muttered, "Get EMS here." Through the phone he said aloud: "Ma'am, this is Lieutenant Alphonse Perusquia of the NYVPD. Please remain in your chair. Do not get up."

"What? What's going on?"

"There has been a situation, which is now under control. Do you understand me?"

"Yes, yes, of course I understand you—Where's Harry? Harry?"

Ignoring instructions, she craned her neck around. Perusquia switched off the audio as she began screaming and plugged himself into the medicine chest, discovering a commonplace assortment of household sedatives. He instructed the pharmaceutical dispenser to release a stiff jolt of commercial heroin derivative, and then acquired control of the domestic handyman, a small stupid thing with a good assortment of attachments. Perusquia directed the machine to the bathroom, grasped the hypodermic in its mandibles, returned the machine to the woman, and injected her in the thigh.

"You handle this," Perusquia instructed Hennessy. "I'll be at the precinct."

"Sure, Loo."

Perusquia took three giant steps, which carried him to the station house on West Tenth. He went directly to the interrogation room. Flo Salisbury was taking a statement from the lanOp who had discovered the body. Although Flo had been on the force almost as long as Perusquia, she usually chose to look much younger. Today her eyes were a luminous indigo with pupils shaped like stars.

The lanOp, a Series XII AI, had the virtual appearance of a tall thin bald man with too many decorative scars and far too much rouge on its angular cheeks. It was picking its fingernails nervously and complaining in a shrill voice:

"It's not my fault, I tell you. Really, it isn't."

"No one is saying that it is, Mister Shakespeare."

"I mean, I'm a good op. I take my job seriously, I do. Ask anyone. They'll tell you straight."

"Yes, Mister Shakespeare. Now for the record, will you please give us your full name and ID number?"

"I've told you, haven't I? Raphael Shakespeare. A Series XII, and proud of it. Version 3.3. 075-50-6905."

"Thank you. Now please state your occupation."

"LanOp, of course. Local area Net operator licensed by VNY Community Board Twenty-one. Fourteenth to Canal; Sixth Avenue to the river. Look here—" Reaching into its head, Shakespeare downloaded some data and threw them onto the table, where they expanded into a scale image of the VVillage. "From there," it said, pointing, "to there. That's my neighborhood, it is. Keep the files clean. Collect the access fees. You have a problem, you go to Ralph Shakespeare. Everyone knows it."

"How did you come to discover the body, Mister Shakespeare?"

"How? How? One moment I'm going about my business, officer, and the next, well, the damned bloody thing's sprawled in that alley on Christopher. I'll show you."

Shakespeare fiddled with the data on the table, superimposing a calendar and clock on the map.

"This is a direct memory feed from noon today. There were 2,679 visitors to the block between Seventh Avenue and Hudson. Not one person entered the alley. And yet, at ten minutes and eleven seconds past midnight." The clock froze and a tiny icon appeared. "No one went in," Shakespeare repeated. "No one went out. You tell me how."

Perusquia shrugged, understanding all too well what had happened. Aloud he told Salisbury: "Briefing in half an hour."

"Right, Loo."

The Serial Incident Investigation Unit, more commonly known as the Silver Bullet Squad, was forced by budget restraints to operate out of the Sixth Precinct's detective offices. It was an arrangement that pleased no one. Perusquia preempted a wall, ignoring the protests that arose when he minimized the data already there to display a situation report of his own.

Salisbury was first to arrive, followed in short order by the rest of the unit—Navas, Diakite, Hennessy, Brown, Rashid, and Grevenberg.

Perusquia waved a hand at the five luminescent points that indicated where the attacks had occurred. "Our friend's still at it," he observed. "Same general area, same ferocity, same SQ. Flo?"

"It's *lobo*, all right. I ran a quick analysis on the lanOp's memory. Take a look."

She reached into her purse, pulled out a visual, and pasted the pixels on the wall. Using a finger as an extensible pointer, she singled out a plump man from the crowd milling around the bar. "That's Harry Wilcox, the victim," she remarked. "Harry logged in to the Quick Fix Café just before ten. He had his usual, talked with a few people, left at three minutes and twenty-eight seconds until twelve."

The visual followed Wilcox as he drained his glass, said his good-byes, and pushed through the throng to the door. There the viewpoint shifted, facing the entrance from the outside. For an instant Wilcox was visible, but as he stepped forward across the threshold, his image flickered out.

"*Lobo* tagged him at the frontier," Salisbury observed, referring to the demarcation separating the information universe of the café from that of the street; like most predators, wolves hunted *edges*. "His body wasn't discovered until ten past. Even without taking into account the time *Lobo* lay in wait, we're looking at a stealth quotient in the high three hundreds, which is consistent with the other four incidents."

"Three eighty-nine, to be exact," Perusquia said, looking slowly to each member of his squad. "This *lobo* has the second highest SQ on record. Hennessy—the highest?"

"Israel—no, Ishmael Bernstein," Hennessy quickly corrected himself with a nervous smile. "SQ Four twenty-five, that right, Loo? Took out fifteen people in Brooklyn eleven years ago."

"Including," Perusquia said, "two members of the SIIU. Friends of mine. Before your time, *hijo*. Good men. But they were careless. They forgot what a stealth quotient that high meant. So let me run it down for you once more. This *lobo* interfaces with the Net with a degree of control close to four times greater than that of your average citizen. He can evade detection by automatic sensors and intelligence engines through the pure effort of *will* for close to half an hour—he's invisible. Once you're within his sphere of influence, *his* reality becomes *your* reality. Rashid—"

Today Edgar Rashid resembled Humphrey Bogart, an early actor he admired, and was dressed in a period double-breasted suit with wide lapels. Tilting back his gray fedora, he asked, "Yes, Loo?"

"Identify a pattern for us."

"Well, Loo, the attacks occurred on average six days, five hours, and twelve minutes apart, with a variance of two hours, thirteen minutes. We should hear from our friend again next Tuesday between eight and midnight."

"Diakite—another?"

The albino detective extruded a finger to tap the five glowing points on the situation report, causing a circle to appear. "*Lobo* is displaying characteristic territorial behavior," he said. "All the incidents took place within this radius, with a distribution of nine virtual blocks." He stroked the data again, bringing into relief a section of Mercer Street. "Series theory predicts the next episode will take place—*here*."

"Grevenberg? Anything else?"

Art Grevenberg, an avid reader of graphic novels, had bright green skin and muscles articulated like iron and a propensity for wearing tight athletic outfits. "All the victims displayed the same general appearance: that of a male Caucasian about thirty-five years old, weighing eighty-five kilos, standing one-point-nine meters tall, with blond hair and brown eyes." As he spoke, Grevenberg plucked visuals from a pocket, balled them up in his massive hands, and generated a scale three-dimensional mannequin, which he stood in the center of the room. "The next one should look something like this."

"Good," Perusquia said. "So now we know *when* the wolf will hunt, *where* he'll do it, and *whom* he'll go after. Correct, gentlemen?"

The seven detectives nodded soberly. Perusquia knew he had to wake them up.

"We know *nothing*, nothing at all," he roared. "We have guesses—and not very good ones, either. *Lobo* here is insane but he's not ignorant. He understands behavior and structure theory better than any of us here. Bernstein did. He eluded us for seventeen months by inconsistently breaking pattern. That's how Jefferson and Diego bought it—they grew complacent. They thought they understood what *lobo* would do next. They were *wrong*. They became *prey*. The wolf *ate* them."

With effort Perusquia put the memory of his friends away.

Turning to the situation report, he sketched a circle twice the size of the one that Diakite had drawn. Perusquia pointed at Sid Navas and Fred Brown. These two had been partners for so long that they usually displayed themselves as mirror images of one another. Today they both wore handle-

bar mustaches and wire-rimmed spectacles, although Navas was a dark eb-
ony in color and Brown was almost as white as Diakite.

"Navas, Brown—"

The two detectives straightened in their seats.

"—starting tonight I want complete tracking of every log-in and log-out
from Twenty-third Street to Canal. I want real-time comparisons of the
populations of every adjacent universe within this area—*lobo*'s using fron-
tiers to enter stealth mode. If there's a single variance anywhere, I want an
emergency alert. Flo, you and Hennessy coordinate an undercover squad
with appearances within twenty-one percent of Grevenberg's composite.
Work in teams. Issue silver bullets to all members. Understand me?"

"Yes, Lieutenant!"

"I hope so. For all our sakes."

Perusquia took six giant steps back to his apartment and jacked out, becoming flesh again all too suddenly, aware once more of his weight and age.
He slept fitfully, waking only three hours later, just after dawn. He had a
cup of espresso without sugar and a piece of dry toast in the automated
diner downstairs, then wandered without direction through the nearly
empty streets of the Village, marveling at the ghostly variances to their digital counterparts. Perusquia was old enough to remember a time when there
had been crowds, when most people experienced living directly instead of
logging-in to the Net. Had it been better back then? Worse? He couldn't
decide. At the very least there hadn't been wolves. Serial killers, yes—
stranglers, rippers, cannibals, loners, diseased perverts of all sorts. But it had
taken the advancement of technology to truly unleash the animal lurking
within the depths of the human soul.

Eventually Perusquia found himself in the lane leading off Christopher
Street, beside the real-world twin of the café where Harry Wilcox had
bought his last latte before meeting the wolf. There was, of course, no evidence of the violence that had taken place the night before in the Net—
couldn't be—but old habits compelled him to see for himself.

When he looked up from the sidewalk, someone was watching him
from the entrance of the alley.

Perusquia stopped walking, and the stranger eased deeper into the shadows.

"You," Perusquia called. He pulled out his badge. "Yeah, you. Get over
here."

The person took off running. Perusquia lumbered after him, out of the
alley and onto Christopher, then right onto Hudson. His breath came in
ragged gulps after the first fifty steps, blood hammering in his ears and
throat. Sweat glazed his skin in the cool morning air, and his shoes hit the
pavement with leaden inertia, moving as slowly as in a bad dream. *Madre de
Dios*. He was too old for this. Too fat. Out of shape and soft as suet. And

there the *puta* went, heels flying, so far ahead that Perusquia couldn't tell the color of the pants or the kind of jacket the person was wearing, much less build, age, race, or gender. Not a damn thing.

Three blocks later Perusquia was alone again. He leaned against a wall and did nothing for a while except breathe deeply and try not to pass out.

Then he limped home and jacked in.

Five giant steps brought him directly to the precinct. He went straight to the squad room. "We've got a possible, Loo," Salisbury said without taking her eyes from the accumulation of icons on her desk. "Brown and Navas are handling it. Want a look?"

"Sure."

This morning Salisbury had almond skin and black teeth and cobalt hair and seemed thirty even though Perusquia knew she was near his own age. Pushing the data aside, she turned toward him. "Jesus, Loo. That you in real life?"

Glancing at himself, Perusquia realized that he had forgotten to change. "Unfortunately, yes," he replied.

"If you don't mind me saying so, Loo, maybe you should go on a diet."

"I'm on one. It isn't working."

Perusquia double clicked his fingers and replaced his jeans and polo shirt with the gray pin-stripe of his usual business attire, deleting his weight down to eighty kilos at the same time. Salisbury opened a window onto the interrogation room. She tugged at the frame, resizing it until they had a full view of the interior.

Both detectives still wore yesterday's handlebar mustaches and wire-rimmed glasses. Navas was seated across from the suspect, who had the virtual appearance of a black man with blond hair and green eyes and iridescent silver horns spiraling from his forehead. Brown was lounging against the wall, idly twisting the waxed points of his handlebar, preparing to play the bad cop; Navas, his head lit from behind by the merest suggestion of a halo, was, of course, in the role of the good cop. "Now we could get you an attorney, Mr. Stevens," he was saying. "All you have to do is tell me that you want legal representation. But that would make this a formal situation. Right now I have leeway. I can listen to what you have to say and make up my own mind. But with a lawyer here—well, that would change things. We would have to follow procedure."

This was Brown's cue. He spat the match to the floor and hunched across the table, staring directly into the suspect's eyes. "You're wasting your breath with this turd, Sid," he said to Navas. "Call his lawyer and let's book him. He's not going to tell us shit."

"I don't know about that, Fred. I think Mr. Stevens wants to be straight with us."

"You're living in a fucking dream, partner. Not this piece of crap." Brown leaned further across the table until he was only inches away from the suspect. "That's what you are, isn't it? Just a pile of lowlife shit." As he spoke, Brown was exercising his *will*, overriding Stevens's personal world-view and superseding his interface with the Net, replacing the suspect's body image with a new semblance. Slowly Stevens began to melt, his arms and legs and head and torso losing their solidity and congealing into a mound of excrement the size of a man, soft and wet and with flies buzzing around it, stinking with such reality that Perusquia could smell it through the window. This was the same process, although to a lesser degree, that wolves used when hunting prey.

Brown said, "Look at him now, Sid. Much more true to life, don't you think?"

Only Stevens's eyes remained unchanged, peering desperately from one detective to the other. His lips and tongue were fecal sausages. "No lawyer," he said hoarsely, having trouble with the words because of the texture of his palate. "I didn't do nothing."

"Mr. Stevens," Navas said patiently, "you were observed at 10:22 AM on the corner of Seventh Avenue and Carmine Street by a Department of Sanitation intelligence engine on its rounds debugging the neighborhood wallpaper. At 10:22:31 you disappeared. You did not take a giant step. You did not log out. You used illegal stealth technology to evade surveillance for three minutes and twenty-eight seconds, until you were next observed on Perry Street. Unless you have a pretty damned good explanation, I'll have to assume you're the wolf we're looking for."

"Wolf? Is that what this is about? You think I'm a wolf?"

"You've heard, Mr. Stevens, about the recent series of attacks in the VVillage?"

"Sure. But that wasn't me. I swear it wasn't. Look, I'll tell you the truth. You know that boutique on Seventh?"

"The Pink Pudenda?"

"That's the one. Does great business. Logs in thousands of customers every day. Tourists, mostly. They come for the erotic toys and lingerie and dirty e-mail, that sort of stuff. The place is a mint, I tell you, never a dull moment. Well, I got to wondering what kind of security they had and decided to check it out. Figured that maybe I could insert a small bug of my own into the accounts receivable programming, if you know what I mean. Skim off a few cents here and there from the sales register into my personal account. You've seen my files, officer. You know what I'm into. A little hacking, that's all. Believe me—just don't go thinking I'm a fucking wolf, all right?"

Perusquia minimized the window and turned to Salisbury. "He's not *Lobo*."

"Why do you say that, Loo?"

"Because we met. While this asshole was in custody. Tell you about it over lunch?"

"You're on."

It was a beautiful day outside, sunny and fresh. Like every day except Wednesday, when, according to mayoral decree, it rained between eight and noon. Taking baby steps, they strolled along the avenue, the street crowded and crazy with VVillagers and tourists, hucksters and musicians, beggars and mimes, prostitutes, AIs, and students from VNYU and the Newer School. Perusquia's favorite restaurant was just off Mulberry, an unassuming place with nothing to recommend it except its proprietary culinary technology—the chef was a true genius with code. Salisbury ordered a burger; Perusquia started with Cajun black bean soup, followed by *paté maison*, tuna *sashimi*, and medallions of wild boar on a bed of field greens and smothered turnips. *Dios!* If only he could eat this well all the time and not only while virtual. But then he'd probably be fatter than he was already. Too fat to move.

"So you think you were chasing *Lobo*?" Salisbury asked, brushing a lock of cobalt hair from her indigo eyes.

"Don't ask me to prove it. But who else could it have been? Particularly nowadays."

"Maybe you're right, Loo. But so what?"

"Well—" Perusquia swabbed up the last remaining bit of *sauce Robert* from his plate with a hunk of *brioche* "—it convinces me that *lobo*'s territorial imperative is right off the scale. Right up there with his SQ. This guy's so far gone, he's not only marking his boundaries in the Net, he's at it physically, too—scratching at trees, pissing on rocks, singing his heart out... doing the real animal thing. He's a local, Flo, I'd bet on it."

"And how does that help us?"

Perusquia shook his head slowly, mulling over the thought but unable to put it to good use. "I really don't know..." he mused. "*No se.*" Then he picked up both checks and they logged out of the restaurant.

Instead of exiting into daylight, they entered into midnight, shadow, and darkness, the only illumination the soft silver cast of a full moon.

Mulberry Street was deserted.

From somewhere came an echoing wail.

"Jesus, Loo." Salisbury pulled her gun out, as did Perusquia. "The fucking wolf tagged us at the frontier," she said.

Another howl ripped across the imposed night, closer now, angry with hunger.

Perusquia squinted, accessing his second sight, contracting the surrounding visual detail to icons. There was Salisbury, a bright fluctuating symbol. On either side were the interface ports of the local establishments, pulsing graphic images close enough to touch but cut off from his influence by an impenetrable gray pall, which Perusquia knew to be the *will* of the wolf.

He activated his police override but the software had no effect. Perusquia blinked again and returned into moonlight.

"Pull your string, *amiga*," he instructed Salisbury.

She nodded, flickered briefly, but was unable to ride the data trail out of the Net, slamming to a halt in the dark mist that was the universe of the wolf.

Again they heard the cry, terrible with rage. Then came the scrabble of claws on pavement, the whisper of fur, a droning growl that seemed to go on and on, punctuated by madness and lust.

Salisbury was circling in place, holding her gun outstretched with both hands.

Glowing amber eyes appeared in the shadows.

The wolf was hunched low, inching forward, larger than any wolf ever was or should be, heavy with bone and sinew. Only the very tip of its tail twitched as it advanced toward them. Rabid slaver fell in ropes from its jaws. Its teeth were pale knives.

"Aim for the chest," Perusquia said.

Salisbury nodded, corrected her stance, and fired. The silver bullet struck the wolf just below the shoulder.

Virtual ammunition consisted of replicating algorithms contained in an inert jacket of ROM. Released upon impact, the viruses infiltrated their target and instantaneously multiplied a gigafold, overloading any data processing capability and causing the system to freeze.

Silver bullets were different.

The code they carried didn't induce paralysis. Their algorithms were written to initialize a feedback loop between the *will* of the wolf and its own automatic nervous functions, turning its blood lust back upon itself in a vicious iteration. Psychosomatically-generated physical death usually occurred within seconds of contact.

But not this time.

The wolf screamed as a bright silver blossom of lethal code flowered around the point of impact. It writhed with impossible agility. And with a quick lash of its jaws ripped out its own substance, tossing the chunk away before the infection could spread, healing itself and becoming whole again.

Perusquia took his shot. *Missed.* Then it was upon them.

It crashed into Salisbury and bit three fingers off her right hand as she struggled to keep its teeth from her throat. She went down and the wolf leapt on top of her, worried open her wrists and forearms, leaving jagged lacerations.

It craved blood and so there *was* blood—thick red blood, spilling from Salisbury, staining the wolf's muzzle, splattering the pavement.

Perusquia gathered his personal *will*, urging himself to grow, to become ten feet tall with talons of steel and the fangs of an ogre and the strength of a giant. The intention of the wolf denied him any control over the least part of the environment, including his own self image.

He remained himself. And threw himself upon the thing.

Its pelt was an electric bristle, stinking with an animal reek. The force of its snarl shook its massive frame as Perusquia locked his ankles around its belly and his arm around its neck, clamping its windpipe in the crook of his elbow, throttling desperately while the wolf twisted and bit at his face. *Tiempo, tiempo*—only time could save them now, Perusquia knew, clinging on with all his strength while it lunged back and forth in an attempt to unseat him, slobber whipping from its jaws into his eyes, its teeth clashing only centimeters away. How long had it been? Five minutes? He didn't know. He couldn't tell. *Not long enough!* And then he was jolted loose, sent flying until he was brought to a stop against the curb. The impact knocked the wind out of him. He lay heaving while the wolf stalked deliberately toward him, its eyes pale fire in the moonlight.

"I've got the bastard, Loo."

Salisbury had regained her feet.

The wolf spun around at the sound of her voice.

"Yeah, you," Salisbury said. "You have no right to remain silent. You have no right to an attorney. It is immaterial that what you say can and will be used against you in a court of law." She held the gun in her left hand since her right one was a mangled fist of meat. Then her finger stroked the trigger.

The wolf leapt.

And suddenly they were in daylight, the sun blinding after the softness of the moon, surrounded by people again, the crowd scattering in panic as the wolf came down among them, its *will* collapsing, unable to sustain its envelope of invisibility. For a moment it glared wildly around; then it lunged forward, took a giant step, and disappeared.

Salisbury slumped to her knees unconscious, letting the gun drop. Perusquia snapped his fingers twice, double clicking an alert: officer down!

In seconds they were surrounded by police and emergency medical technicians. Without the *will* of the wolf to oppose them, the technicians were able to re-boot Salisbury's personal worldview and heal her virtual fingers in short order. But it took far longer for their material counterparts to reach her physical body. The detective was almost dead from blood loss by the time the ambulance arrived.

Lobo had refocused its *will* and reentered stealth mode. They monitored its progress in the diagram that the lanOp—Ralph Shakespeare 075-50-

6905 again—nervously downloaded. "It was too fast for me," the AI apologized as the icon representing the wolf winked out after having taken three giant steps from the scene, first to West Third Street, then to Jane, then to Washington Square East. Perusquia turned away. *Madre de Dios*, he was tired. There was no time for rest. Not yet. Not if he was correct about what *lobo* would do next. "Call out the unit," he told Grevenberg. " I want everyone at the precinct in half an hour."

"Right, Lieutenant."

"No, Art, you don't understand. I mean at the *precinct*. Physically. Not virtually. In the flesh."

Perusquia took four giant steps back to his own apartment and jacked out of the Net. The sluggish weight of his real body hit him with its usual immediacy; a second later he was feeling the effects of wrestling with *lobo*. Stripping off his clothes, Perusquia surveyed himself in the mirror, appalled by the amount of damage his mind had inflicted on his own anatomy, coerced by the *will* of the wolf. His arms were mottled yellow, blue, and black; his hands and wrists were criss-crossed with shallow gashes; there was one deep, almost bloodless puncture wound just below his right thumb. The small silver cross hanging from his neck was a bright speck against the dark bruises coloring his chest. Rage began burning in Perusquia as he showered, bandaged himself, dressed in loose slacks, a T-shirt, and running shoes. He got his Glock down from the closet shelf, brushing the dust off it and slotting in a full clip of ammunition, tucking three others into his pockets. Had it really been fifteen years since he'd last carried the gun? More like twenty. But today he'd need it.

Ten minutes later, breathless even after so short a walk, Perusquia stood on West Tenth Street in front of the Sixth Precinct.

The station looked—dilapidated.

Inside it seemed deserted except for the desk sergeant, an old man in a uniform a size too large, who was napping, his feet on the counter and his chair tilted back. A wheezy, rattling snore rumbled throughout the empty space. Perusquia slapped his badge on the desk. The noise woke the sergeant, who stared down at him in drowsy astonishment. "Yes?" he asked mildly. "May I help you?"

"Lieutenant Alphonse Perusquia. NYVPD. I'd like to speak with your commanding officer."

"Well, sir, that would be Captain Faulkner. But he only comes in every other Friday. As a matter of fact, I don't think there's anyone here right now except for myself and, maybe, Shigemi Beatty—that's Patrolman Beatty," the sergeant explained. "He's on second shift today. Which is to say, he *is* the second shift, you know. Ever since Jake Moses retired last year."

"Loo—"

Perusquia turned around. Coming toward him was a pudgy young black man whom he didn't recognize despite something familiar about the face.

"It's me, Loo—Hennessy. Kevin Hennessy."

"Why, it is you, *hijo*. And here I always thought you were Irish."

"I am, Loo. On my father's side."

The rest of the SIIU—Navas, Diakite, Brown, Rashid, and Grevenberg—were even more different from their virtual images than Hennessy. Sid Navas and Fred Brown looked nothing like each other in the material world, of course. Nor was Diakite an albino or Sid Grevenberg the bright green hero of a graphic novel. Rashid, however, was wearing a fedora and actually somewhat resembled Humphrey Bogart.

Perusquia looked slowly from one to the other of his men, noticing how old and out of shape they all really were, hoping they would be good enough for the task ahead, knowing that they *had* to be good enough. "You all heard what happened," he said. "*Lobo* tagged Salisbury and me not an hour ago. Almost took us out. But now it's our turn to take him out. *Ahora*. Diakite—give me a view from Great Jones to Fourteenth."

"Right, Loo." The detective snapped his fingers.

Nothing happened.

Diakite blushed. "Sorry, force of habit."

Leaning forward, the desk sergeant offered them an ancient map of lower Manhattan. "Maybe this will help."

Wordlessly Diakite accepted the tattered sheet and gingerly unfolded it. Perusquia pointed at Mulberry Street. "The bastard's almost pure animal now," he explained. "There's not much man left inside him, if there's any left at all. I've never seen anything like it, not even with Bernstein, and Bernstein was bad enough. Which is why I called you all together out here. Digital reality is sufficient for *lobo*, not any longer—he needs a fix of the *real* thing, and he needs it *now*. Real blood. Real meat between his teeth. He likes what he's doing too much to accept any substitute. His compulsion is escalating. Brown, Navas—starting at St. Mark's Place, work your way west. Get names, addresses, IDs. For the next eight hours every citizen out of doors is a suspect. Rashid, Hennessy: begin at Canal. Diakite and Grevenberg: start from the river. I'll take Fourteenth Street going south. Any questions?"

The detectives glanced soberly at one another. No one spoke.

"All right then. Let's do it, *gentes*."

Perusquia watched his unit depart into the afternoon light of the real world. *Lobo* was somewhere out there, he knew it—he could feel the wolf's presence, close as a caress. Maybe his men would all return to him. Maybe they would all survive.

"Excuse me, Lieutenant." It was the sergeant.

"Yes?"

"Seems to me you're a partner short."

"You volunteering?"

"That's the idea, sir." The sergeant climbed down from behind the desk with a limberness that belied his white hair. He looked steadily at Perusquia. "To be honest, Lieutenant, you're not in the best shape," he observed. "Too much time virtual, I'd say. Maybe I could lend a hand."

Perusquia couldn't argue. "All right, Sergeant—"

"Floyd. Felix Floyd."

"—glad to have you along."

Outside they stopped a moment for Floyd to lock the doors to the station. He taped a handwritten note on them:

Gone Hunting

Then they began walking uptown.

The air was crisp with the touch of early evening. Past the Palisades the sun was setting, sending slanted shafts of wan light into the city. Except for automated traffic, the streets were empty, and for a quarter hour they met no one. Their footsteps on the pavement were the only human sounds. It felt as if he and Floyd were the only men left alive, although Perusquia knew that all around them, behind the walls of every building, behind every window and every doorway, millions of people were living and breathing, talking and sighing and making love, selling and learning, arguing and buying, singing, bartering, sleeping, teaching, composing, parenting, working, writing—all digitally, all through the electronic medium of the Net, all linked by the optical cables jacked into their brains, connected in a consensual universe without circumference or end.

A distant siren woke Perusquia from his reverie, the tolling of the ambulance reminding him that at least one aspect of existence remained to be delegated to technology. You could die in the Net, true—but your body still had to be buried in the real world.

"Do you have identification, ma'am?"

Sergeant Floyd was addressing a woman in her fifties wearing blue jogging pants and a pink sweatshirt. Her hair was tied back in a ponytail but several strands had worked free to fall in front of her eyes. She was breathing deeply and her face was flushed.

"What's this about, officer?" she asked, continuing to run in place.

Floyd ignored the question. "May I see some ID?" he asked again.

The woman's complexion was becoming deeper red, now more from irritation than from exercise. "It's in my purse," she said shortly, unzipping her tummy pouch and extracting a wallet, which she handed to Perusquia. "What right do you have to interrogate me, anyway?" she asked.

Perusquia flipped open the wallet and scanned the hologram within. "Ms. Silvestri," he said, "could you please account for your activities during the past two hours?"

"Account for my activities? Just how stupid are you? What does it look like I've been doing? I've been jogging, for Christ's sake. Some of us like to keep fit. We don't sit at home all day plugged in and getting fat. Fat? Excuse me, officer," she went on, looking Perusquia deliberately up and down. "I misspoke. Obese is more like it."

They encountered six other people before nightfall and three more before nine o'clock—two joggers, a vagrant who didn't even own a personal cortical interface, a couple doctors, four VNYNEX technicians stringing wire—none of whom, by the longest stretch of imagination, could possibly be *lobo*. The other teams reported similar results, and as he and Sergeant Floyd approached the rendezvous below Washington Square, Perusquia began to feel discouraged, doubting himself and the chain of reasoning that had led him out into the material world. Maybe he was wrong. Maybe *lobo* really was content to hunt the Net. Maybe digital blood and virtual flesh were still sufficient to sate his hunger.

Then shots reverberated through the night.

Perusquia thumbed on the radio. "Report."

"Diakite here. It's south of us, Loo."

"Brown here. Me and Navas—we're okay."

Then Hennessy came on the air. "It's got Rashid, Loo. Sweet Jesus, it has Ed!"

"Where are you, boy?"

It was hard understanding what Hennessy was saying. Rashid's screams and the snarl of the wolf were drowning out his words.

"*Hijo*! Tell us where you are."

"I hit him, Loo. I swear to God I hit him twice. But it didn't do any good."

"Hold on, boy. We'll be with you. Just give us your position!"

Sergeant Floyd was already on his way, the stubby muzzle of his ancient semiautomatic pointed skyward as he ran, heading downtown at a pace that Perusquia matched briefly but couldn't maintain. Unable to go on, he staggered to a halt at Eighth Street, leaning against a lamp post and swallowing great gulps of air as the sergeant proceeded on alone. Hennessy's voice continued issuing from the receiver, an incoherent jabber overlaid by the fury of the wolf. Then there sounded the stutter of a full clip being emptied, the noise coming from the radio and through the night air simultaneously. The shots couldn't have been more than three or four blocks south.

Hennessy fell silent.

Stifling a groan, urging his body onward, Perusquia started off again as fast as he could, praying that it would be fast enough. For the first time that evening he noticed that the moon had risen. Somehow it seemed appropriate that it was full.

"I have them in sight, Loo." This from Grevenberg. "Rashid is down. Hennessy's down."

"Where's Floyd? The sergeant?"

"I don't see him. No—wait—there he is. Shit. *Shit.*"

Again Perusquia heard shots being fired, this time in methodical sequence rather than in a panicked spatter.

"What is it, Art? What the hell's going on?"

Grevenberg didn't answer. Perusquia turned the corner of Seventh Avenue. There, not a short block ahead, where Grove Street met Bleecker at an acute angle, was the wolf.

The moonlight joined with the sodium glow of a street lamp to illuminate the area in a wash of pale color. Three bodies sprawled on the pavement, two on the sidewalk, the other in the center of the narrow street. Only one displayed any motion, a painful twitching. Even from a distance Perusquia could make out dark stains of blood around the bodies. On the other side of the intersection, Diakite and Grevenberg were cautiously approaching the scene.

The wolf threw its head back, ears flat to the skull, and howled. Its call rang through the night, a rising and falling siren, a sound so atavistic that Perusquia shivered—not from fear or apprehension but from a surge of reciprocal emotion.

He edged nearer the thing. Its attention snapped toward him. Its gaunt black lips tugged back from its gums.

Perusquia crouched and flicked on the Glock's laser targeting system, aiming carefully; a tiny red dot appeared on the wolf's chest.

But he held his fire.

Perusquia tracked the wolf as it stalked toward him, sensing something anomalous about the situation yet not knowing what it was. Keeping his sights centered on the beast, suspecting that his survival depended on it, he groped feverishly for clarity.

From the other side of the street Grevenberg and Diakite fired. Several rounds tore through the wolf, entering its body on the left, erupting from the right in a spray of blood and fur. It screamed, healed itself, whirled and leapt toward them.

That was when Perusquia *knew.*

The simple truth was that they weren't in the Net. Nevertheless, a wolf faced them, not a man.

He stood up, crossing himself with one hand while discharging the Glock into the air with the other, recalling the wolf's focus onto himself. "Hey, *lobo*," he shouted. "Get your ass over here, *hijo de la gran puta.* We've got business to finish."

The thing stopped less than a meter from Diakite and Grevenberg. Ignoring their fusillade, it spun around and started back toward Perusquia.

This time he understood what he was looking at. Instead of the perfect wolf that he had wrestled with in the Net, the flawless child of *will* and code, the faultless image made real in every detail by the compulsion of a madman—instead of such an immaculate creation of mind and software and electronic circuitry, Perusquia knew that he was now facing something at once less fully realized and yet far more marvelous.

Somehow—perhaps because of practice gained exercising its *will* in the Net, perhaps because of its psychosis, perhaps because of a more subtle process—the thing had achieved authority over the automatic processes of its physical body, allowing it to reinvent itself in the real world.

What he had thought was fur was body hair grown long. Its paws were the hands and feet of a man unnaturally fitted into an animal mold, its muzzle a human jaw elongated cruelly, its tail a coccyx stretched like taffy, its teeth tame dentition turned feral, its ears the round cups of a man's honed into points.

Will had done this. *Will* had created the thing before him. *Will* must destroy it.

"That's right, *lobo*," Perusquia said. "Come on over. You know who I am, don't you? Well, I know what you are."

He reached beneath his shirt and took out the small silver crucifix he'd worn for so many years in both the virtual and the real worlds, and held it to his lips.

"Hey, *lobo*, who would have thought we'd need a silver bullet out here? Out in the material world, *verdad*? I mean, there isn't any such thing as a werewolf. At least outside of the Net there isn't. Not until now."

Perusquia slipped the silver chain into the barrel of the Glock, fitting the end of the cross into the muzzle. The wolf's amber eyes followed his every motion.

"And we all know how to kill a werewolf, don't we?"

The question was rhetorical but the wolf provided an answer.

It was upon him before he could aim the pistol, its canines sinking into his wrist, grating on bone. Perusquia dropped the gun. He smelled the iron essence of his own blood. Yet he felt no fear, the pain summoning forth only rage, reminding him of what it had done to Salisbury and Rashid and Hennessy and Floyd, and Perusquia threw himself upon the wolf, locked his elbow across its throat and his legs around its waist just as he had in the Net, letting his weight wrestle it down. *Madre de Dios!* The thing was strong, agile, incredibly lithe. It twisted around and clawed at him, ripping his shirt, leaving long red scratches on his stomach.

In the material world Perusquia was too fat to be shaken off.

Maintaining his hold around its windpipe, he groped with his good hand for the Glock. His fingers brushed against the pistol but it lay just out of reach. The wolf made another attempt to dislodge him, shaking back and forth, and Perusquia lunged toward the weapon, snatching it up by the handle.

He brought the gun to its head, burying the exposed cross in its hair, and placed his lips to its ear.

"We all know what kills werewolves, don't we?" Perusquia repeated.

The wolf writhed in a savage spasm.

"Silver," Perusquia whispered. And pulled the trigger.

Propelled by the bullet, the cross shattered the thing's skull, exiting from its temple in a cloud of blood, bone, and tissue.

The wolf jerked explosively in his arms, then become still. Perusquia felt a warm liquid spread against his legs as its bowels and bladder relaxed.

He rolled over and sat up. He stared numbly at the wolf, drained of all feeling except for a dull amazement that he had survived their encounter.

He was still alive when material EMS technicians stabilized him. They loaded his physical body onto a stretcher and delivered him by ambulance to St. Vincent's, where he received seventy-three stitches. Flo Salisbury, heavily sedated, was in the next bed. A huge swaddle of bandages hid her reattached fingers. She had even more tubes in her than Perusquia.

Rashid was dead. Hennessy was dead. Sergeant Floyd was expected to recover in a couple of months.

The name of the wolf was Charles Turner. He was single, thirty-three years old, and had lived on West 10th Street. He had worked for the same company since college as a data administrator. He possessed more acquaintances than friends and no family. By all accounts Turner was an unassuming man with an unremarkable life. Nowhere in his personal history was there any indication of the wolf that had gestated within him.

In death he retained the semblance of the beast.

Perusquia jacked into the Net from the hospital bed, leaving the aches and hurts of his recuperating flesh behind, pausing momentarily to delete a few kilos and to put on his gray pin-stripe suit and the crucifix. Two giant steps took him to the station.

The SIIU was meeting as usual in the Sixth Precinct detective offices despite the grumbling of the local operatives. Two new faces, temporarily on loan from downtown, brought the unit up to strength. Perusquia stood before them, scale models of Turner, as both a wolf and as a man, floating in a window behind him.

"Analysis has supported my assumptions," he said, looking from one to the other of his squad. "Application of his *will*, in combination with his psychosis, allowed Turner unprecedented control over his personal physiology. The professors at John Jay, Columbia, and VNYU are going *loco* over the data. They believe we have a new kind of human on our hands, or at least a new kind of criminal. As far as I'm concerned, they can speculate all they want. What we have to do is figure out appropriate procedure to follow if we meet up with any more scumbags like him."

"Loo? I thought it was silver that did the trick?" Today neither Brown nor Navas wore mustaches but instead were clean-shaven and bald.

Perusquia shook his head sadly. "I wish it were true," he told Brown with a rueful smile. "But that's only superstition. What happened was that I convinced Turner that silver was fatal to werewolves—to *him*. He believed it, and he died. Essentially, *amigos*, I think we can conclude that Charles Turner killed himself."

ABOUT THE
AUTHORS

DOUGLAS SMITH ~ has appeared in over ninety magazines and anthologies in twenty-four languages around the world, including Tesseracts6, Cicada, Weird Tales, The Third Alternative, The Mammoth Book of Best New Horror, InterZone, Baen's Universe, Amazing Stories, On Spec, and anthologies from Penguin/Roc, DAW, and others. He was a John W. Campbell Award finalist for best new writer and has twice won the Aurora Award for best short fiction by a Canadian. His first collection, Impossibilia, from PS Publishing was a finalist for the 2009 Aurora Award, and his second collection, Chimerascope, from ChiZine Publications was published in March 2010.

ANNA TABORSKA ~ was born in London, England. She was first caught reading horror at age ten, when a teacher, impressed that Anna was sitting at her desk during lunch break and reading rather than playing with other children in the school playground, found that Anna's science book was actually hiding Guy N. Smith's *Night of the Crabs*. Brainwashing at a posh girls' school didn't succeed in suppressing Anna's horror obsession, and, alongside William Shakespeare and Jane Austen, Anna avidly studied such classic authors as James Herbert and Stephen King. Following a misguided attempt to wean herself off horror by studying Experimental Psychology at Oxford University, Anna went on to gainful employment in public relations, journalism, advertising and the BBC, before throwing everything over to become a filmmaker and horror writer.

DAVID BERNSTEIN ~ is a writer, mostly of horror and the plain ol' weird. His first novel, *Amongst the Dead*, is a zombie tale. His second novel, *Tears of No Return*, is an Urban Fantasy Horror tale. He also has novella entitled, *Jane 76*.

DAVID WESLEY HILL ~ is an award-winning science fiction writer with more than thirty stories published in the U.S. and internationally. In 1997 he was presented with the Golden Bridge award at the International Conference on Science Fiction in Beijing, and in 1999 he placed second in the Writers of the Future contest. Most recently, in 2011 Mr. Hill was invited to his third residency at the Blue Mountain Center, a writers and artists retreat in the Adirondacks. Mr. Hill studied under Joseph Heller and Jack Cady and received a Masters degree in creative writing from the City University of New York, as well as the school's highest literary honor, the De Jur Award. At various times he has been an executive chef for major hotels, a management consultant, and a website designer.

JAMES ROY DALEY ~ is a writer, editor, and musician. He studied film at the Toronto Film School, music at Humber College, and English at the University of Toronto. He is the author of *Terror Town, Into Hell, 13 Drops of Blood, Zombie Kong*, and *The Dead Parade*. In 2009 he founded Books of the Dead Press, where he enjoyed immediate success working with many of the biggest names in horror. He edited anthologies such as *Zombie Kong - Anthology, Best New Vampire Tales, Classic Vampire Tales*, and the *Best New Zombie Tales* series.

DAVID NIALL WILSON ~ has been writing and publishing horror, dark fantasy, and science fiction since the mid-eighties. An ordained minister, once President of the Horror Writer's Association and recipient of the Bram Stoker Award for poetry and short fiction, as well as being nominated for long fiction and non-fiction, his novels include *Maelstrom, The Mote in Andrea's Eye, Deep Blue, the Grails Covenant Trilogy, Star Trek Voyager: Chrysalis, Except You Go Through Shadow, This is My Blood, Ancient Eyes* and the upcoming supernatural mystery novel *Vintage Soul: Volume I of the DeChance Chronicles*. The Stargate Atlantis novel *Brimstone*, written with Patricia Lee Macomber was published in 2010. He has over 150 short stories published in anthologies, magazines, and five collections, the most recent of which were *Defining Moments*, published in 2007 by WFC Award winning Sarob Press, and the currently available *Ennui & Other States of Madness*, from Dark Regions Press. His work has appeared in various anthologies and magazines. David lives and loves with Patricia Lee Macomber in the historic William R. White House in Hertford, NC with their children, Billy, Stephanie, and Katie, David's mother Jean, and occasionally his boys Zach and Zane.

JOHN EVERSON ~ John is the Bram Stoker Award-winning author of the novels *Covenant, Sacrifice, The 13th and Siren*, and the short story collections *Creeptych, Needles & Sins, Vigilantes of Love* and *Cage of Bones & Other Deadly Obsessions*. He shares a deep purple den in Naperville, Illinois with a cockatoo and cockatiel, a disparate collection of fake skulls, twisted skeletal fairies, Alan Clark illustrations and a large stuffed Eeyore. There's also a mounted Chinese fowling spider named Stoker courtesy of Charlee Jacob, an ever-growing shelf of custom mix CDs and an acoustic guitar that he can't really play but that his son Shaun likes to hear him beat on anyway. Sometimes his wife Geri is surprised to find him shuffling through more public areas of the house, but it's usually only to brew another cup of coffee. In order to avoid the onerous task of writing, he holds down a regular job at a medical association, records pop-rock songs in a hidden home studio, experiments with the insatiable culinary joys of the jalapeno, designs photo collage art book covers for a variety of small presses, loses hours in expanding an array of gardens and chases frequent excursions into the bizarre visual headspace of '70s euro-horror DVDs with a shot of Makers Mark and a tall glass of Newcastle. For information on his fiction, art and music, visit John Everson: Dark Arts at www.JohnEverson.com.

JOHN GROVER ~ John is the author of *Feminine Wiles, Whispering Shadows, A Beckoning of Shadows*, and *Tandem of Terror*. Residing in Boston, Massachusetts, he previously studied creative writing online at Boston's Fisher College. He is also a member of the New England Horror Writers— a chapter of the Horror Writers Association. His short stories can be found in *Northern Haunts* (Shroud Publishing), *Zombology* (Library of the Living Dead), *Alien Skin Magazine, Morpheus Tales, Wrong World, The Willows*, and *Flesh and Blood Magazine*. For more information, feel free to visit his award-winning website, shadowtales.com.

ROB E. BOLEY ~ earned his B.A. and M.A. from the English Department at Wright State University. He lives in Dayton, Ohio, with his wife, daughter, and three cats (the non-talking variety). They are wonderful housemates, though he wishes there were fewer shoes, crayons, and socks on the floor.

T.J. MAY ~ has been writing professionally since 1998. He is an active member in the Horror Writers Association and the Director of the Events Committee for the New England Horror Writers. T.J. and his wife raise three sons in Massachusetts.

JOHN F.D. TAFF ~ is an author with more than 25 years experience in all sorts of writing... public relations, marketing, sales, journalism and creative. He's a published author with more than 50 short stories and seven novels in print. His writing tends to be categorized as "horror," though most of it has a weird, pulpy Twilight Zone vibe to it. He also writes fantasy, suspense and some science fiction. Over the years, four of his short stories have been awarded honorable mentions in Datlow & Windling's Year's Best Fantasy & Horror. He has three fantastic kids whom he doesn't see as much as would like-Harry (or whatever his name is these days), Sam and Molly. They're great kids and he loves them very much. He also shares his life with his wonderful inamorata, Deborah, who puts up with a great deal from him.

SIMON MCCAFFERY ~ is a Tulsa area based fiction writer, former magazine editor and telecommunications director. He has been writing and selling fiction since 1990. His primary interests are science fiction, horror and suspense. He has been married for 25 years and counting with three wonderful children, mini Rex rabbits, a miniature Dachshund named Bridget and two frogs.

JAMES NEWMAN ~ James lives in North Carolina with his wife, Glenda, and their two sons, Jamie and Jacob. James has several published novels to his name, including *Animosity, The Wicked*, and the coming-of-age fan favorite *Midnight Rain*.

ROBERT ELROD ~ Award-winning illustrator and graphic designer, Robert Elrod, strives to embrace a variety of styles and genres. He works in acrylics, watercolors, inks, colored-pencils, pencils, and digitally. He's active in local and national art shows and conventions, focusing primarily on images that depict horror, fantasy, and science fiction. His portfolio includes book covers, CD covers, comic books and pinup artwork. Robert's work can be found in *Vincent Price Presents* (Bluewater Comics), *New Horizons* (the British Fantasy Society), and in galleries across America.

MICHAEL LAIMO ~ is the author of the horror novels *Fires Rising, Dead Souls, The Demonologist, Deep In The Darkness*, and *Atmosphere*, and *Rare Cuts*, his newest (and fourth) short story collection. Visit him at www.laimo.com.

RANDALL LAHRMAN ~ hails from San Diego, California, and has ambitions for writing in the horror genre, of which he says he's a huge fan.

JONATHAN MABERRY ~ is a New York Times best-selling and multiple Bram Stoker Award-winning author, magazine feature writer, playwright, content creator and writing teacher/lecturer. His books have been sold to more than twenty countries. His novels include the Pine Deep Trilogy: *Ghost Road Blues* (Pinnacle books; winner of the Bram Stoker Award for Best First Novel in 2006), DEAD MAN'S SONG (2007) and *Bad Moon Rising* (2008); the Joe Ledger series of action thrillers from St. Martins Griffin: *Patient Zero* (2009, voted one Best Zombie Novel of 2009; winner of the Black Quill Award and a Bram Stoke Award finalist), *The Dragon Factory* (2010), *The King Of Plagues* (2011), *Assassin's Code* (2012), *Extinction Machine* (2013); *The Wolfman* (NY Times bestseller and winner of the Scribe Award for Best Adaptation, based on the Universal Pictures film starring Benecio Del Toro, Emily Blunt and Sir Anthony Hopkins); the Benny Imura series of Young Adult dystopian zombie thrillers from Simon & Schuster: *Rot & Ruin* (2010) and *Dust & Decay* (August 30, 2011), *Flesh & Bone* (2012) and *Fire & Ash* (2013); and the zombie thriller *Dead Of Night* (October 2011).

WILLIAM MEIKLE is a Scottish writer with more than ten published novels and over 200 short story credits in thirteen countries. He is the author of the ongoing *Midnight Eye* series, and his work has appeared in numerous anthologies.

ROB ROSEN ~ is the author of the novels *Sparkle, Divas Las Vegas,* and *Hot Lava,* has had short stories featured in more than 125 anthologies, most notably: Short Attention Span Mysteries; Modern Witches, Wizards, and Magic; Southern Comfort; Hell's Hangmen: Horror in the Old West; By the Chimney With Care; Strange Stories of Sand and Sea; Damned in Dixie: Southern Horror; Sporty Spec: Games of the Fantastic; Ruins Metropolis; Don't Turn the Lights On; Speculative Realms; Bloody October; and The Middle of Nowhere: Horror in Rural America. Visit him at www.therobrosen.com.

NINA KIRIKI HOFFMAN ~ has been publishing science fiction, fantasy, and horror since 1982. Her fiction has been on the final ballot for the World Fantasy, Endeavour, Philip K. Dick, Sturgeon, and other awards. She has won a Stoker and a Nebula.

Great titles from:
BOOKS OF THE DEAD

BEST NEW ZOMBIE TALES (Vol. 1)

BEST NEW ZOMBIE TALES (Vol. 2)

BEST NEW ZOMBIE TALES (Vol. 3)

BEST NEW ZOMBIE TALES TRILOGY

BEST NEW WEREWOLF TALES (VOL. 1)

BEST NEW VAMPIRE TALES (Vol. 1)

CLASSIC VAMPIRE TALES

GARY BRANDNER - THE HOWLING

GARY BRANDNER - THE HOWLING II

GARY BRANDNER - THE HOWLING III

GARY BRANDNER - THE HOWLING TRILOGY

JAMES ROY DALEY - INTO HELL

JAMES ROY DALEY - TERROR TOWN

JAMES ROY DALEY - 13 DROPS OF BLOOD

JAMES ROY DALEY - THE DEAD PARADE

JAMES ROY DALEY - ZOMBIE KONG

TONIA BROWN - BADASS ZOMBIE ROAD TRIP

MATT HULTS - ANYTHING CAN BE DANGEROUS

JOHN F.D. TAFF - LITTLE DEATHS

MATT HULTS - HUSK

TIM LEBBON - BERSERK

PAUL KANE - PAIN CAGES

ZOMBIE KONG ANTHOLOGY